"The humour and action
are joy-filled and entertaining.
It should win something for being
such a pleasure to read."

Starburst Magazine on *Pax Omega*

"Ewing's bizarre, legitimately post-
modern, tongue-in-cheek contribution
is from a different world. It's brilliant
– there's no doubting it – but it's
a disturbing, over-the-top,
self-reflective type of brilliance.
Men punch bears, and then go on
chapter-length explorations of the
nature of authorship. Cross Joe Lansdale
with Grant Morrison, and you start to get
close to Ewing."

Pornokitsch on *Death Got No Mercy*

"This is real pulp material, the stuff of
brooding humour, gritty violence and all-out
action, with rugged (super)heroes and sarky
dames. There's a lot to love here."

Total Sci-Fi Online on *Gods of Manhattan*

"Does Ewing succeed? Of course he does.
Ewing is the kind of writer who loves a
challenge and is up to the task of delivering.
Pax Omega is about leaving you really
thinking about what you just read."

Graeme's Fantasy Book Review on *Pax Omega*

GREENBOX
ALL
EWING
IN A BOTH
TOGETHER
WOULD
NO
BE THEY HERS
SUCH / SUCH
THAT GROWN
FIRST TO AGREE
FROM
ALLOBLIGATION

First published 2013 by Solaris
an imprint of Rebellion Publishing Ltd,
Riverside House, Osney Mead,
Oxford, OX2 0ES, UK

www.solarisbooks.com

ISBN 978-1-78108-094-8

Copyright © Al Ewing 2013

10 9 8 7 6 5 4 3 2 1

A CIP catalogue record for this book is available from the
British Library.

Designed & typeset by Rebellion Publishing

Printed in the US

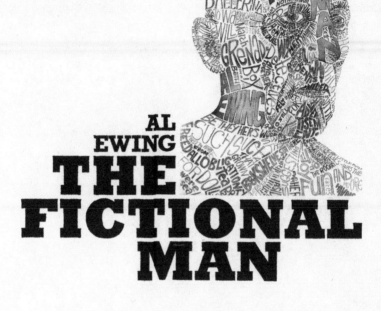

AL
EWING

THE
FICTIONAL
MAN

SOLARIS

For Sarah,
who helped unlock this when I needed it most.

CHAPTER ONE

RALPH CUTNER WAS fictional, but Niles didn't hold that against him.

THERE WERE ADVANTAGES in having a fictional human – a Fictional – for a therapist.

Niles could still remember the four fruitless months, four and a half years ago, two hours a week, when he'd perched uncomfortably on the edge of a teal suede couch belonging to one Dr Mary Loewes.

She'd done most of the talking. Niles, for his part, would hesitate for long seconds, then nod silently or make small meaningless noises. On rare occasions, he might actually manage to answer one of her questions – though guardedly, with a drawn-out, one-word answer, as if he was sitting in an interrogation cell instead of a tastefully-appointed office.

Inside Niles' head, it was a different story.

"What you don't understand, Mary," the author snapped, (he would narrate to himself) *"is that I was*

attempting a last-ditch attempt to save my marriage. That's why I slept with that woman – to wake my wife up to the problems we were going through before it was too late!"

"Mr Golan, I understand perfectly well," Dr Loewes said, understandingly, *"and I agree completely with everything you just said."*

Niles Golan had a habit of internally narrating his own life story, usually improving on it as he went. Mostly, it was the romance of a juicy internal monologue, a quirk that – like the habit of rolling golf balls around in his palm, which he'd claimed was how he came up with new ideas, at least until he'd lost one of the golf balls – he assumed made him deep. Partly, it was born of a neurotic desire to always be working, or at least pretend to be working – the kind of thing that Dr Loewes could have helped with, if he'd opened up to her for half a second.

Laughing inwardly at the obviousness of her technique, the author deflected her foolish questions with a practiced panache, Niles would think, or something like it. And later, as he signed over the four hundred dollars she required per hour, he would feel a warm glow of satisfaction, as if he'd won a game he was playing with her. Another session finished – another session with the walls of his mental fortress still unbreached.

After thirty-four sessions – coming to thirteen thousand, six hundred dollars in total – he had decided that therapy was too expensive a hobby to pursue any further.

"AND YET..." SAID Ralph Cutner, four and a half years later, as Niles Golan relaxed in the sumptuous brown leather chair he kept for his patients, "...here we are."

"Well, this is hardly the same," Niles muttered, leaning back into the warm recesses of the brown leather. It was the same chair that had been on the show – as far as possible, Ralph had tried to duplicate the set of *Cutner's Chair* to the last degree when setting up his practice, and obviously the chair itself played a large part of that. He'd bought it from a memorabilia collector for twelve thousand dollars and a signed photo.

"Isn't it?"

"Well, no. I mean, it's different, isn't it? The sessions with Doctor Loewes... they were something I promised Iyla I'd do. Before the divorce, I mean."

"Right, right. This would have been after the thing with Justine." Ralph smiled. Like most Fictionals created specifically for the small screen, he was a handsome man – a little craggy, perhaps, not quite as unnaturally gorgeous as some of the soap-opera Fictionals, but definitely the better looking of the two men. Not that Niles had much to worry about – obviously his chin was weaker, and he'd been going bald for some time, and his nose was perhaps a little long, but all that added character.

And he was real, of course. That made a difference.

"Whereas this, on the other hand," he said, ignoring the mention of Justine Coverly – he really didn't want to talk about *her* today, or any of the others, or his ex-wife – "these weekly sessions with you... that's something I came to of my own accord. It was *my* decision to come and see you, I wasn't pressured into it by anybody, so..." Niles shrugged, waving a hand idly. "There we are. Completely different situations."

Ralph half-smiled, raising one eyebrow – the imperfections of which had been discussed by the studio's design team for some days. He paused dramatically for a moment before speaking.

"That's the *only* difference?"

Niles swallowed. "Well, yes. Absolutely." He coughed. "The only difference that matters – to me, I mean." He leaned forward, scratching the back of his head. Ralph's arms were folded now, and Niles had a feeling he'd seen that particular fold of the arms on the 'very special episode' of *Cutner's Chair* where Ralph Cutner had analysed a Grand Wizard of the local Klan.

"Do, um... do *you* think there are any other differences?" Niles tried to make his voice as innocent as possible. "Between you and her? That matter?"

Ralph raised his other eyebrow and said nothing.

Niles sighed. "It's going to sound insulting."

"How so?"

"It's going to sound as if... well, as if I don't consider you a real..." He swallowed. "You know."

Ralph's eyes crinkled just so, in a way that hadn't been designed into him but was encouraged by the director all the same, particularly for close-ups. The crinkle of Ralph's eyes was a happy accident for the translation team. "No, I don't know. You're going to have to tell me." He chuckled. "A real therapist? A real jerk? A real human being? What?"

Niles shifted uncomfortably in the chair for a moment. "...A real *therapist*," he finished, weakly.

Ralph leaned back against the wall, lowering and raising his eyebrows in a little ballet. His eyebrows were very expressive, when he wanted them to be. "Hesitation. That's very interesting."

The author stared Ralph Cutner right in the eye as his ridiculous eyebrows waggled like caterpillars. With one insouciant glare, he dared the man to make his accusation and be done. Instead, the Fictional crumbled, utterly defeated.

Niles didn't look at Ralph. He looked at the floor. The silence stretched on.

"Here's the thing, Niles." Ralph suddenly grinned, showing teeth. "I'm *not* a real therapist – I mean, I made that clear when you started coming to see me. Technically, I'm a life coach. Because to call yourself a therapist, you need to get certain degrees. I don't have those. I never went to college – I was never the age you go to college at. I've always been thirty-five – or able to *play* thirty-five, I should say. In real terms, I'm nine." He leant forward, jerking a thumb conspiratorially at the certificates on the wall. "The moment I came out of the translation tube, those degrees were waiting for me. They're not real, either. Just props, from the show." Another dry little chuckle. "But you knew that."

Niles flushed red. Of course, he knew all about the show: *Cutner's Chair*, a one-hour weekly drama about a curmudgeonly psychiatrist with a heart of gold who (with the help of a clutch of beautiful interns) solved one crippling neurosis per week in time for a montage of learning moments cut to some unobjectionable indie song aimed at the dad demographic. It had run for seven seasons, leaving behind a large albeit steadily shrinking fan base, several dozen tumblr accounts, a small ocean of memorabilia – and the Fictional, Ralph Cutner.

THERE WERE STILL, occasionally, in far-flung corners of the world, people who didn't know what Fictionals were.

Strictly speaking, a Fictional was a cloned and modified human being. If you'd worked in the fast food industry, you'd probably have an understanding of cloning – since the big genetics breakthroughs of the 'seventies and 'eighties, it was where the meat came from. The higher class of restaurant still used 'real' chickens, pigs and cows, but anyone who told you they could taste the difference was a liar, and a pretentious one at that.

The laws of most countries prohibited the cloning and duplication of real people. "Every American has the right to their individual identity" was the line in the US. There were also various bans in place on weaponised and otherwise enhanced humans, but every so often North Korea would crow about men who could see in the dark and lift buses, at which point any country with the technology to achieve that would realise they were far better off just working on a nuclear programme. Which they did.

So really, the only legal or useful place left for human cloning was in entertainment.

They'd already used a cloned shark in *Jaws* – augmenting it to be larger, more vicious-looking, but also more docile and easy to train. Thanks to some wheeling and dealing behind the scenes, it was significantly cheaper than the cost of a model would have been. In the wake of that film's success, a brief spate of creature features with cloned animals followed – *Dodectapus, Piranha, Death Bear* – and, eventually, someone took a close look at the laws on the books and decided to take the next logical step.

George Burns had been in the running for the title role in *Oh, God!*, but the studio made the decision, somewhat blasphemously, to cast a cloned human with a personality programmed by a computer – a computer the size of several rooms, back then – to match the God from the original Avery Corman novel. According to the law, real people could not be duplicated, but fictional people – as confirmed by a fairly contentious ruling from the Supreme Court – were fair game.

(In trying to explain the Supreme Court's working, Warren Burger made a rather confused analogy – that, just as fictions could be translated from English to Spanish, so they could be 'translated' into the language of the human genetic code. It was one of the least coherent statements of his career, but the term stuck.)

God, as he emerged from the translation tube, had a warm, beatific personality and a wickedly dry sense of humour, but what made his performance – as himself, or Himself, depending on how heretical you were feeling – was the essential otherworldliness he brought to the role, that strange touch of unreality. If you were to watch the film today, you probably won't notice it – we're used to Fictionals now – but imagine how it must have been, in 1977, to see a fictional man walking and talking for the very first time...

God made two sequels – one with George Burns starring opposite him as the Devil – and after that, the studio released him from his contract and he was left to his own devices. Over the next year – 1985 – he starred in 'special episodes' of *Magnum, P.I.* and *Cheers* and announced his plans to write a (necessarily short) autobiography. He never finished the book; he was found dead in bed in late December of that year. Physically, he was eight years old.

By that time, eighty-three other Fictionals – most with life expectancies benefitting from the rapid improvements in cloning technology – had been produced by the larger studios. By 1990, there would be more than four hundred, each of them modelled on a fictional character from a novel or a play, or created especially for the big or small screens. By the turn of the millennium, the number of Fictionals in Los Angeles would stabilise somewhere between forty and fifty thousand.

The Fictionals were here to stay.

* * *

"...ALL RIGHT." NILES sighed, looking at the floor. "Maybe I was worried about implying... oh, you know what. The other thing."

Ralph chuckled again.

In a flash, the novelist leaped from the chair. With one expertly-delivered karate chop, the giggling moron's neck was snapped like a cheese straw, Niles thought, as he continued to sit and stare at his shoes.

"What other thing?" Ralph grinned. "Come on, say it out loud. It won't hurt us."

Niles sighed. "You being a... a Fictional." He scowled. "There, happy?"

"A Fictional." Cutner stood up and began walking around the room in a slow circle, staring intently ahead. On the *Cutner's Chair* message boards, this was known as the 'walk and talk' moment. *He stalked his office like a panther prowling a cage,* Niles found himself thinking, *the laser eye of his mind seeking out every last detail of the demons plaguing the inner landscape of the handsome novelist.*

It was comforting, in a way – but at the same time, oddly irritating. It almost felt as if Ralph was flaunting his unreality, shoving it down Niles' throat.

"Say it loud, say it proud. Created, not gestated. My father was a typewriter and my mother was a translation tube." Ralph gave himself another beat, as though following the orders of an invisible director, then turned. "I'm not *real* in the way that you are, Mr Golan. That's a part of it, isn't it?"

"No." Niles scowled. He could see what Cutner was implying. It was arrant nonsense, of course.

There were people who thought that way – *realists,*

they were called. They'd been a serious problem for the movie industry until 1989, when a realist mob had murdered Bernie Lomax, a Fictional created for the *Weekend At Bernie's* franchise, leading to a controversial and arguably gruesome rewrite of the script. Public opinion had turned solidly against realism after that, but there were still plenty of people who felt that a character who'd emerged from a translation tube with a full personality already in place was, if not an abomination *per se,* at least naturally inferior to someone who'd been born from a human womb, who'd acquired their genetic makeup the old-fashioned way.

Niles wasn't one of those people. The Fictionals were *different* – of course they were – but certainly not *inferior.* Not *very* inferior.

He scowled. "I don't know. Maybe."

Cutner smiled, showing his teeth again. *It was the predatory grin of a shark,* Niles narrated, feeling the old desire to shut himself up like a clam rising in him.

"The way I see it," Cutner said, "you couldn't open up to Loewes because she *was* real. She *was* a professional therapist. She was analysing every word and gesture you made – or you thought she was, anyway, and that's enough. Probably seeing things about you that you hadn't worked out yourself yet, right? And that's not a nice position to be in for you. You felt vulnerable." He smiled, pouring himself an apple juice from the whiskey decanter on the sideboard; like many Fictionals, he had an aversion to alcohol, preferring the prop drinks that came on the set. He knocked the drink he'd poured back in one. "You come to me because you feel superior to me."

"Really?" Niles tried not to roll his eyes. "Because I'm a writer? Is that it?"

"Sure, why not? A famous writer, at that. How many books is it now?"

Niles had to admit it was nice to be called a *famous* writer. And he certainly didn't mind talking about his work – in fact, it was one of his favourite topics of conversation. "Eighteen. Nineteen in February. And Doubleday want a new Kurt Power novel by Christmas."

KURT POWER WAS Niles Golan's signature character; a no-nonsense private eye and ex-lawyer who, on the days he wasn't solving cases involving genius serial killers, consulted for the police and anti-terrorist forces. He was divorced, with a drink problem and – the clever touch Niles was most proud of – an autistic six-year-old daughter, whose unique insights often provided the key to a difficult case. The first few novels had done relatively well, before sales settled down to something reasonable but unremarkable – enough to keep Niles in the style to which he had become accustomed, but not enough to put him up amongst the greats, which was where he felt he deserved to be.

After all, what did King or Rowling have that Golan didn't? Why did Gaiman command a Twitter following of over a million, while Niles struggled to reach six thousand? Why had *Bring Up The Bodies* won a Booker while *Pudding And Pie: A Kurt Power Novel* had been so cruelly ignored?

The critics, of course. Critics, Niles Golan believed, came in two varieties – insightful, and jealous. The insightful occasionally compared him to Clancy, or Crichton, which was flattering, although Niles really saw himself as being closer to a young Thomas Pynchon. The other kind of critic, meanwhile – the jealous kind – used words like 'cosy' and 'predictable.' Which was obviously ridiculous, especially after Niles had ended *Down To The Woods Tonight: A Kurt Power Novel* by having the Teddy Bear Killer murder Power's new girlfriend in cold blood, just to cruelly mess with Kurt's head and drive him back to the drink. How could anyone have predicted a finale like that?

No, obviously whichever small-minded hack had called that stroke of brilliance 'predictable' – it was Lance Pritchards, writing in the *Topeka Examiner* – was suffering from a touch of the green-eyed monster. How depressing it must be, Niles thought, to sit behind a desk all day, being called on to write wretched little hit-pieces about wordsmiths who could out-write you in their sleep! No wonder Lance Pritchards so envied Niles that he had to use what meagre power he had to poison the well against him. Lance Pritchards and all those bastards on Amazon, giving their meagre three-star reviews to books like *The Saladin Imperative: A Kurt Power Novel*, even though it had surely completely changed their understanding of Middle Eastern politics.

Bastards, all of them.

CUTNER SMILED. "RIGHT, right. Nineteen books. And, obviously, you know Kurt Power could end up being translated any day now" – he was actively smirking now, in a way Niles didn't much like – "just as soon as the studios realise what a hit they'd have on their hands. Which, I guess, makes you something like a minor God compared with me..."

"I didn't create you."

"No, but you..." He coughed, in a way Niles couldn't help but notice. "You easily could have done. Ahem."

The Fictional's thoughts were as visible to the author as words on a page, Niles thought. Anyway, he could have easily thought up a character like Ralph Cutner – easiest thing in the world. He'd just had his hands full with Kurt Power, that was all. Who, by the way, was a vastly more complex creation, what with his father having been murdered by the leader of the very terrorist organisation he found himself regularly defending the world from.

Ralph read his expression. "Of course, as a writer – a *wordsmith* – you can probably see all my motivations, my inner workings, my tropes and tics, just the way you felt Loewes could see yours. Am I warm?"

Niles grimaced. "Not even slightly. You're stone cold," he said bitterly.

Cutner shrugged. "Well, that's why you come to me, to hear things you can dismiss easily."

"That's not true," Niles scowled. "I just, ah, find you a little more..." – Niles searched for the word, not wanting to be drawn into any more discussions of his supposed realist tendencies – "more *relatable* than Loewes was. That's all."

Cutner chuckled. "Well, of course you can *relate* to me, I'm an acerbic genius who doesn't suffer fools gladly. Relating to me strokes your ego."

Niles gritted his teeth. *It took an incredible display of iron will for the author to resist rising from the chair and punching the smirk off the man. How dare he?*

He forced himself to relax, and pointed to the decanter. "If it's not too much to ask, could you pour me a glass of that?"

"Sure." Ralph poured another apple juice and handed Niles the glass, a look of distaste crossing his face for a moment. "You're not alone, you know – well, when it comes to the ego-stroking, at least. Most of my clients aren't like you. They're real fans of the show – they can quote every line. They don't want treatment, they just come here to re-enact old scenes, or make out we're friends. Very occasionally" – a look of disgust crossed his face – "one makes an appointment just to tell me they're in *love* with me."

Niles was shocked. "Wait, they say this to your *face?*"

"What can I say?" Ralph shrugged. "Some people are freaks."

THERE WAS NOTHING particularly sick or wrong or unpleasant about a human becoming attached to a fictional character. That had been something for writers to aim for since literature began.

No, it was simply a question of degree.

People could fill blogs and tumblrs with adoring gifs of a particular character, a cartoon or comic-book icon – there was nothing strange about that. Nobody saw much difference between a tumblr devoted to Thor or Loki and one devoted to James Dean or Brad Pitt.

Some, admittedly, took it a little further. They might start sleeping with a body pillow or a 'real doll' of their favourite character, touching and stroking it in the night. Or they might photoshop a cartoon horse into their arms or their bed and put the resulting pictures up on Facebook. That might make the general public feel a little queasy.

As it was generally understood, real people could love each other. Real people could have affection for fictional characters. But if a real person *loved* a fictional character – well, then something had gone very, very wrong with them. There was a necessary distance between the real and the imaginary.

And when the imaginary was walking around in the world of the real, it made things even more complicated. Those queasy feelings – pity, revulsion, an overriding sense of creepiness – didn't go away just because the fictional character in question had been translated into a clone body instead of onto a pillow. Fictionals were still imaginary beings. If anything, those feelings of disgust became even more pronounced. The idea of a human being and a Fictional having sex produced an almost phobic reaction in many people, including Niles.

There were, occasionally, human beings who slept with Fictionals, even fell in love with them. On the rare occasions when human/Fictional couplings had been admitted to – only twice since the first Fictional was translated, once in 1991 and once in 2000 – it had been professional and social suicide for both parties. The gutter press had had a field day, subjecting the couples in question to as much muck as they could hurl without fear of litigation, and the public had been happy to lap up every salacious detail. No studio would take a chance on casting a Fictional who'd been subjected to that kind of public gaze, and their human partners tended to be 'let go' for vague and spurious reasons, such as 'bringing the company into disrepute.' Eventually, they'd been forced to leave Hollywood altogether. It was a taboo that had a frightening amount of power to ruin lives.

Fictionals paired off with each other occasionally, although rarely. The ratio of male to female Fictionals – mostly Fictionals were male, white and straight, thanks to the prejudices of the Hollywood system – meant such couplings were few and far between. When they did happen, the press found such 'slash pairings' utterly adorable, like a wedding between two of the cutest little puppies in the world.

Other Fictionals usually didn't comment.

But Fictional sex – no matter who with – was a very rare thing. In the main, Fictionals were carefully designed to sublimate their sexual desires into their roles – there was nothing unusual in a Fictional falling deeply in love with an actor's portrayal of a character, and then treating the actor his-or-herself as a completely different person, a fellow professional doing a job. For a Fictional to fall in love with a human being rather than a fellow fictional character would be a rebellion against everything they knew, against their very nature.

They just weren't built that way.

RALPH GROANED, AND Niles could see the distaste in his face deepening to disgust. "Some days, I wish I *was* a real therapist. Some of these people need help." He shuddered. "Try this on for size – I had a client once who walked in, dropped his trousers and started literally beating off in the chair. I tried dragging him out of it, but that just sent him over the edge. He was calling me his *Daddy*."

Niles blinked for a moment. "Wait. When you say *over the edge...*" He shifted in the chair, nervous.

Ralph had the decency to look embarrassed. He nodded to the chair. "I did clean it. Thoroughly. With bleach. It's been completely disinfected – hell, I'd sit in it myself." Noticing the look on Niles' face, he indicated the chair he'd been sitting in earlier – a stiff-backed wooden chair that looked like it would have been more at home around a dining table. "But feel free to sit in that one."

Niles hesitated for a moment.

The author was a man of the world, of course. He didn't want to give the impression that he was bothered by something as minor as sitting on a chair that had once been –

– he got up hurriedly.

Ralph sighed, looking at the chair with venom, and then returned to the sideboard to pour another drink. Niles opened his mouth to ask for one, but he reminded himself that it was only apple juice. What he needed after that revelation was whiskey.

Ralph took a sip of the drink and smiled. "You're meeting Maurice after this?"

Niles fell greedily on the change of subject. "That's right. I am indeed." He leaned back on the creaking new chair, trying to keep his voice from getting too smug. "Apparently, he's been talking to a studio – one of the big ones, in fact. Talisman Pictures. They might just have some screenplay work lined up for me. According to Maurice, it could – *could* – be the big one."

Cutner raised an eyebrow. "You're kidding. They're doing a Kurt Power movie?" He sounded shocked.

Niles ignored the implicit criticism in the tone. He'd been wanting to see a Kurt Power film for years, ever since he'd created the character in his exciting debut novel, *Power Of Attorney: A Kurt Power Novel.* (He'd dropped the lawyer angle after he'd realised how much research was involved.)

For the leading man, he could just about see Cruise, or Clooney, or Pitt. But those were second choices. He knew there was only one person who'd really be perfect for it.

He could picture the scene now.

The author watched, breathless, as the adult body of Kurt Power grew in the translation tube, day by day.

Like a proud papa, he would lay his hands on the tube, gazing in wonderment at the creation of life taking place before him. A life that could not have been without the first spark of genius that had come from his very pen.

Then the first meeting with him, in some executive's office. *They shook hands, the author smiling paternally. "Welcome to the world," he said, in gentle tones that rang with a hidden steel. Kurt Power could only look upon his Creator in silent wonder.*

Niles knew that Kurt Power, when he emerged, would know all about him – what he'd done, the part he'd played in Power's existence. He'd be grateful for that – intensely grateful. But it wouldn't stop the two of them becoming close friends. After all, Niles reflected, Niles Golan, ground-breaking author, was just the sort of person Kurt Power would count as a close friend. Just the kind of person he'd respect.

"You're a good Joe, Niles," Kurt drawled, in the authentic voice of the American working man. "You sure are a gosh-darned good Joe."

And people would see him on the streets, on sets, in gossip magazines. *"That's Kurt Power," breathed the beautiful stenographer, her full, firm breasts heaving with undisguised admiration. "The new Fictional. Based on the Niles Golan books – have you read them? He's like a young Thomas Pynchon, with just a hint of Ernest Hemingway," she sighed, orgasmically.*

It would be all he'd ever wanted.

Niles couldn't help but smile. Cutner was right - it would be like being a god. A benevolent god.

He chuckled modestly.

"Well... we'll see."

CHAPTER TWO

THE MAN FROM *Talisman Pictures* had the smile of someone intimately acquainted with success, used to getting exactly what he wanted. The easy smile of a winner at the game of life.

The author, not to be outdone, shot back a steely grin, fire glinting in his elegant hazel eyes. He was amused at all the Hollywood game-playing, but he knew he could eat this man for breakfast, if necessary.

Niles smiled back, weakly, his clammy hands shifting to and fro as he tried to work out where to put them. After another few awkward seconds, he stuck out his hand to be shaken, hoping his palm wasn't too sweaty.

"Miles!" said The Man From Talisman Pictures, smiling wider. "Baby!"

NILES HAD MOVED to Los Angeles eleven years earlier, after a brief period in San Francisco. He'd moved to America on a whim, after England lost its appeal for him following a particularly scathing review in the *Times Literary Supplement.*

During his first month in San Fran, he'd met a young and vivacious woman named Iyla Johri, with a smile that – at the time – he'd found captivating. On their second meeting, he'd compared it to the smile of the Mona Lisa, and he'd been able to tell just by her surprised reaction – *"really?"* – that nobody else had had the imagination to make such an off-beat comparison.

By their fourth date, he'd found out that she handled public relations for a publisher of children's books, she liked tea with a dash of honey and lemon, and she had two small moles on the back of her shoulder, like a figure eight. The two of them were soon living together, and when Iyla found a much higher-paying job with an animation studio in Los Angeles, Niles had followed her there. On their first night in the new place, he'd proposed.

Part of him had expected Hollywood to open itself up like a flower within a few weeks, bestowing the sweet nectar of celebrity on him almost the moment he arrived. He'd imagined that people would know him there – know Kurt Power, at least – but, as it turned out, he was just one more D-List semi-somebody in a city that had far more than its fair share of them. Like everyone else in town, he had a screenplay he'd made a couple of desultory attempts to sell – a powerfully erotic thriller centred around the outbreak of an infectious skin disease, which he still secretly believed was a masterpiece. His agent, however – a conservative woman in her sixties named Agnes Cowan who lived in Dorset – was far more interested in keeping the Kurt Power money flowing than in helping his client on any risky changes of career. Before long Niles was back to his old routine, putting out at least one new Kurt Power novel every year and spending the remaining time on other projects, which somehow never included the movies.

And so things had continued for almost eleven fruitful years – punctuated here and there by a little personal stress, but that was life – until the summer of 2012, when Agnes had died suddenly after being gored by a ram during an ill-fated visit to a petting zoo, a tragic event that had forced Niles to take on a new agent. Maurice Zuckerbroth, who claimed to be thirty-nine – and had been making that claim for years – was a short, chubby, slightly oleaginous man with a black moustache, a dyed-black comb-over and a perpetual air of slightly anxious over-enthusiasm. Niles wouldn't have gone to a man like that under ordinary circumstances, but Zuckerbroth was the man who'd somehow sold *The Wizard Games* to Fantasia Films, which had made the original author – Helen something – a household name. If he was willing to do something similar for Kurt Power... well, Niles wasn't about to say no.

Maurice, on their first meeting, had promised faithfully that not only would he keep all Niles' current contracts running smoothly, but he would personally see to it that Kurt Power was given the green light for a big-budget picture within the year.

And now, just over eight months later, here they were.

NILES HAD EXPECTED to be having the meeting in the Talisman offices – he'd had visions of dazzling a trio of sharp-suited executives at a mahogany boardroom table until they rose as one to deliver him a standing ovation – but instead Maurice had taken him to a greasy diner with a badly-painted mural taking up one wall, which was apparently where the man from Talisman Pictures liked to have his lunch meetings. As they sat and waited for their entrées, Niles found himself trying not to look at the poorly-proportioned Elvis, or the lumpy Marilyn, or the Bogart whose arm didn't seem to be connected to his torso in any meaningful way, but he couldn't quite tear his eyes away. They looked disdainfully back at him. "So retro," said The Man From Talisman Pictures, whose name, it turned out, was Dean.

He wore a grey suit of undistinguished cut, close-cropped blonde hair and an uneven tan. Niles wondered if his slightly shabby look was a sign that he had less power within the studio system, or more. "I just can't get enough of the décor here. It's like outsider art. You should try the fries, they're just... like a statement, you know?" Dean already had a bowl of the fries in front of him – they were cold and greasy, thin strips of potato that seemed like they'd been made days before and then left in a dingy corner of a walk-in fridge to congeal. Dean picked one up, looking at it for a moment, and shook his head. "It's the irony, you know? I think Adam Sandler eats here."

"They're fantastic, buddy. I'll get a bowl myself. Oh, waitress!" Maurice lifted his pudgy fingers, trying and failing to snap them. The waitress brought laminated menus, handing them over with a disdainful roll of her eyes. Maurice scanned the plastic for a moment, then shook his head. "I'm gonna have to go off-menu here, honey bun. Give me a hummus wrap, feta salad with aioli and a diet old-fashioned lemonade – no corn syrup." He grinned wide enough to show the gold of his left molar. The waitress looked back at him as if he was an ant.

Niles coughed, feeling sheepish. "I'll, ah, just have a glass of water." The waitress narrowed her eyes.

"Just water?"

Niles smiled brightly. "Ah, yes. Thank you."

She pursed her lips. "I don't know if we do *just* water."

Niles' smile became fixed. "Tap water," he said. "It doesn't have to be bottled."

"*Tap* water." She shook her head slowly. "I can check for it, I guess." She looked at him out of one eye, then slowly shuffled away.

Maurice turned to Niles and nodded, looking impressed. *Power play, bro,* he mouthed. Niles didn't really know what that meant, but it seemed good. Maurice turned his attention back to Dean. "So, is it time to talk turkey here? You got something for my boy? Maybe a little *K-to-the-P* action?" He waggled his eyebrows and grinned.

Dean grinned back, dangling another limp fry between his fingers. He still hadn't put one in his mouth. "'Turkey'! You're on my wavelength, Maurice!" The two of them laughed uproariously. Niles had no idea what the joke was. He felt increasingly lost. Dean dropped the fry back in the bowl, sucking on his finger for a moment, then leaned back in the plastic seat. "Okay, let's do it to it – let's talk for real. Like *real* for real. Okay? Miles?"

Niles shot Maurice a quick, frantic look. He should have corrected Dean the first time, but it was too late now. Wasn't it?

The author coughed, drawing attention. "My name," he said quietly, with a hidden steel ringing in his voice, *"is Niles. With an N." The man from the studio blinked, then shook his head deferentially.*

"I am so sorry, Mister Golan," he said, putting his head in his hands. "I stand revealed before you as a fool. A cringing simpleton, unworthy to even kiss the fingers that created such masterpieces as Murder Force: A Kurt Power Novel. *Please, let us make this grievous error up to you. Let us breathe life into the majesty that is... Kurt Power."*

The author nodded, graciously. "You can make the attempt, I suppose. Of course, I'll have to direct it myself."

Yes. He should say something. The situation was becoming ridiculous. "Um... Dean?" He licked his lips, wondering how to phrase it.

"What is it, Miles?"

"Actually," the author murmured, quietly, so as not to cause a fuss, "my name is Niles –"

For a moment, the studio executive only stared, the veins in his forehead seeming to inflate like balloon animals. Then, eyes bulging, he grabbed hold of the Formica table and wrenched it out of the concrete floor, the flex of his muscles tearing the jacket from his back in two pieces. "You son of a bitch!" he howled, "You hopeless, cringing piece of nothing! How DARE you correct me! I have had pus drained from my genital warts that was more important than you! You couldn't even cut it in this town as a disease!" With that, he lifted the table into the air, spittle flying from his perfect teeth, and slammed it down on the heads of the two cowering men in front of him with enough force to crack their skulls like eggshells.

No charges were ever brought.

"Miles?"

"What?" Niles yelped. His mouth was dry.

"What is it, buddy?" Dean was smiling. "You kind of zoned out there."

Maurice was looking at him strangely. Niles forced his nervousness down. Of course it wouldn't be like that. "Well... it's just that, er..." He tried to hear the hidden steel ring in his voice. "I, um..."

He swallowed. "I just wanted to say how great it is to be working with you on this. Bringing Kurt Power to the silver screen."

Maurice started to make small, jerky movements with his head. It took Niles a moment to realise that he was trying to shake it in a way Dean wouldn't notice. His smile never faded, but there was anguish in his eyes.

Dean tapped two greasy forefingers together for a moment, suddenly looking very serious. "Yeah. Sure. Listen," he said, looking grave, as if receiving news of the death of a close relative, "I have to go potty. Time out, okay?" Then he was up, striding towards a tattily painted door with the words LEADING MEN written on it. In Hobo font.

MAURICE CONTINUED SMILING glassily until one second after the door had swung shut. Then the smile vanished, replaced by a grim scowl of anger. "*Asshole!*" he hissed, keeping one eye on the toilet door.

"What?" Niles gaped. "I thought we were here to –"

Maurice upgraded from a hiss to a quiet yell. "We're here to get Kurt Power into movies! At least, that's what I *thought* we were here to do, but you just – you moved too fast! We had a good deal going on here! We just needed to buy it some drinks, massage its shoulders a little, drop some hints about protection, but no, you had to go straight in there and fuck it! You *fucked the deal,* Niles! You fucked *us!* You *prick!*" He clutched at his head, rubbing his temples as though he was developing a migraine. "Jesus! All right. Calm down. Niles, you know I love you, man –"

"You just called me a prick."

Maurice winced. "Yeah, you made me say that. I didn't want to. It *hurt* me, buddy, to call you that word, but you forced me to do it. It's like you kicked me in the damn balls, making me call you that. But you don't have to apologise, 'cause I still love you. Where were we?"

Niles frowned. "You'd just called me a prick."

"Right, right." Maurice shook his head. "Listen, buddy, you can't just *ask* the man from Talisman Pictures to make your book into a movie for you. There's a process – a *comme-ci-comme-ça*, you know? Scratching backs. You know what I'm saying?"

"Not really."

"This," Maurice sighed, pulling off the trick of making his patience seem infinite but not completely boundless, "is not that meeting. Maybe that meeting comes after this meeting, but this is not *that* meeting. This is the meeting where he tells us how we can *get* to that meeting. He's gonna leave a little trail of breadcrumbs through a little maze. And we're gonna follow it, right?"

He was getting quite animated now. "We're gonna run his maze, and at the end there's gonna be a little button we can hit with our noses that'll deliver food or cocaine, and we eat the cocaine because *this is Hollywood!*" He banged the table. "This is Hollywood, Niles! Fuck the food! We eat the cocaine!"

Niles blinked. "I don't actually do..."

Maurice leaned forward, whispering confidentially. "The cocaine is Kurt Power. It's a metaphor. We're gonna get you Kurt Power on the big screen, with a Fictional for leading man, first refusal on directors, a trailer, hookers, the *works* – you just gotta let me drive, buddy. You gotta let me do my magic." He looked around, as if they were being watched. "Listen, I've got things going on, buddy. I've got irons in the fire, you know? I got things going on you wouldn't *believe*." He stared at Niles for a moment, evaluating. "You ever ghost-written?"

Niles stared back. He wasn't sure if he liked being evaluated. "Not really, no."

Maurice nodded. "Could you write in a kinda Victorian style? You know – *fancy?*"

Niles settled back into the plastic chair, keeping an eye out for the waitress. She seemed to be taking quite a long time, considering he just wanted a water. "Well, I *suppose...*" he said, trying to change the subject, "but, um, one thing at a time. Is this how things usually go? With meetings, I mean?"

Maurice shrugged. "Who the hell knows? We're in the jungle here. I don't make up the rules about which bugs we eat to get stars, y'know?" The toilet flushed, and Maurice quickly re-assumed his glassy smile.

DEAN RETURNED TO the table, rubbing his nose with the back of his hand. Niles decided he was just being paranoid. Dean probably had a cold.

"Kurt Power," he said, in an odd, strangled voice. "Kurt. Power." He let the words hang in the air for a few seconds, rocking in his chair, then spread his hands wide, conjuring an invisible movie screen. "Open on the rain."

Or not, thought Niles.

On the other hand, Dean was at least discussing Kurt Power, which was more than Maurice had led him to expect. *"Well, I suppose this is the meeting," the author smirked, casting a sideways look at his fatuous agent, who clearly knew nothing about the very business he claimed to work in, as well as being disarmingly short and quite ugly.*

"Open on the rain. Kurt Power. He's... he's wearing a coat." Dean stared into the middle distance for a moment, his jaw clenching and unclenching. "No! No coat. He's stripped to the waist! Rain coursing down his back. Female thirty-five-to-fifty-fives go wild!"

"I suppose..." Niles murmured, brow wrinkling slightly. "I mean, I never thought of Kurt Power as a sex symbol *per se,* more as the wounded dignity of the disenfranchised working man, but..."

"*Yes!*" Dean yelled, slamming his hand down on the table. "Wounded dignity! He's been shot! Stabbed! With a pitchfork! Wait – that's third-act stuff. Okay, okay, okay, so Kurt Power is in the rain, he's shirtless, he's wounded, like, emotionally, and with a pitchfork... the camera angles around... "

Niles leaned forward, his breath caught in his throat. This, at last, was the moment.

"The camera angles around, and he's... he's balls deep in a hen."

The breath in Niles' throat expelled itself in a coughing fit. "*What?*" he spluttered, reaching for the glass of water that still hadn't arrived.

Dean stared fixedly at him for a moment, then relaxed completely, leaning back in his chair as though nothing had happened. "Actually," he said calmly, "I don't know if now is really the right societal moment for a Kurt Power movie to really *thrive,* you know? I don't think the culture's ready for it."

"Did you just say –"

Dean waved the question away. "There's a right time and a wrong time, and this is *nearly* the right time, but it's the *wrong* time, you know? It's like – Kurt Power is really *now,* but it might be just a little bit *too* now. Like maybe we should just hold off a little, just until it's a little bit *then,* just to really maximise the whole now-ness of the property..." He tailed off, staring into the distance again. Niles looked over at Maurice, who was grinning and nodding as if all this made perfect sense.

After a moment, Dean steepled his fingers and looked straight at Niles. "I'm going to get real here, Miles. I mean, like, for *real* real. I *love* your stuff. The whole wounded-dignity-of-the-working-man thing, the whole Kurt Power thing, the whole..." He thought for a second. "Ordering water. Old school. I love it."

Niles looked around. The waitress was nowhere to be seen. Apart from the three of them, the restaurant seemed to be completely deserted.

"I love *everything* you do," Dean continued, "but what I want to do is *share* the love. Introduce my guys at Talisman Pictures to the *real* Miles Goland – the man, the writer, the total package. Really sell them on you, show them you've got what we need, you know? You with me?"

Niles wasn't sure he was, but he nodded anyway.

Dean grinned, leaning back. "I mean, right now, we've got this project that's almost at the screenplay stage, so I'm looking for people to send in pitches – I mean, you've written screenplays, right?"

Niles thought of the unsold screenplay for *Sinfection*, lying at the bottom of a box of ancient tax paperwork in his study, and nodded again.

"Do you remember *The Delicious Mr Doll?*"

Niles didn't nod this time. He grinned like a kid.

THE DELICIOUS MR DOLL, made in 1966 and still available in DVD bargain bins today, was one of many attempts by various studios to spoof, supplant and otherwise ride on the coattails of James Bond. It was also the thirteen-year-old Niles Golan's favourite film of all time.

The Talisman Studios of 1966, having failed to anticipate the secret agent boom, had looked at Connery's Bond in a slightly desperate attempt to work out what could possibly be missing in the formula, and decided that the answer was camp. Enter Dalton Doll, Agent of Y.V.O.O.R.G. (Young Valiant Operatives for Order, Right and Good, which a grown man had at one point been paid real American currency to think up.)

Doll was, by day, the lead singer of swinging pop combo The All Together, which was made up of himself and five glamorous female assistants in bikinis – his 'Dolly Birds,' numbered one through five. By night, he retired to his sumptuous 'pleasure pad' to lounge about in a kimono awaiting orders from Y.V.O.O.R.G. – which, in this film, involved infiltrating an organisation made up entirely of beautiful women who planned to blackmail the world with an inhibition-lowering gas.

Niles Golan, age thirteen, had loved it.

It was an oddity he'd discovered late one night on Channel 4, long after his parents were in bed. Later in life, when the question of his favourite film came up at parties – usually dull ones – he would claim that it was *Apocalypse Now*, and would even go so far as to pretend to like the music of The Doors. But first, his mind would travel back in time to *The Delicious Mr Doll* – in particular, the scenes with Anouska Hempel in a tight-fitting black latex cat suit. While embarrassment had prevented his adult self from actually owning a copy, the teenaged boy inside him still nursed a phantom erection over the movie, and would always be listening for the creak of parental feet on the stairs.

*　　*　　*

NILES SWALLOWED, NOT wanting to give his excitement away. "I... I think I might have seen it. Once."

Dean nodded. "Fantastic! Okay, let's go in close. Now, what we do *not* want – absolutely, positively do not want – is a remake, okay?"

Niles nodded.

"Hollywood is lousy right now with that – remakes, reboots, whatever, it's just like... like digging up graves and stealing corpses, you know? It's all these bland, imagination-free assholes admitting that there aren't any original ideas left in the world, that all there is is this endless going back to the past... I mean, everyone hates remakes. Remakes are *over*. When a studio says they're doing a remake it makes me want to be sick, actually physically sick." He stared balefully at Niles for a moment. "So what we're doing here – and I want to make sure you understand this – is *not* remaking a movie. What we're doing here is taking a movie from the past and *making it again now*." He leaned forward, looking Niles right in the eye. "Only *better*."

"Um," Niles coughed. Maurice shot him a warning look.

"We're looking," Dean said, warming to his theme, "for a complete re-imagination of the core concept here, okay? Like, all that camp stuff, the 'sixties stuff – get rid of it. Junk it. Everything that's not relevant to here and now, to 2013? Toss it out. It's crap." Dean scowled, as if the idea of camp was a rotting carcass someone had left on the table.

"Bang up to date. Right." Niles nodded, wondering when exactly he'd accepted the job of writing a new *Mr Doll* film, and whether he should clarify things like his contract or the rate of pay. "So just to be clear, you want me to –"

"But that doesn't mean we don't want retro," Dean said, leaning forward. "I mean, retro is very big right now. It's huge. Like, the whole 'sixties stuff – the *cool* 'sixties – that, you keep. You know, with the Dolly Birds, that revolving bed, the suits, the army of chicks, all that stuff. Keep it in. It's what people come to see. You could kind of do it ironically, maybe..."

Niles nodded. "Right. So, a spoof? *Austin Powers* type stuff?"

"No," Dean shook his head impatiently, "no spoofing anything. This is going to be a dark take, a serious reflection of the times we live in now, okay? Like, the chick army – what are they called?"

"F.L.O.O.Z.Y.," Niles said automatically, without thinking. "It stands for Feminist Liberation Of –"

Dean cut him off, wincing. "Christ, lose that."

"I suppose it does sound a little –"

"You put feminism in there and you lose the guys. Now they're, like, Occupy, like they want to kill all the rich people and blow America up. But they still wear bondage gear. Dudes love that."

Niles would have wondered if someone had slipped something into his water, if it had ever arrived. "I'm sorry?"

"Bondage gear, leather, latex, all that stuff. Everyone loves it. It's edgy, you know? And maybe our guy, Doll – is there a way we can make that less gay? – maybe our guy has, uh, some drones he can use? Predator drones. That way we can get into that whole debate about whether we should use drones to take out terrorists safely and cleanly or allow them to invade America and murder our kids." Dean looked painfully earnest as he dangled another fry, swaying it to and fro for emphasis. "Like, maybe there's this lady lawyer who Mr Doll's banging who says the drones are killing too many terrorists or something, some bullshit, but it turns out she's one of the lesbian Occupy chicks so he kills her. With one of his drones. Like, just put the conversation out there in dramatic form, okay?"

"Right. Let me see if I've got this clear," Niles said, slowly. "You want me to write a new version of *The Delicious Mr Doll –*"

"Current title is just *Mr Doll*," Dean said quickly.

"A new version that isn't a remake, but is a... re-envisioning..."

"See, that's a great word. That's why you're the writer, Miles."

"...which is very 'sixties retro but also bang up to 2013. And you want to keep the Dolly Birds and the leopard-skin bed that revolves but you want to handle it all in a very serious and dark way. But with lots of latex and leather outfits. And at some point the main character has to engage in a debate – I *say* debate, but more of a physical fight – about the use of drone warfare." He paused, feeling his temples throb.

"Yes," Dean said, smiling widely. "That's exactly right."

Blazing with fury, the author drew himself up to his full height. "The Delicious Mr Doll *is not my favourite film,"* he intoned, in a voice of thunder, "not anymore. That would be Apocalypse Now. All the same, I will not assist in the desecration of what I'm sure some people would call a work of art, and one that helped them, I assume, through a very difficult adolescence. You have wasted my time, my agent's time, and your own time, and furthermore the water I ordered has still not arrived and the décor in this hole is hideous beyond description. And now,"* the writer continued, picking up the man's

bowl of cold, glutinous fries and upending it on his head,
"you may go. I wish you satisfaction, sir, in mangling Mr
Doll to your heart's content – for you will never do the
same with Kurt Power!"

The man from the studio gasped, shocked at the sheer
unfettered machismo of the author's gesture of contempt
– and then clutched his hand to his heart and slumped
to the floor. The scene had been too much for the frail,
black organ.

He was dead!

"Justice is done," the author murmured, in a tone of
cold contempt.

"I suppose I could do that," Niles said, slowly. "When did you want the pitch, exactly?"

Dean thought for a moment. "I'll need something for the day after tomorrow."

Niles frowned. It was quicker than he'd like, but he was confident he could throw something together. "Can we, um... talk about pay?"

Dean waved the question away. "We can 'talk turkey' later" – he did finger quotes and winked at Maurice – "on the basic rate for the screenplay, but if we ended up using yours for the translation, you'd get incentives for this film plus any new ones in the franchise, so..."

Maurice sat up straight and grinned, showing his gold molar again. Niles looked at him, then back at Dean. "I'm sorry, translation?"

"Talisman Pictures is taking this whole *Mr Doll* thing very seriously, Miles. We're creating a brand new Fictional for the franchise." He chuckled. "I mean, I say *we*, you know, we'd handle the look of him, but..."

"But I'd create him." Niles said, leaning forward. "I'd create Dalton Doll's personality. Something I wrote would enter the world as a living being. Something I created..."

"Well, technically something some guy in 1966 –" Maurice started to say, and shut up. Niles was staring into space.

Dalton Doll reached out a hand. His creator took it in a firm grip and pumped twice. Then Doll turned to the window, looking out at the beauty of the world he had been given. As the studio executives looked on, in awe of the creative talent that had brought this new being into existence, Doll took a deep breath, savouring the sweetness of the air.

"You're a good Joe, Niles," he breathed, in the authentic voice of the working man of the mid-'sixties. "You sure are a gosh-darned good Joe."

Niles smiled, reaching out to shake Dean's grease-coated hand. "Well, then. Let me just say that it's a pleasure to work with you."

CHAPTER THREE

THE BAR WAS called The Queen Victoria. Occasionally Niles found himself wondering if the owners had been at all inspired by *Eastenders*.

It seemed unlikely, somehow – the people who ran it were a friendly gay couple from Oregon, rather than ex-pats wanting to create a taste of home – but at the same time, the dark, wood-panelled walls, the charmingly imperial decor and the faintly musty carpeting might have been pulled in from a fictional reality.

Which was, he thought, oddly fitting. After all, The Victoria was where Niles went to drink with Bob.

Aside from Ralph, Bob Benton was the only other Fictional Niles knew. Which made it all the more curious that, over the course of the past ten years, he had assumed the post of Niles' best and only friend.

BOB BENTON'S FICTIONAL biography went as follows: he was a 'bio-chemist' – an update from the original origin given to him in the early 'forties, when he'd simply been a pharmacist – who'd discovered a concentration of 'formic ethers' that had given him fantastic strength. Donning a costume with a skull and crossbones on the chest, a yellow cape, and a domino mask, he set out to protect the citizens of Bowery Bay – a city invented especially for the television series Benton had starred in – as The Black Terror.

Benton's real-world origin story was significantly more complex.

As a character existing in the public domain, The Black Terror could – within reason – be used by anybody, with no fear of legal action. As with Frankenstein or Charlie Chan, anyone could put out a Black Terror comic, or a Black Terror movie. The Black Terror TV show in the 'sixties, starring Lyle Waggoner as Benton and Peter Deyell as his young ward Tim, had been popular enough to create a wave of 'Terrormania' across the United States, and while there were plenty of attempts to cash in on the situation, only the official merchandise and tie-ins – starring copyrighted characters and locations created for the show like Commissioner O'Driscoll, Terrorgirl and Swing City – shifted significant units.

More than twenty years later, ParaVideo Entertainment examined the phenomenon and decided that it might be worth making a Black Terror movie, complete with the kind of big budget and big stars that would, hopefully, re-ignite the 'Terrormania' phenomenon. After all, while they couldn't hold the copyright on The Black Terror, they could certainly hold the copyright on a Fictional for at least as long as his contract lasted, if not longer – and it would be that Fictional on whom the action figures, T-shirts and other merchandise would be based. Legally, it was foolproof.

So the first Robert Benton – chemist for a pharmaceutical firm, general polymath and citizen of a dark, neon-lit and grimly camp metropolis named Cryme City – was born, in early 1988. The next year, *The Black Terror* earned almost $500 million at the box office, and nearly twice that in merchandise, making a continuing franchise inevitable. Over the next nine years, Robert Benton made three more films, although as time went on the direction became increasingly shoddy. The later episodes pushed the formula so far towards camp comedy – of a particularly ill-conceived sort – that the fourth film, *The Black Terror And Tim,* barely made a profit on the domestic front. It was decided that Robert Benton would be released from his contract, but given first refusal on any new sequels, should the studio ever feel the need to make them.

One year later, the first Robert Benton committed suicide. He left no note.

When the second Robert Benton – Bob – heard the news, he felt as if he himself had died.

"SEE, I ALWAYS knew." Bob said quietly, taking a long sip of his beer – he preferred the real thing, rather than ginger ale or apple juice.

He'd picked up the taste after *The New Adventures Of The Black Terror* was cancelled – since then, he'd grown a thick beard and let his black hair grow rougher and shaggier than it had been, but he was still unmistakably TV's Terror, beloved by a generation who'd been glued to his exploits even as the first Benton's star had faded. He'd made a career for himself as a relatively well-known voice actor, and had even managed to get small roles in independent films and – his proudest moment

– as a mass murderer in an episode of *CSI: Miami*. But for the most part he was still thoroughly typecast from the role that had created him. Even the voice work had started to run dry.

He put the half-empty bottle down with a grimace. "I always knew the studio – Nestor – created me because of *him*. Because of Robert. Because he was so successful, he made them so much money. I was just the... the cheap knock-off. There were times when I hated him for that – which is crazy, because he was me." He scowled, and took another swig. "But for a few minor details – city names, supporting cast – we were the same person. At the very least, we were close enough to be brothers. Born from the same father – that platonic ideal Benton, the one who only exists on paper." He chuckled to himself. "Or Richard E. Hughes. I had to look him up. Died in 1974, or I might have found him and given him a piece of my mind. I don't know why more of us don't do that – confront our gods."

Niles coughed nervously, wondering when the right moment would be exactly to tell Bob his news. He didn't like interrupting Bob while he was having one of his existential crises, but at the same time this was hardly a new topic of conversation.

"So," Bob said, "when I heard Robert was dead – killed himself, for fuck's sake, totally out of character – I felt like... like the reason for my existence was gone. Like another side of *myself* was gone. I started wondering if he'd done it because of me, because when I was translated he lost any kind of uniqueness, any individual status he had. Never mind what the judge said." He looked into the distance for a moment. "I mean – look, my show was cancelled before his last film, sure. But that was an *artistic* choice. We wanted to quit while we were ahead,

I thought I could have a career, the writers thought they could have another big hit with their show about the guy who can turn invisible in water..." He sighed heavily, shook his head again, and drained his bottle in a few gulps.

Niles shrugged. "*Sea-Thru* did all right. It got a full season."

Bob snorted. "On DVD, sure. Well, anyway... we ended on a high note, at least. A lot better than what happened to Robert. I mean," he said, warming to his theme, "can you even imagine what it's like to be rejected like that? By the public, by the people you were created for, to be told you don't *matter,* while all the time there's another version of you... *basking...*" He spat the final word like a curse.

Niles looked over at his friend, hesitated a moment, and then ventured a question. "This wouldn't be about Rob, would it? Benton number three?"

Bob snorted. "For fuck's sake, Niles. What do you think?"

THE SECOND BOB Benton – the man who would, in the fullness of time, become Niles' best friend – was created to cash in on the second wave of 'Terrormania' by filling a void the first one, somewhat foolishly, had not. There were three things that hadn't occurred to ParaVideo: firstly that the general public might want more Black Terror after they left the movie theatre, secondly that they could provide a supply for this demand by producing a regular Black Terror TV show, and thirdly that someone else might have the idea first.

In 1991, the Nestor Communications Company became that someone. Their television arm had been debating the best way to spend their translation budget, and – with a second Black Terror movie on the way and the character still very much in the public domain – another Bob Benton, just different enough to avoid copyright claims, seemed like an ideal use of the money. What had to be changed would be changed for the better – they'd re-introduce Tim as the Terror's sidekick, but change him to a her, a vivacious brunette who'd remind the Dads in the audience of the long-missed, never-forgotten Terrorgirl. In place of Furst's chilly, art-deco Cryme City, with its endless darkness and neon, they'd set the action in Bowery Bay, an ersatz San Francisco with as many sunny days as gloomy nights. Most importantly, instead of the cold, calculating Robert Benton – whose humour seemed limited to the occasional barbed quip and who seemed quite willing to kill criminals as long as their bodies could be immediately hidden off-screen and forgotten – they would create a warmer Benton, more melancholy, carrying an inner sadness in place of the frozen heart of the movie version.

Not so much a 'Robert,' the memo said. *More of a 'Bob.'*

Bob Benton was the first 'duplicate' Fictional, and his appearance on the Hollywood scene caused a stir in the gossip magazines and – once ParaVideo were informed – in the courts. The landmark ruling – that duplication of public domain characters contravened neither ParaVideo's established copyright nor the right of all Americans, Fictional or otherwise, to their own unique identity, just as long as there were definite physical and psychological differences between the different versions – opened the door to a fascinating world where Zorro could fence against Zorro outside Mann's Chinese Theatre, or two entirely different Draculas could sit under parasols on the beach, discussing the relative merits of a third and fourth in their thick Transylvanian accents.

It also opened the door to Rob Benton, the third Black Terror, whose newest film – a nastily half-baked examination of modern politics wrapped up in a superhero cape, of the kind that Dean had clearly been attempting to get Niles to rip off – had just shattered all known box office records. Rob was angry, conservative, over-muscled, given to putting on a ridiculous voice when in the mask, and apparently almost impossible to have a real conversation with. Audiences couldn't get enough of him.

BOB STARED AT his empty bottle with an air of loathing. "Did you see the clip online of that little bastard screaming at the sound man? And *that's* The Black Terror now. Christ. I had a voice gig for a Terror videogame last year – they wanted me to do it in that stupid voice of his, that dumb croak. They kept saying, *no, make it deeper, make it growlier* – eventually nobody could understand what the hell I was saying. They said it wasn't working, paid me for the morning and threw me out. Not even the full day. Assholes."

"Well, did I tell you my news?" Niles smiled, telling himself it'd be a good idea to get Bob's mind off his problems. Bob had been created to be somewhat morose – morbid, even – and Niles felt a distraction from his ever-present black cloud would be welcome. Besides, it was big news, and it wasn't like he hadn't heard this particular song and dance from Bob before.

Bob sighed, rolling his eyes. "Is it happening at last? Am I finally going to get to meet Kurt Power – is there going to be a *team-up?* I mean, I've heard so much about the guy."

Niles was vaguely hurt by the tone. *Bob was obviously jealous, the writer reflected, smiling inwardly at the depth of his insight into the human condition. But even in a world where Kurt Power existed, Bob would still be a valued friend. Less valued than Kurt Power, admittedly, but still valued for all that.*

"Not quite," Niles said, getting the barmaid's attention. "Two more over here." He turned back to Bob, smiling genially. "You're in the ballpark, though."

Bob looked up as the beer arrived, narrowing his eyes slightly. "Seriously?"

Niles smiled, paying for the drinks and adding a hefty tip. "Have one yourself while you're at it." The previous beer had put him in a magnanimous mood, and there was a small part of him that was considering buying a round for the house to celebrate recent events. But aside from himself and Bob, the only other customer was a very striking woman with red hair and a glass of white wine watching the TV, and Niles felt that the gesture might be misinterpreted. And if a gesture like that was going to be misinterpreted, he thought to himself, he'd rather Bob wasn't around to get in the way. He smiled, admiring her dress – 'sixties retro, a multi-coloured op-art pattern. A good omen.

He turned back to Bob. "Seriously what?"

Bob frowned, picking up the new bottle and taking a brief swig. "You get to create a human being?"

"A Fictional, yes."

Bob shot him a look. "You don't need to say it like there's a difference."

Niles frowned, puzzled. It was the second time today he'd been accused of realism, and he was starting to resent the implication. If there was any realism going on, it was reverse realism – these Fictionals assuming every womb-born human automatically thought less of them.

"You're the real realist here," the author murmured, drawing himself up to his full height. The Fictional, caught by his logic, could only stare at the bar top and reassess his entire life. He immediately apologised and left, allowing the author to get to know the fascinating red-haired woman unimpeded.

"You're the..." Niles swallowed. "I mean, you're not being fair. There *is* a difference – quite a few differences, actually. You've not aged a day in all the time I've known you, for a start." Niles lifted a finger to his receding hairline, pointing to the grey hairs that were starting to come in. "Not a problem for you. One shave and a haircut and you'd be in your mid-twenties again."

Bob shook his head, looking pained. "God, don't talk about that." He spoke through gritted teeth, clutching his bottle of beer so hard that Niles feared it might break. "If I got a grey hair tomorrow, it'd be the happiest day of my damned life."

Niles' brow furrowed. "I don't see how that's possible..."

"You don't! Why am I not surprised?" Bob took a swig, looking bitter, and then stared at his drink for a moment. "Sorry. It's been a rough couple of days. I should thank you for the beer."

"Yes, you should," Niles muttered reproachfully.

Bob gave him a wan smile. "Come on, then, Niles. Let's hear it. Who is it you're translating? One of your own? You've got that other detective character –"

"Madeleine Sorrow." Niles winced as he said it. Madeleine Sorrow had been a forensic pathologist and ex-porn star with an estranged daughter who solved violent crimes in Edinburgh. Niles had never been to

Edinburgh for longer than a day visit, but he felt he knew it intimately after watching *Trainspotting,* and Irvine Welsh's trick of writing phonetically had appealed to him.

He'd written two books with her, the second of which, *The Cursed Moon* – about a serial rapist who targeted menstruating women – was filled with the kind of searing social commentary and powerfully erotic sexual content that Niles had created Madeleine Sorrow to better express. It was still held up occasionally in places like *The Guardian* and *The London Review of Books* as being one of the worst books ever written by a human being. *Private Eye* had devoted three pages and a particularly well-realised cartoon to ripping it apart. It had only been published in England, and was the main reason he'd left.

Niles had never written a single word featuring Madeleine since, although part of him still considered that decision to be the literary world's loss. *"They made their choice," the author sneered as he set the match to the unfinished manuscript – a manuscript that could have ended sexism forever. "Let them live with it as best they can."*

"No," Niles mumbled, "not Madeleine Sorrow." He cast a quick glance over at the red-haired woman, as if the mere mention of Madeleine Sorrow would send her running from the bar in disgust – then hurriedly cast his eyes down to the wood of the bar top when he saw she was looking back at him curiously. "Not one of mine at all."

Bob nodded. "Don't keep me in suspense."

"It's, ah... have you ever heard of *The Delicious Mr Doll*? It's a kind of secret agent film..."

"Sure. I think you told me about it once – kind of swinging 'sixties stuff. *Austin Powers,* right?"

Niles smiled tightly. "Probably one of the main influences on it. I never saw *Austin Powers,* myself." He'd looked at the poster for the film and had the uneasy feeling that the film would have been laughing at him as much as the secret agent genre, and he'd never watched it to find out if he was right. "Anyway, they want to make a new *Mr Doll* film, and they've asked me to pitch. If they like what they see... well, they'll get out the translation tube and I'll be shaking hands with Dalton Doll himself."

Bob took another long swig of his beer, eyeing Niles carefully. "I need to visit the bathroom," he said, after a pause.

Niles blinked quizzically. "What? Why?"

Bob laughed. "Because I need to piss. Jesus, come on."

Niles pouted, irritated at Bob's reaction. He'd expected a different one – not awe, exactly, but congratulation, at least. For goodness' sake, he was about to have a hand in the creation of a living being – one of Bob's own! A *little* bit of awe wouldn't go amiss. "You're not changing the subject," he said officiously. "I want to know what you think."

"All right, fine." Bob thought for a moment. "Okay, let me try and put it into words. What I said earlier about confronting our gods..." He paused, frowning. "I actually did know the guy who created me – on the writing side, anyway. A guy called Malcolm Stuyvesant – he was the head writer, they call it *showrunner* now, on the *New Adventures.* On *Sea-Thru* too, plus I think he wrote a few episodes of *Buffy* or *Angel* or one of those, but... the mid-'nineties were his time to shine. He's not done too much since. Anyway, he's the guy who wrote the series bible, the personality description, everything the technicians worked from. I mean, obviously when you're translating a new Fictional, you put a little more thought into it than you do if you're just making up a protagonist... right?" He looked at Niles pointedly.

Niles nodded briskly. "Oh, of course." He didn't like the implication that he hadn't put a great deal of thought into Kurt Power. He knew everything there was to know about Kurt Power's life, from his eye colour (a steely blue) to his favourite song (it varied) to where his daughter went to school (it varied).

"So this guy Malcolm, the lead writer... I got to know him pretty well. I mean, we worked together for as long as the show was on. He'd bounce ideas off me, let me ad-lib a line – towards the end, he was practically letting me co-plot the thing. He'd throw situations at me and ask me what my next move was, we'd write episodes that way. I wonder why more shows don't do that."

Niles smiled. *The New Adventures Of The Black Terror* wasn't really his thing – it was a little too camp for his liking, and the whole premise of a costumed adventurer felt like a trope designed for pre-literate children – but he had to admit that every episode he'd watched had rushed along splendidly, and there'd never been any point where he thought Bob wouldn't have said or done what was on the screen. Contrast the fifth season of *Cutner's Chair,* in which the viewer was asked to believe Ralph Cutner was mesmerised by the romantic charms of a female patient who clearly bored him senseless – Niles could hear the raging arguments on the set between Ralph and the writer in question in every line of dialogue – and you did, indeed, start to wonder. Some people, Niles thought, just didn't know how to use Fictionals properly. "So," he said, taking a sip of his beer, "you had some filial feeling towards him?"

"I never said that."

Niles blinked, confused. "But surely you thought of him as a father figure –"

Bob shook his head. "No, no. Jesus, Niles, I know what *filial* means. I've already got a father – Rex Benton. Criminologist, gunned down by racketeers, left me his secret lab, yadda yadda. I mean, he wasn't *real*, sure, and he's dead, but the guy was still my dad. No, Malcolm was my *creator* – my main one, I mean. There's a big difference. That's what I think you don't realise." He got up off the bar stool, towering over Niles. "He was a nice guy, but the thing is that we never really got on well – not outside of work, anyhow. As soon as the show finished, we pretty much stopped talking to each other... listen, I *really* need to go..."

Niles blinked. "Why?"

"Because my bladder feels like it's going to explode. Back in a second."

"No, I mean –" Niles started, but Bob had walked away, towards the toilets. On the way, he stopped to take a look at a flyer for something called META MEET – probably a band. Obviously not in that much of a hurry to pee, Niles thought bitterly.

He sighed, taking another sip of his pint, then looked over at the redhead. She was still looking at him, her head tilted, and he found himself risking a smile and a nod. There was something about her that was very striking – something about her hair and her eyes – but he couldn't quite work out what. It wasn't that she was beautiful, exactly – beautiful women were ten-a-penny in LA, and in that context she was nothing particularly special – but there was something in the way she held herself, in the retro clothing. Something oddly distanced – artificial, even. Every movement she made looked like a performance.

He suddenly realised he was staring, and shifted his eyes to the news report playing out on the TV above her head. The words SHERLOCK HOLMES MURDER leapt out at him. He nodded to the barmaid. "I'm sorry, can you turn that up a little?"

"– coming to you live from the scene of the murder." A reporter in a dark suit was speaking to the camera in front of a pawn shop of some kind, as police attended to a taped-off area behind him. "We're not sure what Sherlock Holmes – and to avoid confusion, I'll reiterate that this is the modern-day Sherlock Holmes, the one whose new show finished its first season on HDI just a few weeks ago – we're not sure what he was doing on Camerford and Vine exactly. There is a Subway here, he might have wanted to eat something – what we do know is that at around seven-twenty he was brutally struck from behind by an unknown attacker who, ah, crushed his skull with repeated blows from some kind of heavy object –"

The reporter was interrupted by the woman at the news desk. "I'm just going to stop you there, Phil – do the police have any idea of the motive for the attack? Why kill the new Sherlock Holmes?"

"It's hard to say, Joanne –" The reporter looked around, as if trying to seek someone out. "It's possible that the attacker might not even have known he *was* Sherlock Holmes. Remember, this was a modern incarnation of the character, so unlike most of the more, ah, historical Fictionals, he would have been dressed quite normally..." He seemed to catch sight of someone off-camera, and made a quick beckoning gesture. "Actually, we have some people here with ideas on that – Sherlock Holmes and, uh... and Sherlock Holmes. If I could just ask you guys to step over here a moment –"

Niles blinked as two more Sherlock Holmeses wandered into shot – one tall and thin, with a roman nose and the full deerstalker-and-pipe outfit, the other shorter, moustached, and looking altogether more pugnacious, wearing a loose-fitting shirt in a vaguely Victorian style. Niles recognised the second from recent movie posters – he was a more action-packed, violent Holmes, who'd been dreamed up by the Nestor Brothers studio to put a new spin on the mythos. He vaguely recalled another, earlier Holmes working as a consultant on that film – probably the taller one, who looked more like the classic model.

"Mr Holmes," the reporter turned towards the shorter Holmes, before pausing to rethink the question. "Mr Holmes of 2009... I understand you've been discussing the situation with the investigating officers –"

"I have been discussing the situation with the officers," the taller Holmes said in an icy tone. "My companion has been taking notes on the deductive process. Unfortunately the budget for his translation did not extend to inculcating him *in utero* with the proper degree of intelligence to apply my methods –"

"Steady on, old chap," growled the shorter Holmes in a wounded tone. Niles noted that his accent had some American undertones – either poor programming in the voice, or an attempt to sway the US audiences.

"My dear fellow, each to their own," the taller Holmes said, sucking contemplatively on his pipe for a moment before removing a magnifying glass from his cape and studying the asphalt beneath his feet. "Were we engaged in a situation calling for use of the fistic arts, or the commandeering of a runaway horse-and-carriage, I would gladly cede authority to you. But this is a matter of deduction and in such matters I remain your superior... ah!" The taller Holmes paused, bending down and studying the ground carefully for a long second.

The reporter opened his mouth to ask another question, but thought better of it as the taller Holmes rose to his feet again, holding what looked like a human hair. "Almost invisible against the tarmac. Sherlock, my good fellow" – he nodded to his fellow Holmes – "what do you make of this?"

The shorter Holmes peered at it, frowning. "A thread of some kind. Tweed, I'd say. Where do you suppose it came from?"

"First, consider the murder weapon. A large, heavy object, almost certainly metal, but also containing enough glass to provide the slivers we found by the body earlier. If we add that to the grains of pipe-tobacco we discovered on the dead man's clothes..."

The shorter Holmes shook his head impatiently. "The thread, man! Where did it come from? A blazer, perhaps?"

The taller Holmes smiled paternally. "Who would wear a tweed blazer in Los Angeles in the middle of an unusually hot spring? No, my dear fellow, it's quite elementary. In fact, I can answer you off the top of my head." He calmly lifted off his deerstalker, holding it next to the thread. "You see? It could almost be from this one. It's not, of course – the pattern is subtly different – and besides, you are my alibi."

The shorter Holmes took a step back, staring in horror. "Holmes, you're not saying the murderer is –"

"One of us, my dear Wat –" The taller Holmes hurriedly corrected himself. "My dear fellow. We have eliminated the impossible and what remains must now be the truth. The killer smoked a pipe, he wore a deerstalker hat, the murder weapon was a heavy magnifying glass – ergo, either he was engaging in a particularly outré means of throwing the police off his scent... or the killer was none other than Mr Sherlock Holmes."

He turned back to the reporter, but the reporter was unable to do anything but stare.

"Jesus," Bob said, and Niles realised that he'd returned from the toilet a minute or two before. He'd been so absorbed in the drama unfolding on the screen that he hadn't noticed. He quickly looked around for the red-haired woman, but she was nowhere to be seen.

"It doesn't seem real," Niles said, taking a long pull on his pint. "It's like a spoof broadcast. Insane."

Bob chuckled dryly. "That's what happens when you invite fictions into the world. They bring fiction with them. This isn't much different from that Dexter Morgan business."

"Well, they got to him in time," Niles muttered. Bob gave him a sideways look. "What?"

"See, this is my point," Bob said, choosing his words carefully. "I'm just wondering if you understand what you're getting into. This isn't some literary fantasy where you get to meet your own character and have a beer with him while he tells you how great a god you've been. Bringing someone imaginary into the real world isn't a thing you can predict." He pointed his bottle at the screen, where the reporter had finally recovered his wits enough to go back to the studio. Needless to say, the hunt for the killer Holmes was now the top story. "Look at this. Because somebody decided to translate me, even though there was already a 'Bob Benton' out in the world, we get this, this knock-on effect. And now we've got a situation where there are about fifteen different Sherlocks running around LA and one of them might be a killer. I guarantee that's not how Malcolm and the rest of the bright boys at Nestor saw this whole thing working out."

"We-ell..." Niles considered. "It's not like there's already a Dalton Doll. And if I make one, there aren't likely to be any more..." He frowned. "So really, I'm not sure how this applies."

Bob sighed. "I'm just saying that your actions are going to have consequences. The guy you invent is going to exist in the world – the real world, not just some movie where the worst thing that can happen is you get a bad review. I mean..." He pointed at the screen. "Let's say Sherlock Holmes did just kill someone. I'm betting you can trace that back to some bad writing on somebody's part. Whoever translated that guy is going to get lawsuits up the wazoo." He hurriedly threw up his hands, noticing the look Niles was throwing him. "Not that I'm saying you're a bad writer..."

"No, of course not." Niles scowled. "Since when does The Black Terror talk about people's wazoos?"

Bob smiled. "Well, there you go. Bad characterisation. Like I say, Niles, you've got to watch what you put in here." He tapped his head twice, then turned and signalled the barmaid. "Same again over here, please."

CHAPTER FOUR

From the screenplay for THE DELICIOUS MR DOLL
(1966), by Hutton H Hopper & Jean-Paul Vitti:

<u>INT. DOLL'S "PLEASURE PAD" - NIGHT.</u>

DOLL opens the door to usher KITTEN into
the room. She slips off her MINK COAT,
holding it in the air until the AUTOMATIC
COAT-STAND rises out of the floor and hooks
it. Underneath, she's wearing a very short,
VERY low-cut MINI-SKIRT DRESS made from
GOLD COINS and GOLD-EFFECT GO-GO BOOTS. We
get a GOOD LOOK. Doll SMILES.

DOLL:

Somebody oughtta put you in Fort Knox,
sweetheart.

KITTEN:
Fort Knox couldn't afford me.

DOLL presses one of the studs on his WRIST
COMMUNICATOR and a ZEBRA-SKIN LOVE SEAT
lowers itself FROM THE CEILING.

DOLL:
I'll bet. Take a load off those
dynamite stems, baby - drink?

KITTEN nods. As she SITS, DOLL moves to the
AUTOMATIC DRINKS CABINET.

DOLL:
One Old-Fashioned. Substitute White
Horse for Bourbon, hold the cherry.

(He looks her over, particularly HER LEGS)

And a Pink Squirrel for the little
lady.

A hatch in the device OPENS, revealing THE
TWO DRINKS. DOLL takes them both, handing
the PINK SQUIRREL to KITTEN.

KITTEN:
You know my drink. Impressive.

DOLL:
Some things you can tell about a woman.

KITTEN:

Oh? Like what?

DOLL:

Like maybe somewhere along the line
she's gotten her pretty head all filled
up with a load of fancy doubletalk.

KITTEN:

And I suppose you're just the man to
talk me back around?

DOLL:

Baby, anyone who says lips like yours
were made for talking is a grade-A,
certified nut.

KITTEN:

You're quite the charmer, Mr Dalton
Doll... Agent Of Y.V.O.O.R.G. That's
right, I know a few things about you,
too.

KITTEN reaches into her BEE-HIVE HAIR-DO
and removes a SMALL BUT DEADLY PISTOL. She
AIMS IT at DOLL.

KITTEN:

Don't move an inch.

DOLL:

Until a moment ago, I was moving
several. That's a pretty gun for

a pretty girl, but don't think I won't take it away from you.

KITTEN:
You'd be wise not to try, Mr Doll. A single explosive bullet from this gun can kill a charging bull elephant - I'd hate to waste one killing you.

DOLL:
Well, I'm kind of like an elephant myself - in the trunk department. Listen, sweetness, you're playing a dangerous game here and unlike that dress, it's way too big for you. Why don't you quit now before I have to get tough?

KITTEN:
Don't be a fool. You honestly think you stand a chance against the might of F.L.O.O.Z.Y.? You're nothing but a worm under our heel - and just like a worm, you're for the birds, Dalton Doll. Now - take off your clothes.

(She smiles, EVILLY)

I want to personally search you for weapons.

DOLL:

(Hand moving to his CUFFLINK)

Start with this one, gorgeous -

He triggers the DART GUN hidden in his
CUFFLINK and shoots a PARALYSING DART into
her wrist.

KITTEN:

My arm! I can't move it!

DOLL:

(taking the GUN from her)

That's enough of that - now, talk!
Where are F.L.O.O.Z.Y. holding the
Dolly Birds? I know you're up to your
pretty green eyes in this caper, so
spill!

(he SLAPS her, hard)

Come on, spill it! Talk!

(he SLAPS her again)

I said talk, sister! Tell me! Now!

(he SLAPS her again)

- at which point the phone rang.

* * *

THE FIRST THING Niles had done after coming home from the bar the night before was to download a copy of *The Delicious Mr Doll*, which he hadn't gotten more than fifteen minutes into before falling asleep. The next morning, after breakfast, he decided to tackle it fresh, with his notebook in hand. He made a couple of vague notes during the credit sequence, a self-consciously psychedelic affair involving each member of The All Together playing their instruments over a flashing pastel-coloured background, but after that he'd become absorbed in the story – such as it was – and in his own memories of adolescence. The notebook lay forgotten on the coffee table in front of him.

When Dalton Doll's 'pleasure pad' first appeared on the screen, with his mini-harem of Dolly Birds fussing about him in their oddly shapeless 'sixties dresses, Niles found himself smiling fondly, if a little ruefully. As a teenager, it had been his idea of a dream home – at the time he might as well have wanted a base on the moon, but now that he looked around his apartment, at the striking minimalist furniture and the Richard Hamilton prints on the wall, he had to admit he'd come fairly close. He might not have a hat stand he could summon from the floor or a zebra-skin love seat he could drop from the ceiling, but he had an espresso machine and a lava lamp, and if he didn't have a harem yet it was hardly for want of trying.

The thought jarred. *Was* he trying? Not to get a *harem*, for God's sake, that was ridiculous, but just to – well, get involved with someone? Meet new people? To, to put it bluntly, get laid?

It had been three years since the divorce – and the unpleasantness that had triggered it – and the realisation hit him that he hadn't made a serious effort to meet anyone in all that time, which was... bizarre, considering how he'd behaved before then. He'd mostly been working on his novels, or spending time with Bob and – some of his other friends had stuck around, surely? – or he'd been having his therapy sessions with Ralph. What social life he had aside from that consisted mainly of launch parties and publicity junkets, and while he did plenty of looking – ogling, even, this was still LA – he always seemed to have an excuse not to 'seal the deal.'

"Good God," he muttered to himself. "Seal the deal." He sounded like one of those idiots who wrote seduction manuals. *How To 'Neg' The 'Hotties': A Kurt Power Manual.* That was a bad sign. Something was obviously starting to curdle.

Now that he thought seriously about it, the woman he spoke to most regularly – and also the last woman he'd been in any way intimate with – was Iyla, which seemed... off, somehow, in a way he couldn't quite put his finger on. He'd have to speak to Ralph about it at their next session.

He sighed, shaking the thought off and allowing his mind to return to the movie. It had reached one of his favourite parts – the casino scene, featuring the first appearance of Joi Lansing as the delectable Kitten Caboodle. Niles found himself perking up. As she leaned forward over the roulette table to serve Dalton Doll his Old Fashioned – "hold the cherry" was evidently thought by the screenwriters to be a serious rival for "shaken not stirred" – Niles reflexively did the same, as if he could somehow peer further down her top than the cameraman had managed to, and when Doll got her back to his pad and she revealed *that* dress, his hand began, almost unconsciously, to reach down and unbutton his fly –

– at which point the phone rang.

"Damn it," muttered Niles, flushing slightly as he scrabbled around for the smartphone buzzing on the table in front of him. Surely the studio couldn't need their pitch yet? Or was it Bob, ringing to apologise about his rudeness last night? They'd ended the evening amicably enough, but Niles had spent the taxi ride home fuming, recalling Bob's tone when he'd referred to Kurt Power and the future Dalton Doll. How *dare* Bob imply that Niles wasn't a good writer?

Niles blinked at the display. It was Iyla.

The synchronicity unnerved him. He considered ignoring it, but his thumb, seemingly on automatic pilot, slid across the display to answer the call.

"Hello, Iyla?" He already regretted answering, but he was committed now. He put the film on mute – he could always come back to where he'd been later, and besides, his putative erection had gone back to sleep at the first sight of her name. He wondered exactly when it was that she'd begun having that effect on him.

"Niles, hi. Listen, it's not a biggie – were you working?" Her voice was brisk and rich, with a slight hint of the stronger accents of her parents. They'd hated him, of course, particularly at the end when she'd finish most nights by retreating to the spare room and calling them in floods of tears. Her father had once threatened to beat him to death with a tire iron, and it had taken a lot of restraint and understanding for him not to call the police.

"*Yes, I was working,*" the author said, as if speaking to a child. "*I'm always working. I can never turn it off, not for a second. To me, breathing and writing are the same. When you plunge me into the cold waters of our dead*

love, stop my work, stop my breath – I begin to die."
With that, he crushed the phone with a single clench of his
powerful hand, and returned to making his copious notes.

Perhaps he would thank her at the Oscar ceremony –
for nothing.

"No, no, nothing I can't..." he tailed off. On the screen, Doll and Kitten – now naked but for a discreet op-art bed sheet – were locked in a passionate embrace. She was mouthing the words *"real man"* into his earlobe. That bit, he realised, might have to be updated for modern audiences. "Nothing important. How have you been?"

"I've been fine. Things are great. Look, the reason I'm calling is that I was opening up one of the boxes..."

Niles frowned. "Still? It's been years."

Iyla sighed. "I've been busy, okay? And – look, I don't know if you noticed, but that was kind of a painful time for me. I mean, I couldn't even look at those damn boxes for a year – I bought a whole new wardrobe, new furniture..."

"I thought you looked different that time..." They'd met for coffee on New Year's Day of 2011, more than ten months after it had all fallen apart – that whole ugly business. Niles hadn't wanted to, but Iyla had insisted they make some attempt to mend fences. Her therapist was telling her to forgive and forget – or try to, anyway.

"Yeah, I had that pixie cut. Don't know what the hell I was thinking, I walked out of that salon thinking I'd made the mistake of my life – well, present company excepted." She laughed, letting him know it was a 'joke.' He frowned. "If you'd said anything about it then I might have killed you, but fortunately you just droned on and on about this terribly original idea you were working on about some terrorists who'd actually got hold of a nuclear bomb..."

He could hear the sarcasm in her voice. "For your information, *Edge Of Doomsday: A Kurt Power Novel* reached number 19 on the US bestseller lists last September."

There was a pause. "You didn't." Niles heard her laughter on the other end of the line. Once upon a time, making her laugh like that would have been the highlight of his day. "You did! You put it out on 9/11!"

"9/10," Niles replied, stiffly. "The Monday. And it was an arbitrary date, nothing more."

"I cannot *believe* you sometimes," He could hear her take a drink of something to calm the fit of giggles. "Ohh, boy. Every time I think I've hit the limit with you, you still manage to surprise me, you know that? It's kind of adorable now I don't have to live with it."

Niles pursed his lips. "Listen, Iyla, when I said I wasn't working – well, technically speaking –"

"Sure. Sorry. I'll get back to why I called." She was still smiling – he could hear it in her voice. He could remember the first time he'd seen that smile – a launch party for Linda's book, the one about the wolf-girl, or possibly the one with the family of otters. Iyla had seemed so exotic to him – was that racist, he wondered? No, of course not, it was a compliment – exotic and alive, wearing a sharply-cut skirt-suit that showed off her legs, while Linda flounced around in a grim floral sundress that came down to her ankles and seemed designed for a commune in the 'seventies. He'd spent the whole evening finding little excuses to talk to the fascinating Indian girl – *Indian-American,* he corrected himself, *as opposed to Native American, that's Red Indian* – and avoiding Linda, who'd eventually made a noisy demand to leave. She'd been in floods of tears as he'd driven her home – he didn't remember formally ending it then, but then he hadn't really needed to, given the circumstances. Realistically the whole thing had ended long before, anyway, before she'd even moved to San Francisco with him. It was when she'd stopped smoking and started putting on the weight.

Of course, eventually Iyla ceased to be the exotic other and became the woman who caused fusses at perfectly innocent flirtations, but he wasn't to know that then.

On the screen, Joi Lansing and Anouska Hempel were about to do their big dungeon scene. Kitten was at that moment being chained to the wall by two well-built black women in red and yellow spandex, while the evil Ms Harridan, leader of F.L.O.O.Z.Y., waited in the wings. Niles lip-read the words *"honey-chile"* from one of the henchwomen and winced. Best to get rid of that, too. "Sorry, I was distracted for a minute. You were saying about the box?"

Iyla sighed. "It's not that big a deal. I can call back later."

"No, tell me now." Niles said, pausing the film. "You were unpacking a box, and..."

"And it's one of yours. It's got a whole bunch of your old CDs in it. And no offence, but I'm not having your shit taking up space in my life. I figured I'd give you a chance to take them off my hands – I'm home all Wednesday."

Niles thought. "I've got a therapy appointment on Wednesday."

"What, for the whole day? Look, I'm not paying postage. Either you come get them or they go to the Goodwill. Actually, it's not like anyone uses CDs any more, I'll probably just throw them away –"

"Don't be hasty," Niles said hurriedly, "I could import them onto my laptop. It might save me some money on iTunes. Which albums are they? Are you sure they're mine?"

He heard the sound of cardboard being dragged across carpet, and then the click of plastic on plastic as she sorted through them. "Let's see... Gustav Holst, that's yours. Mike And The Mechanics, Dire Straits, U2... Josie And The Pussycats, that's definitely yours... *Terrordance...*"

Niles winced again. "That's not mine –"

"I've got *Purple Rain* here, and that's absolutely one of yours. Your music taste was frozen in ice with the woolly mammoths."

"Not *Terrordance*, though." Niles rubbed his temples. "I mean, God. *Terrordance*. Where did *that* come from?"

There was a brief pause. "I have no idea," Iyla said, although from the sound of it she probably did. Some impulse buy she now regretted. "That goes to the Goodwill, I guess."

"If they'll take it." Niles sighed. "All right, might as well go through the lot. I'll stop you if there's anything I don't want." He leaned back on the couch, staring at the frozen image of Joi Lansing, caught in mid-writhe, listening to Iyla reel off a short list of albums he remembered buying, most, if not all, from the time before he'd met her. He found himself wondering if this particular box had ever been unpacked during their time together. Maybe it was a metaphor for their relationship – although if it was, it was a metaphor that included him buying *Terrordance* on CD, and that wasn't a metaphor he was quite prepared to accept. "Hold on," he said suddenly. "What was that last one?"

Iyla sighed. "The *Donnie Darko* soundtrack. That's definitely yours, it's all 'eighties music."

Niles shook his head, sitting up straight. "No, I remember you buying that. We'd just gone to see the film – you remember, it was 2001, we were still living in San Francisco –"

Iyla scoffed. "I hated that film."

"You only hate it now because you saw the Director's Cut. When you saw it in the cinema you thought it was great. And you *loved* the music, you thought that was the best part –"

"Where are you *getting* this from?" Iyla sounded incredulous. Did she really not remember?

"After the showing," Niles said, surprised at the urgency that had crept into his voice, "we headed down to that restaurant you loved, the Italian one, and we walked because it was all downhill and on the way there was a Best Buy, and – and you'd been talking about the soundtrack, about how great those old Tears For Fears songs were and how they felt really fresh in a lot of ways and you wanted to hear more of them, and we passed a Best Buy and you just went right in and bought the album. I *remember* it. You actually jumped up and down when you found it, you had this big smile, your eyes were shining –"

"Okay, okay," Iyla said down the line, sounding a little disturbed. "It's not yours. I'll give it to the Goodwill."

"And afterwards, in the restaurant, you kept taking it out and looking at the track listing, and you were in such a good mood –" Niles couldn't seem to stop himself talking. "You were in such a good mood because of the film, and, and because you'd just had a job offer in LA for twice the salary you were on, enough for us to get a really nice apartment, and... I remember the way you said *us*, like it was a given, not like... like you were asking if there was an *us*, if I was going to leave. Like it was... well. A given." He paused, taking a breath, but Iyla didn't interrupt. He knew he should just stop talking, but the words just kept coming out. All of a sudden they seemed very important to say. "And after dinner, we went back to your place and I, I stayed over, and..." He swallowed. "And the day after, I said I'd walk back to mine, not take a cab, since it was such a mild day. And on the way... on the way I saw the ring in the jeweller's shop window. And I had to buy it."

There was silence on the other end of the line.

"Because... because you were the one." He said it quietly, flatly. There was a lead weight in his gut.

More silence. He could hear her breathing – steady, controlled.

"Iyla?"

"How many other women did you screw while you were married to me, Niles?" she said, quietly. "I counted at least three, but I'll bet there were a lot more."

Niles groaned. "Iyla –"

"I remember there was Bobbi," she said, methodically, like she was making a list of the types of birds native to California. "Now her I wrote off as an early mid-life crisis, like getting a motorcycle or hair plugs. It was pretty obvious you weren't serious about her, it was just... I don't know, proving to yourself you could get a twenty-year-old into bed. Jacking off your ego. You were already bored of her by the time I found out." Her voice was cold, the tone she'd had then. He felt sick.

"Iyla, that didn't mean –"

"Save the clichés for your crappy books, Niles." That one stung. He felt a flush of anger spreading over his face, mixing with the guilt. "So I just figured you were a little boy who needed a little toy, and maybe now you'd, whatever, sown your oats, maybe that was it. And maybe I decided to myself that the fact that you didn't just scrape me off like shit on your shoe and run to the newer model, the way you did with Linda – and yes, I know I was an idiot to even start with you after that – meant that maybe, *maybe* I was somehow special to you."

"Iyla, you... you were, I mean you are –" he stammered, then cursed himself. More clichés. He slumped back on the couch, holding the phone out in front of him, staring at it, at her name, while her voice echoed hollowly from the plastic.

"And then two years later along comes Justine. Justine the fucking *Head of Marketing,* so you don't so much screw her behind my back as in front of my fucking face –"

"You never said anything –" Niles muttered, rubbing his forehead. He'd honestly been surprised to find out that she'd known about that – he'd assumed he'd covered his tracks perfectly. That had been part of the thrill, the adrenaline rush from the sneaking around. He remembered it had already started seeming like hard work when she'd found him out, but Justine hadn't wanted to end it. She'd been too old for him anyway. Once he realised how much effort she put into looking attractive for him – how saggy and lined she was under normal circumstances – most of his interest in her had died.

"Maybe I am a cliché," the author thought to himself. And then he ended the call, because there was no point continuing it. He simply switched his phone off and went back to work. The end.

"No, I never said anything. For three months. I spent two and a half months telling myself it was nothing, that she was ten years older than you, not your fucking *type* – and then my folks were visiting and I couldn't say anything in front of them and you were sneaking off to fuck her *while they were sleeping in the fucking apartment* – and then when I finally, *finally* get the courage together to tell you I know, after I've seen you fucking her with my own eyes, and thanks for *that*, you son of a bitch, you told me *how hard for you it was!*" She was screaming into the phone. He found himself wondering if the neighbours could hear it, if they thought it was part of the film.

"It was hard," Niles mumbled. *The writer ended the call. He put the phone down and ended the call, and then he dropped his phone in the toilet. All it took was the smallest movement of his thumb and the whole ordeal was over.*

The thumb didn't move.

"'Oh, she's so clingy,' you said. 'It was supposed to be this casual thing and she wants more, I don't know what to do...' I had to leave my *job,* you fucking asshole! You were so fucking cowardly about it I had to *end your affair* for you! Your affair with *my fucking boss*! I couldn't stay! I had to go back to *children's books*!" Niles could tell Iyla was crying now, although she was almost managing to hide it. He moved the phone back to his ear, feeling numb. "I should have left you then. I should have just fucking kicked you out right then..."

Niles remembered – the couples' counselling they'd tried for half a year, until Niles had called it off, unable to deal with the implied judgement Dr Alder loaded every single sentence with. Then the sessions with Dr Loewes, on his own – what a waste of money *that* had been.

Eventually, he'd come to the realisation, after Justine had stalked his Facebook page with vague threats to go to the press and tell them everything – threats she thankfully never carried out – that he'd been a fool. Possibly even a sex addict. LA was the town for it, after all. Somehow, the marriage had survived, and for a couple of years – and yes, during that time there had been the occasional one-night stand, but if he was a sex addict it couldn't be helped – it had been almost healthy. Not quite the blissful time of old, but he'd been happy, and for all he knew she had been too.

And then, of course, he'd met Danica Moss.

"Listen, let's not... let's not talk about this anymore," he heard himself pleading, his voice weary, drained. He couldn't bear it if she brought up Danica. Not now.

There was a white-hot moment of silence on the other end of the line.

"Please," he said, hearing how hollow it sounded in his ears.

Iyla let out a long, slow breath. "All right. Let's not," she said, her voice shaking, and then Niles could hear the wet, snuffling sound of her blowing her nose. Eventually, she spoke again. "So you're getting therapy now?" Her voice still had that edge of bitterness. "Still think you're a sex addict?"

"No," he said quietly.

"So who is it?" she asked. "Anyone I know? Who knows, maybe we're going to the same one."

Niles hesitated a moment. "Um, probably not. Do you... do you remember Ralph Cutner?"

"Not really. Was he a friend of yours, or –" She tailed off. "Ralph *Cutner?*"

Niles said nothing.

"*Cutner's Chair* Ralph Cutner? You're seeing a Fictional for therapy? Is he even licensed?" She sounded like she didn't know whether to be disgusted or find it hilarious. Or both.

"Yes," he replied, "As a life coach." He could feel his cheeks growing hotter, though he didn't know why he was so embarrassed – about this, at least. It was her problem, not his. She'd always had a nasty streak of realism inside her, buried down deep – at least he'd always thought so. He remembered the way she'd treated Bob.

He cleared his throat. "Listen, there's no need to be *realist* about –"

"Oh, fuck you, Niles. As far as I'm concerned, you and he deserve each other. And I'm throwing all this shit away." There were four brief pips and the line went dead. Iyla's name vanished from the phone display.

Niles looked at it for a long moment, wondering if he should call her back – it'd be a shame to download all of *Beggar On A Beach Of Gold* again – and then he put the phone on the table, picked up his notebook, and restarted the film.

INT. F.L.O.O.Z.Y. DUNGEON - NIGHT.

KITTEN:
You can do what you want with me,
Mizz Harridan. But you'll never turn
Dalton Doll into one of your limp-
wristed half-men!

Niles sighed, making a quick note. Get rid of that.

He's one hundred per cent male -
an A-1 swinging stud! He knows the
truth about what a woman wants -
that every 'no' on a lady's lips is
just a plea for a real man to make
her say 'yes'!

"Oh, Christ," Niles moaned, grimacing. Definitely get rid of that. Who wrote this, anyway? What were they *thinking?*

```
            MS. HARRIDAN:
    I see. It seems Mr Doll is the one
    who's turned you, Miss Caboodle. Well,
    perhaps I can convince you to come
    back to the winning side.

    (she cracks her WHIP in the air.)

    I can be very persuasive.


            KITTEN:
    You twisted monster! You're no woman
    - you're a devil in drag!

MS HARRIDAN TAKES HOLD OF KITTEN'S FACE,
TURNING HER HEAD so that their EYES LOCK.
Then she SLOWLY DRAWS HER THUMB over
KITTEN'S LIPS.


            MS. HARRIDAN:
    My my. Such a spitfire.


SHE MOVES AWAY, and a LARGE PLASTIC TUBE
SLIDES OUT OF THE WALL to ENCLOSE KITTEN.
Inside, she STRUGGLES HELPLESSLY. We get a
GOOD LOOK.
```

Niles felt his cheeks burning. He felt like an adolescent again – a stupid adolescent watching the only pornography he could find. He kept expecting his mother to burst in. The fact that his erection was starting to come back only made him feel worse.

```
          MS. HARRIDAN:
     I hope you retain your passion when
     you come to serve me again - as a
     woman should serve a woman. Release
     the gas!
```

There is a HISSING SOUND as the INHIBITEX GAS begins to FILL THE TUBE. PSYCHEDELIC LIGHTS flash in KITTEN'S EYES and SINISTER THEREMIN MUSIC PLAYS. She RESISTS, struggling HARDER.

```
          KITTEN:
     No! I'll never be - like you! You're
     sick - evil! Something's twisted your
     mind, turned you against nature! Women
     weren't meant to rule the world - we
     need men, don't you see? Only a man
     can truly fulfil a woman! Only a
```

"God." Niles angrily switched the TV off. "Get rid of it," he muttered. "Get rid of it all."

CHAPTER FIVE

"Bob?"

"What?" Bob groaned. "What do you want?"

The author shook his head sadly. The Fictional's voice sounded truly wretched, limping out of the phone and into his head like a wounded soldier emerging from a bombed-out trench. Obviously, the man had continued to drink late into the night after their parting – perhaps to dull the guilt he felt at his snide insinuations about the writer's craft. "I'll forgive him," the author thought, magnanimously. "His own nature has proved punishment enough."

"Late night?" Niles asked, trying to keep the grim smile out of his voice.

"No later than yours." Niles could hear Bob gritting his teeth. "Just a sick headache, that's all. Probably a migraine coming. What do you *want*, Niles?"

"Well, to tell you the truth," Niles said, "I'm not having that fantastic a time myself. I'm completely blocked on this *Mr Doll* thing and... well, I'm just having a terrible morning." He decided not to tell Bob about the row with Iyla. They'd always acted a little strangely around each other, probably because of Bob's Fictional status. Iyla's reaction to the news about Ralph Cutner had only confirmed her closet realism in his mind.

Best not to burden Bob with it, anyway. "So I was thinking... lunch? My treat."

Bob groaned wearily into the phone. A bad sign. "I can't, Niles. Not today. It's not a good day." He sounded like a man on the verge of collapse.

Niles frowned. "You're sure? It might take your mind off your troubles. I, ah, I can pay..." He tried to be as delicate as he could about the fact that Bob had no work coming in at the moment, and increasingly limited funds. He'd freely admitted to Niles the week before that he wouldn't be able to pay the rent on his place past August. Niles had offered Bob the couch, but Bob had declined, saying that he'd have somewhere he could move into if the need arose. He was fairly tight-lipped about where that was – Niles hoped that didn't mean it was under a bridge somewhere.

"Not a good day, Niles. Not a good day. I'm staying in bed." He coughed, a great hacking mucus cough that made Niles yank the phone away from his ear as if some of Bob's snot would come tumbling out of an app. "Jesus, I hope I'm not getting flu..."

"Can, um, can Fictionals get flu?" Niles asked, and immediately wished he hadn't. "So, you're, you're absolutely sure you're not coming out?" He blustered on, before Bob could respond. "Because I really could use a listening ear –"

"Well, that's why God invented therapists. Or in your case, life coaches. Ow." Bob groaned. "Listen, do me a favour and let me die in peace, will you?"

Niles laughed, trying to get Bob engaged in the conversation. "I think I missed the part of the Bible where God invented the life coach..." It was a weak joke, and he knew it. Still, he was confident if he could keep Bob talking, he might agree to –

"God died in 1985," Bob muttered, and ended the call.

Niles stared at the phone for a moment, then scrolled through his contacts for another number.

"Buddy! How is every little thing?" Maurice seemed to be feeling much more chipper than Bob was.

Niles smiled to himself. Maurice's enthusiasm always had an uplifting effect on him, and he was starting to feel a little better already. *The agent sounded eager to treat the author to a lavish meal – a meal well deserved after* Pocketful Of Posies: A Kurt Power Novel *had been delivered a mere six weeks after the prescribed deadline.*

"Well, it's been a bit of a pisser of a morning, if I'm honest," he said. "Had a blazing row with Iyla – my ex-wife –"

"Hey, don't talk to me about ex-wives," Maurice interrupted, "I got two of them and let me tell ya, the day Aline becomes number three cannot come soon enough. You ever meet Aline?"

"Once," said Niles, wincing. It wasn't a pleasant memory.

"Well," Maurice chuckled, "don't you worry about me, buddy. I got wife number four lined up right now. She's a massage therapist – you get my meaning?" Another chuckle. "So anyway, how's the pitch going, huh? What's your genius idea for *The Dangerous Mr Doll?* That's your new title, by the way. No need to thank me, it came to me in a dream. The universe wants this to happen, buddy."

Niles bit his lip. "Well... funny you should ask about the pitch, because..."

"Because it's done! I knew it! Lay it on me, Niles. Tell me how you're bringing the swinging 'sixties screaming into the right now." Maurice lapsed into an expectant silence on the other end of the line.

Niles marshalled his thoughts. "Well."

"Don't leave me hanging here! C'mon, start us off the way God intended. 'We open on,' dot dot dot..." He paused, evidently waiting for the magic to happen.

Niles wasn't feeling particularly magical. "The thing is, Maurice," he said, picking his words with care, "I've realised *The Delicious Mr Doll* may, perhaps, not actually be... well, very good. At all."

He waited for a response from Maurice. There wasn't one.

"I mean, obviously I loved it when I was younger. I still do! It's a camp classic – of its kind, anyway. But when I, ah, look at it with a *writer's* eye... well, to start with, it's a bit unreconstructed."

Nothing.

"When I say unreconstructed, I mean sexist. Aggressively. It's, it's very misogynistic indeed."

Still nothing.

"And I think it might be a little bit homophobic as well, at least when it comes to gay men. And, um, and lesbians. Also it's racist. A little bit. Probably. It's, it's hard for me to tell, but now I come to think of it I'm reasonably certain that it probably almost definitely is quite racist." He swallowed hard. Still nothing. "Maurice?"

"Wait, that's it? That's everything?" Maurice's voice echoed from the speaker. "I thought we had a real problem. Just tell anyone who asks it's hard-hitting and controversial, you'll be fine. Listen, buddy, I've got faith in you, I know you're going to turn this around, you're gonna make everybody very happy, but I got a, uh, a *massage* to arrange, so sayonara and all that jazz. You can give me what you got in a couple hours. Or tomorrow. Make it tomorrow. I got some, uh, *business* I need to take care of, you get me?" He chuckled in a way that made Niles think of filthy raincoats.

"Maurice, I don't even know where to start with –" Niles began, but he was already talking to a dead phone. He turned on the TV again, opening *The Delicious Mr Doll* in his queue and then idly scrolling to a random point somewhere after he'd stopped watching. Maybe he could get that sense of excitement back.

GUARD:

Ooooooooh, ducky!

"Fuck this for a game of soldiers," said Niles, crisply, turning it off again. "I need a drink."

"CAN YOU TURN it up?" Niles said to the barman, taking a fortifying gulp from his pint glass. "I want to see if there's any more news about this Sherlock Holmes killer."

The barman shrugged, turning the volume on the TV up a little louder. There was nobody else in the Victoria – unsurprising, since it was lunchtime and there were somewhere around a thousand places in that particular part of LA that would serve food better, cheaper and with more regard for the basic health regulations. Anyone coming to the Victoria for food – people without tongues, the suicidal – would have been treated, presumably in the interests of preserving a fictional 'Englishness,' to overdone sprouts, burnt steak and kidney pie with week-old gravy and a basket of greasy, heart-attack-inducing 'chips' that were to your average British chip-shop chips what Piltdown Man was to Homo Sapiens: primitive, embarrassing and fake.

Niles found himself vaguely hoping Dean would come in to sample them. While Dean choked on his inedible meal, Niles could inform the coked-up cretin of a few salient facts about Mister Dalton Doll.

"For instance," the author snarled, spitting his words into Dean's bulgy-eyed, powder-nosed little rodent face, "giving Mister Doll a fleet of Predator Drones to blow up Occupy Wall Street with is actually, believe it or not, fundamentally less 'dark' and 'edgy' and 'serious' than leaving the woman-beating little cherry-hater exactly as he is! Seeing that right now he's wandering the casinos of the world telling every woman who walks past him in a dress made of precious metals that the word 'NO' has always been at war with fucking Oceania!"

He grabbed Dean in two meaty hands, tore his head from his body, and crushed his skull to a fine white powder.

"Snort that, you freak," Niles muttered.

He stared at the TV, keeping a tired eye on the running news ticker for reports of the on-going Holmes controversy while some sports scandal played out above it. Partly, he was honestly curious about whether he'd dreamed the whole affair, but he also wanted to know if the murder would mean any changes to the laws that might affect future work. This was the first time a Fictional had killed anyone, after all. Although the victim was a Fictional too – did that make it less newsworthy, or more? He had a feeling that even asking himself the question had some realist undertones.

He sighed heavily. Thoughts of realism brought Iyla back to mind, and her reaction to Ralph. He'd have a lot to say to Ralph when they saw each other again. But would Ralph have anything to say back? Or would he just act like he did? Was he capable of anything else, in the end? Was Bob?

Niles shook his head, draining the rest of the glass, and tried to concentrate on the television. Suddenly, he didn't care about Sherlock Holmes or Ralph Cutner or Bob or any of the rest of them. He wanted to empty his head, not think about Fictionals for a while, about their endless existential issues. He probably was being a realist, but he didn't care. He focused on the screen across the bar. The Sports Desk. Excellent. That was still an arena for real people.

"– and finally," the sportscaster grinned from the screen, "we've got a story that takes us from the world of the stage and screen to the wide, wide world of sports with the news that the New York Yankees have signed none other than Joe Hardy, the Fictional baseball legend of the musical stage and screen, who most recently appeared in a performance of *Damn Yankees* at the Shaftsbury, London, England –"

Niles gave up. "Another pint of the usual," he said, shoulders slumped.

The sportscaster turned to a tanned, healthy young blonde man, seven feet if he was an inch, his body seemingly perfectly designed for the sport of baseball. "Joe Hardy – can I call you Shoeless Joe?"

"From Kokomo?" The big man on the screen laughed. "Just don't sing it, you'll have to pay royalties. Trust me, I know." Of course, his voice – speaking and, Niles assumed, singing – was a perfect baritone.

"I'll be sure to remember that," the sportscaster chuckled. "Joe, not all of the people watching are going to be, heh, *familiar* with musical theatre – can you give us a quick run-down of how you came to be and what makes you the perfect pick for the Yankees this season? A lot of people are calling this a stunt casting, so to speak."

Joe grinned – Niles could see that he spent most of his time grinning. A healthy glow seemed to radiate from him, out of the screen. Niles found himself scowling in response, like a vampire exposed to the sun. One of those would probably walk in to get out of it in a minute.

"Well, truth to tell, Sir, there's not much to it. The fellas at ParaVideo got the rights to the musical, decided to make a film of it, and, well, the short version is it's about a guy makes a deal with the Devil to be the perfect baseball player. So they figured they'd just go ahead and make the perfect baseball player, and then once the film was made I could hire myself out for stage versions and they'd get a big cut, and that'd justify translating me. And, well, here I am." He laughed again. "I don't just sing musical numbers. I've, uh, got a record out at the moment that might be a little more up folks' alley, uh..." He seemed genuinely shy about promoting himself – undoubtedly part of his character as a big, gentle lummox.

"Adorable," Niles groused, taking another big swallow of beer.

"'Take Me Out To The Ball Game,'" the sportscaster smiled. "Out on mp3 as we speak. It's a classic, I'm sure our viewers will agree. Now, Joe – as I'm sure you know – in the musical, you're actually a Washington Senators player. In fact, you actually play *against* the Yankees." His face fell, as if discussing news of the utmost gravity. "As you can imagine, this business of signing *with* the Yankees hasn't sat so well with your fans – not to mention the Senators themselves, who of course are now the Minnesota Twins. They're launching some kind of legal action, I believe?"

Joe showed his other expression – confused misery. From what Niles could remember of the musical, he pulled that one a fair amount, and his face certainly seemed built for it. "Well," Joe said, "I don't know much about that, I'm not the best with contracts or legal stuff, as you know..." He sighed heavily. "But, uh, folks seem to figure that... well, because I was created, uh, genetically, to be the best baseball player in the world... well, they figure, and I ain't sayin' they're right, but they figure that that's, uh..." – he swallowed hard, as if trying to gulp the word down before it could leave his mouth – "cheatin'."

"Not the first time you've been accused of wrongdoing on the diamond," the sportscaster said, sympathetically.

"No, sir, it ain't." Joe breathed another sigh of abject misery. "But before it was always just part of the show." He slumped down further in his chair. "Now it's real. I ain't sure I like that. Hell, I never wanted to sign for the damn Yankees anyway – why would I? I'm a Senators guy, through an' through! But... there ain't no Senators any more..." He sighed again, and the sportscaster looked nervously around the studio, as if expecting some hidden orchestra to burst into a song about hopes, dreams and devil's bargains.

"Oh, God, turn it off," muttered Niles, draining his second glass. "That was just depressing. And get me another, please." Behind him, he heard the creak of the door swinging open.

He looked over his shoulder, and froze.

It was the red-haired woman from the previous night. She was smiling at him.

She was wearing a blue summer dress, what looked like a grey faux-fur bolero jacket, and a pair of flat shoes. Niles wasn't someone who paid a great deal of attention to fashion – *"it ain't about the skirt, baby, it's about the gams underneath,"* the author heard Dalton Doll leer in the recesses of his mind, *"and those sweet stems go all the way up"* – but even he could see that it was an outfit that paid little or no attention to it at all. It seemed like an attempt to create the fashion of another era, far in the past, with whatever she could find. And who on earth wore fake fur on a hot spring day like today?

She had to be mad.

"And whatever the lady wants," he heard himself say.

The red-haired woman smiled a little wider, showing unnaturally perfect white teeth. "Thank you," she said, in a prim, English accent – pure Received Pronunciation – that might have seemed real to someone who hadn't grown up in Surrey. "I'll have a pink gin, please." Niles could hear the California hiding underneath her voice. He realised he was staring again, and began digging in his wallet for the necessary notes.

"Thank you," he said to the barman as the fresh pint and the gin arrived. The red-haired woman picked the glass up carefully, little finger crooked, as though she was drinking a cup of tea in some Victorian play, then placed it down again in the exact same spot before turning and smiling sweetly at him.

The performance seemed so mannered and artificial that Niles honestly didn't know how to respond.

The author smiled, fixing the striking girl's dazzling green eyes with a piercing gaze. "I'm not sure," he said, his voice betraying the subtlest hint of amusement, "that I caught your name."

Well, that would do. Niles wasn't sure he could get any subtle hints of amusement into his voice – not after two pints of pale ale – but he could at least try not to sound like he was in the middle of a minor meltdown.

"I'm... I'm not sure I caught your name," he stammered, and then forced a brittle smile. The smile the woman returned was quite dazzling.

"Liz Lavenza," she trilled in her artificially cut-glass accent, "from Geneva. An absolute pleasure to meet you, Mister..." She offered her hand in a way that suggested it should be kissed.

"Niles Golan." Niles took hold of her hand, shaking it a couple of times in a way that might, now that he thought of it, have been the most awkward physical act he'd committed with a woman since he lost his virginity. And he couldn't quite get his mind off the fact that neither the accent she was faking nor the one he could occasionally hear underneath it were in any way Swiss. She was a very strange person, this Liz Lavenza.

But she did have lovely eyes.

"I'm an author," he said, the words tumbling out of nowhere. "I write books. And, um, screenplays." Oh, God, where was this coming from?

She sniffed at his idle boasts, rising from the bar stool and leaving the place immediately, her gin barely touched. The author was left alone with his beer and his loneliness, to contemplate the utterly atrocious screenplay – singular – that he'd completed, and the pitch for the other that he was having trouble even contemplating. Realising the futility of his existence, he smashed his glass on the wood of the bar top and slit his throat in a single motion.

Get a hold of yourself, he thought.

"Oh, that's marvellous," she beamed, her face lighting up. "Do you know, I had a feeling you were – I heard a little of what you were saying to your friend the last time you were in here." She grinned. "It sounded like fun."

"Last night," Niles murmured. The coincidence of her coming back to the Victoria so soon – at lunchtime, when nobody came within a mile of the place – unnerved him in a way he couldn't quite put his finger on. Was she stalking him? No, that was insane. Paranoid.

Was she a regular here, then, like him and Bob? He didn't think he'd met her before, but then it wasn't like they were in every night of the week. Her name seemed familiar, though. Had he seen it before somewhere?

"It must be wonderful to be a writer," she said, interrupting his thoughts. She took a moment to sip her gin and look at him – a sly look, as if she was talking in a code he should know how to crack. "Making up all those characters. Inventing every little quirk of personality for them, then making them flit about the page and do whatever you want. Having complete control over every single little aspect of their lives." She smiled brightly, placing the gin back down, again in that very mannered way. "Without you, all those people would just be empty little dolls. Just sitting there with no story – well, they wouldn't even be that, would they? They'd be nothing." She tilted her head, looking at him like a cat looking at a mouse she'd caught. "Nothing at all. Tell me, does it give you a feeling of power?"

He stared at her for a moment, then shook his head, looking away. "Um, no. No, it doesn't, not really. Mostly it's just... very hard work." He took a long swallow of his beer. "Ah, mostly, you find out what your characters are going to do at the same time they do. You sort of write a sentence and... well, there's only really one way for it to end. So that's what the character ends up doing." It was an old speech, hard-worn from various interviews, and not fully true, but the truth of it was too complex to really put into words. Especially after two pints of pale ale.

Make that two and a half. He looked at his beer – already half gone, while her gin remained practically untouched. And this was his third, and it wasn't even half past one. Liz would think he was a drunk.

"Like life, then," Liz said, softly. She was looking at him playfully. "I'm not sure I like the sound of that."

"Well, not exactly like life," Niles said, smiling despite himself. "It's a bit more exciting. Beloved side characters die, and there's lots of sex and infidelity – and only a few locations, if you're on TV, because there's not much of a budget. And it'll probably end with someone learning some kind of lesson – you know, the moral of the story."

Liz burst out laughing. "That's *just* like life," she said, the California overtaking her voice a little, "you only have a few locations in that, when you think about it. *And* you've not got much of a budget." Her real accent made her sound far more attractive. "And every paper you pick up tries to tell you what the moral of the story is."

Niles shrugged, smiled, and drank. She *was* very attractive – there, he'd admitted it – but on the other hand this was turning into exactly the sort of unsettling conversation he'd switched off the TV set to avoid. Ever since he'd made the mistake of agreeing to pitch for that damned remake... ever since he'd taken on the responsibility for a new Fictional...

He paused, as an unpleasant thought struck him. Then he set his drink down again, and turned to look at Liz. She looked back at him guilelessly, her expression empty. His stomach lurched.

Was *she* a Fictional?

No. Surely not. He'd *know.*

Anyway, if she *was* a Fictional, surely he'd have heard of her? Unless, of course, she'd given him a false name. Maybe, on some subconscious level, he recognised her face. Was *that* why she seemed so interesting to him?

Oh, God, he hoped not. He didn't want to be a pervert.

He took another sip of the beer. Was she one of those 'manic pixie dream girls' he kept hearing about, the ones who were always popping up in TV shows these days? She might headline a sitcom, for all he knew – that would make sense. Why not just ask her?

"Are you a Fictional?" The author asked, quietly.

"Oh, my God!" The girl screamed, eyes wide with horror. "You actually think I'm a Fictional? Why, I've never been so insulted in my life, you foul, wretched little man!" She slapped him hard across the face before turning on her heel and walking out of the author's life forever. Later that day, her father, hearing of the insult, had him killed.

Niles decided he'd have to ask anyway. Although maybe not quite so directly. "Have I... have I seen you somewhere before...? Maybe on the television?" He felt like he was playing twenty questions. "A sitcom?"

Liz looked at him, with those green eyes of hers, and he felt his mouth go dry, his throat closing up. She leaned forward, looking very deeply, very seriously, into his eyes.

"Perhaps," she said slowly, "I'm from one of *your* novels." She grinned, standing up straight again, her red hair bouncing around her flushed face.

"What?" Niles blinked.

"Maybe I got out. Stranger things have happened. *Maybe,*" she teased, "we're going to fall in love. Despite ourselves. *That's* the kind of thing that happens in stories, isn't it?" She tilted her head again, looking mischievous. "But the question is, am *I* the kind of person who happens in stories?"

Niles just stared at her.

"Oh, look at the *time!*" Liz gasped, grabbing her pink gin and knocking it back in one gulp, then slamming the glass down and hurrying to the door. A moment later, she was gone.

"She's quite mad, of course," the author said to the barman, who nodded soberly.

"I've seen the type before, sir. Manic pixie dream girls, we call 'em. They're nothing but trouble, mark my words." He spat into a glass for emphasis, before wiping it with a dirty rag.

The author nodded, sucking ruefully on a briar pipe. "Still, she did have the most wonderful eyes..."

"Not to mention gams, sir. Dynamite stems, as Dalton Doll would say."

Niles winced, shaking his head. His habit of self-narration was starting to get out of control. The barman came over as he finished off the rest of his third beer. "You want another?"

Niles shook his head. "No, I shouldn't. I've got to..." He tailed off, staring into his empty glass. What did he have to do this afternoon?

Oh, yes. He had to watch *The Delicious Mr Doll* again and try to think of a version of the lead character that wouldn't feel like he was unleashing a cross between a men's-rights-advocating baboon and a two-fisted plague of syphilis into the world of human beings.

"Set 'em up," he sighed.

CHAPTER SIX

```
DOLL PUTS KITTEN over his KNEE and
SPANKS her - for her part, she SQUEALS
and WIGGLES DELIGHTFULLY. We get a GOOD
LOOK. RAUCOUS MUSIC PLAYS. Eventually,
DOLL PULLS HER ROUGHLY back to HER FEET.

              DOLL:
So what do you say now, sugar?
Any more big ideas in that pretty
little brain of yours about world
domination?

              KITTEN:

(breathily)

Not a one... Mister Dalton Doll,
sir.
```

They KISS as the DOLLY BIRDS CHEER.
Behind them, F.L.O.O.Z.Y.'s VOLCANO BASE
EXPLODES.

THE END

NILES SLUMPED INTO the couch, groaning. Get rid of that.

After the fifth pint, he'd made his way home, steeled himself, and started the movie again. With the alcohol in him, it was actually kind of enjoyable, or enjoyable enough – lurid trash, but no more lurid and thoughtless than some things that had come before or after it. Now that he wasn't being distracted by the ghosts of erections past, he could even see the things in it that had made it his favourite film – yes, even counting *Apocalypse Now*: the avant-garde direction, the high-fashion costumes, the gorgeous op-art of the sets. Joi Lansing's pitch-perfect turn as the admittedly problematic female lead – even Anouska Hempel turned in one of the better performances of her career, although she'd still done her best to get the film removed from sale in the UK. And Duke Mitchell brought a surprising amount of nuance to the part of Dalton Doll, adding a patina of irony that smartly blunted the worst of the dialogue. Maybe the drink was re-applying the rose-tinted spectacles he'd come to it with, but now that he'd gotten used to watching it with adult eyes Niles had to admit that it was a fascinating piece of work.

The real problem was that he had no way to make Dalton Doll interesting. Maybe – if he took the overtones that Mitchell had supplied as far as they could possibly go – he'd end up with some kind of post-ironic send-up of 'lad culture,' twenty years too late to be relevant, or a bargain-basement version of Seth MacFarlane or the Wayans Brothers. If he played it straight – unless it fell into the hands of some kind soul who'd rewrite it and take all credit and blame – it would pretty much kill his screenwriting career stone dead, which would essentially mean no living, breathing Kurt Power, or at least not one that hadn't been filtered through another writer's sensibilities.

And the *real* problem – the *really* real problem, to quote Dean – was that either direction would loose a monster onto the world. Oh, Dalton Doll the Fictional would have some safeguards in his personality so he wouldn't be utterly sociopathic – people had learned their lesson after the first Dracula had died from a garlic allergy, and learned it again after the *Dexter* debacle, and presumably this Sherlock Holmes business would lead to even more safety features – but he'd still be a creep. He'd give interviews and sound bites to the press about feminazis and legitimate rape. He'd write books about how to pick up women by 'negging' them in clubs and doing cheap little magic tricks. He'd run for Governor of California.

And if Niles sanded off every last rough, unpleasant edge... what made him interesting? What were his flaws? He couldn't just be a spy with a drink problem and a voracious sexual appetite – that was James Bond. He couldn't just be a spoof James Bond with 'sixties overtones – that was Austin Powers. The serious, dark Bond was Jason Bourne, or possibly Ethan Hunt – although nobody talked about him any more, not since what had happened on the set of *Mission: Impossible II*. Aside from Bond as socially backward misogynist – more so than usual – it had all been done, and the misogynist direction was the one Niles was having so much trouble with. It was a mess.

Idly, he let the closing credits wash over him, soothing his mind with the jangling of psychedelic guitars. Was that The Chocolate Watchband? It'd be about the right period... Niles leaned forward, shaking himself awake, studying the credits to see who'd provided the music.

He blinked, rewound the credits a second or two and paused the film.

SCREENPLAY by HUTTON H HOPPER
& JEAN-PAUL VITTI

Based on "THE DOLL HOUSE"
by FRED MATSON

'Based on'?

FROM THE PARSNIP AV Clubhouse '*TV Review*' section:

DOOR TO NOWHERE, "The Doll House" (Season 1, Episode 27, originally broadcast 12/5/1961)
AV Clubhouse Grade: **A-**
Community Grade: **A** (Sign in to vote)
Reviewed by **Marcus Trowbridge**

So what have we got here?

Well, we've got William Shatner ramping up his natural tendency to play to the back row just enough to deliver one of the all-time great performances of his career. And we've got a guest director in the shape of Christopher Barry – fans of our Classic Who Review will remember that name – who allows Shatner to be Shatner when the script needs it, matching him beat for beat as the intensity rises to the final climax, but pulls him back for the quieter moments, including the haunting final shot of Shatner's soldier turning his wooden rifle over and over in his hands as the sound of cannon fire grows in the distance. (But we're getting ahead of ourselves.) It's some of the director's earliest work, and something of an oddity in that it's the only work he ever did for a US production company. (For those interested in the bizarre intricacies of the relationship between the BBC and Talisman TV, including the full story of how Barry came to direct "The Doll House" and the ideas it gave him for his work on "The Daleks," there's a fascinating blog entry here.)

So with Shatner and Barry we already have lightning in a bottle. But what elevates "The Doll House" to one of the greatest half-hours in television history – if, tragically, one of the least watched – is the writing. Fred Matson, on only his second script for the programme, produces what is easily his best work. proving for the first time that *Door To Nowhere* can be more than just *Twilight Zone Lite*, that it can actually ask the kind of heavy social and existential questions that will go on to make it a distinct show in its own right in the upcoming seasons.

On first glance, the plot relies on a fairly simple 'twist' of the kind that *Twilight Zone* has already done better: William Shatner plays a soldier –

dressed somewhat incongruously in the manner of a British redcoat - who finds himself, without explanation, in the grounds of a large mansion, run - and ruled - entirely by beautiful young women. There are other redcoats already there, but they seem brainwashed, content to drink tea with the women and take them for promenades around the grounds, while Shatner is keen to return to the war, fighting with his fellow 'captives' and even - in the episode's most queasily visceral moment - driving his bayonet into the stomach of 'Barbara,' the Mansion's apparent ruler. (Barry zooms in sharply at the moment the bayonet plunges in before cutting to Shatner's face, glistening with sweat, horrified at his own actions. When we cut back to the face of Diana Millay as Barbara, utterly unperturbed - of course, there's no damage, no sign of any wound - it's as big a shock to the viewer as the violence itself.)

The incident with the bayonet - Shatner's first real exposure to the power of the weapon he constantly carries - creates a change in him, and over the second half of the narrative he comes to accept his imprisonment, finally agreeing with his fellow soldiers that an endless life of platonic pleasure in the Mansion is a far better option than returning to a war that he knows almost nothing about.

Of course, no happiness in an episode of *Door To Nowhere* can last for long - its willingness to go for the bleak ending was what marked it out from its rivals even in these early days - and all

too soon the soldiers start vanishing from the Mansion one by one, and Shatner learns from Millay that "the one who had you first" has discovered his presence in their idyllic retreat and he must now leave them forever. Shatner tries to resist expulsion – railing against the force that controls him in what has to be one of the most Shatnerian performances of all time – before we cut to an argument between a young brother and sister in a suburban home. The brother rescues the last of his wooden toy soldiers from his sister's doll house, where she's been using them to provide romantic companions for her Barbies (or 'Barbaras' – presumably Mattel didn't approve the use of their product). The brother returns the red-painted soldier to his own room, after extracting a solemn promise from his sister that she won't use his toys for "sissy stuff" ever again. As the boy gloats over his reformed army, talking to them about how he's gonna "make 'em fight," we cut to Shatner, marooned on a misty, featureless battlefield, staring at his rifle and the deadly bayonet, listening to the sound of war coming closer. Unlike the very early episodes, when *Door To Nowhere* was still aping its spiritual father, there's no closing narration here – no cuddly homily to see us into the next programme. We simply fade to black.

It's not perfect, of course. In some ways, the episode is a victim of the times – in particular, toy fashions of the period. Barbie had just arrived on the doll scene, but her counterpart for the boys' demographic – GI Joe – had yet to appear,

and it's hard to watch "The Doll House" in the present day and not feel his absence. (Although having said that, I don't believe that GI Joe came with a rifle and bayonet permanently attached. The scene where Shatner tries and fails to put the rifle down is one of the most brilliant - and symbolic - moments of the episode.) I'd have liked it if Matson had been slightly more subtle with his names, too - not only does the title of the episode give the game away to an extent, but Shatner's soldier is actually called 'Sgt Billy Doll' in the credits, which is cringeworthy. Thankfully, he's never fully named in the script.

Probably the biggest problem is the acting. Not all the performances gel - Shatner is obviously magnificent and Millay strikes just the right balance between the peppy innocence you'd want in a "Barbara" doll and the otherworldly qualities you'd expect from the matriarch of a mysterious, possibly alien culture, but the rest of the acting is a little wooden (no pun intended) and in places quite shrill. I'll single out Ron Howard as "The Boy" - he misjudges the tone of the piece badly, playing the ending as almost upbeat and blunting some of the tragedy in the process. (Though it's hard to blame a seven-year-old for fumbling such a complex character beat.) More importantly, there are some frankly awful moments with Horace Keefe, easily the worst of *Door To Nowhere*'s regular 'background players,' as he overplays the subtext and reads the part of Shatner's 'brainwashed' fellow soldier in an excruciatingly camp lisp, which breaks the

tension so badly – as well as being pretty offensive to modern ears – that it drags the episode down from what would have been a solid '**A**.'

For the most part, though, this is up there with the best of *Door To Nowhere*'s three seasons, and it's where we start to see how those seasons are going to shape up. We've got the anti-war sentiment that dominated second season episodes like "<u>A Round Of Liar's Dice</u>" and "<u>What Is That Which The Breeze</u>," and while it might be stretching things a little to credit Matson with predicting America's involvement in a ground war in Vietnam, the idea of young men being called to fight in wars they don't understand the history or even the point of – all at the bidding of overlords who consider them little more than toys to be smashed against one another – is a powerful image that resonates strongly. We also have, arguably, the first of the existentialist questions that grew to take over the programme and inform some of the proto-psychedelic excesses of the third season – "<u>Puppet On A String</u>," "<u>Eyes Down</u>" and "<u>A Man Of Substance</u>" all draw more than a little influence from this episode's examination of what human life might look like from a different perspective, and Matson's Season Three opener "<u>The Fox At Bay</u>" feels almost like a direct sequel, with Jack Warden replacing Shatner as the man lost and alone on a seemingly endless plain as the noises of terrible violence close in on him.

Where this episode stands alone, though – exploring territory no other episode would

dare to for the entirety of *Door To Nowhere*'s run – is in its examinations of gender, sexuality and the meaning of masculinity in a world that was on the brink of an explosion of social and sexual freedoms. When Shatner first arrives, he's belligerent and aggressive, accusing his fellow soldiers of cowardice by leaning on the idea of the 'real man' – and here's where Keefe's ham-fisted performance does some real damage, shoring up 1950s attitudes of what a 'real man' looks and sounds like at exactly the moment the narrative is starting to knock them down – and the clash with Millay, that ends with Shatner essentially attempting to murder her, begins because she offers him a doily for his tea. All through the first act, Shatner is more willing to listen to an absent 'father' – the 'superior officer' who he believes is waiting for him outside the grounds of the Mansion – rather than the 'mother' figure, Millay, who wants nothing more than to see him happy, content and in love. Even after he's realised that he's better off in his new surroundings, he openly wonders what he is, if not a soldier. What makes the tragedy of "The Doll House" so acute is that it's not until Shatner fully accepts the 'sissy stuff' he's been fighting during the whole half-hour, embracing his new identity as one of what Millay calls "the beautiful boys," that it's all ripped away from him and he's brought back, weeping, to what he once thought he wanted.

Best lines/Random thoughts

- "There's a war on. We have to fight. Hell, do you want them to win?" "Depends who they are."

- "Now, don't be a silly, Billy. You can't hurt anyone with that. It's just a stick, that's all, just a silly little stick."

- "I didn't know what happy was until I came here. Happy is not being afraid."

- "You can marry me every day, if you want."

- "Whoever you are – I'm unarmed! It's just a stick! *Just a stick!*"

- The meltdown Shatner has midway through the plot would fit in perfectly with <u>this YouTube of classic Captain Kirk neurosis</u>. "I've lost control!"

- Fans of trash culture might see some similarities between the plot of this episode and cult "classic" *The Delicious Mister Doll*. Hutton Hopper – best known for his ultra-gory schlock horrors *The Girl Flensers* and *Cannibals Of 44th Street* – attempted early in his screenwriting career to turn "The Doll House" into a James Bond/Derek Flint style 'spoof spy' film. The result was basically what would have happened if all originality and nuance had been surgically drained from the episode and then Horace Keefe commissioned to play all the parts. (Even the women.) Director Jean-Paul Vitti added some additional camp and psychedelia, including a fantastic sequence set in a spinning op-art 'gravity room,' but the dialogue remained mostly unchanged and – by all accounts – pretty diabolical. (Vitti did add a heaping helping of his own well-catalogued perversities, as personified by Anouska Hempel in a performance somewhere between the evil queen in *Barbarella* and her own role in *Blacksnake*.) Someone braver than me has attempted to review this atrocity <u>here</u>, but frankly it's something that needs to be seen to be believed, assuming you have three bucks to spend on eBay. Just don't believe the people telling you it's somehow 'ironic.'

Next week: Burgess Meredith plays one of the creepiest Santas on record as we review the Christmas episode, "<u>A Lump Of Coal</u>."

THE SMILE ON Niles' face was so wide it almost hurt. This was *perfect*. Absolutely perfect. He did a quick search for the episode itself – maybe he could download it, or even torrent it - but evidently it wasn't available on anything later than VHS, and any pirates interested in the show had been taken down by Talisman's lawyers long before. Still, he had everything he needed in that review.

'The Doll House' was the starting point he'd been looking for. Rather than adapt Hutton Hopper's material

– and it was nice to put a name to the shame – he could simply follow Hopper's example and layer an exciting spy thriller on top of an already-existing story concept that the studio happened to own. Except unlike Hopper, Niles Golan was not about to *completely* miss the point of 'The Doll House' and reverse its entire message.

Briefly, he wondered if there was more to that on Hopper's part than just cluelessness. It'd be great to talk to him – actually, no, it probably wouldn't be. It'd be nice to talk to Fred Matson, though, get his side.

The old screenwriter puffed on his pipe, eyeing the author carefully as they relaxed with a tumbler of whiskey on the older man's sumptuous veranda. "You know," he said, after a moment, "all I've ever really wanted in this life is for someone to do 'The Doll House' right – to do it as an action-packed secret agent thriller with a dark, serious edge and some powerful eroticism." Matson leaned forward, giving the author an affectionate squeeze on the shoulder with his strong, fatherly hand. "You're a good Joe, Niles. You're a gosh-darned good Joe."

Niles smiled. He knew exactly where he'd gone wrong earlier – because Hopper had made Dalton Doll the authority on what the definition of a 'real man' was, a mouthpiece for Hopper's Neanderthal viewpoint, Niles had assumed that that was all the character could be, that Doll's misogynist machismo was an essential part of him, without which he just couldn't function. But of course, that was nonsense.

Why not have Doll searching for the definitions of masculinity himself, the way Shatner's character had been? (That was, he was certain from reading the review, what 'The Doll House' had been about.) Put him on a mission to find his own identity, both as a man and as a secret agent with a revolving leopard-skin bed and an automatic drinks machine. He'd be trying to be a new kind of man, a sort of 'new man' – Niles had to admit, it sounded like a wonderfully original take on the male protagonist in general, and he was pretty sure nobody had tried to do it with a stereotypical sexist spy character before. He could even throw a little comedy in.

Of course, as in Matson's original work, the moral would be that sometimes being a man meant having to shoot some people. You could sort of have a cry about it and still be a man, but sometimes you just had to get things done.

He tried calling Maurice, but the phone went straight to voicemail. Presumably he was still having his 'massage.' Well, all right, he could go right to the studio with it – pitch something to Dean right now. He'd had five pints, admittedly, but he'd watched a whole film since then, and besides, it'd probably help the pitch. And if Dean didn't want to take the pitch over the phone, that was fine too – he was probably okay to drive over there.

He really wasn't that drunk at all.

The phone was ringing. He psyched himself up, quickly, staring at his reflection in the glass of the coffee table. He was going to *destroy* this pitch. Fucking *destroy* it. He was a *tiger*.

Rarr.

The noise of a handset leaving a cradle. "Shoot."

"Dean? It's Niles. Listen, I've got something –"

"I'm going to have to stop you there." The voice on the other end was young, female. Had he been given the wrong number? "Dean's not available at the moment –"

"Ah!" Niles smiled. "You must be his secretary. Listen, I've got a wonderful pitch for him. Sort of a statement against misogyny, everyday sexism, that kind of thing –"

"Sounds awesome," the voice said dryly. "Like I was *saying,* Dean's calls are being routed through to me for now. He won't be available for some time."

Niles nodded, eager to get to the pitch. "That's fine, but maybe I could leave a voicemail for –"

"He's been arrested for having sex with livestock."

"*What?*" Niles stared at the phone, as if expecting it to bite him. He slumped back down onto the couch, the air draining out of him like a balloon. "So... so what does that mean for the pitch?"

"Well, obviously, the studio had to fire him, so... it's probably dead. I mean, I've taken over most of his projects, but I've got to admit, what I've been hearing... it's not *best-of-breed,* you know?" She enunciated the words *best of breed* as if she was trying them on for size, like a hat. "I really can't afford to give the green light to things that aren't *best-of-breed,* and... well, a guy who sleeps with poultry is not a good judge of what's *best-of-breed,* and what's just... whatever a guy who fucks hens wants to hear. Anyway, he's out and probably so are you. Sorry if that's blunt, I prefer to just rip the Band-Aid off, no false hope, you get me?"

Niles nodded, glumly. "No, I appreciate that. It's very kind, really." He sighed. "So *Mr Doll* is dead. Well, thank you, um..."

"Jane Elson." The voice responded. "Hey, did you say *Mr Doll?* Are you the guy Dean wanted to pitch on that? Because, listen, I'm not going to be able to get onto that tomorrow, but if you can pitch for that in a couple of days..."

Niles sat up. "I thought you said –"

"No, that's one of his I liked. I'm pretty sure with the right script we could make some big numbers on that. It's the whole retro thing – that's what I think people are really going to go for, except if you could make it kind of an early 'noughties retro instead of a 'sixties retro? You know, *Arrested Development*, Brangelina, the Patriot Act, iPods, that whole vibe – that's going to be the next big thing after 'nineties retro burns out and I feel like if we catch that wave we could really make something that's, uh..."

"Best of breed," Niles murmured.

"Right, right. *Best-of-breed*. Listen, you've got my number, I've got your number, give me a call in a few days when you've got something and we'll get the wheels in motion, okay? Ciao for now."

The phone went dead.

Niles put it down on the coffee table, staring at it for a moment. For some reason, now that the pitch was no longer urgently required – or *as* urgently required, anyway – all his ideas had deserted him. He knew he had to start from 'The Doll House' and build on it, and he had a vague mental picture of Mr Doll crying a lot underneath a running shower, but beyond that...

He slumped back on the couch, a wave of weariness washing through him, washing him out. He fumbled for the television remote to put *Mr Doll* on again – maybe now that he knew a little more about where it had come from, the film would open itself up to him, reveal some hidden depths...

But he was already asleep before the opening titles finished.

CHAPTER SEVEN

WHEN HE WOKE up again, it was dark, and the phone told him it was past one in the morning.

Niles lifted himself off the couch and headed to the bathroom. He knew he should call Maurice about the pitch and the new circumstances, but there was no point calling him this late – besides, he had a feeling Maurice would be a little pissed off that he'd called Dean, or rather Jane, without consulting him first. Still, he had an extra few days now to work things out, so it was all to the good.

As the toothbrush buzzed away at his gum lining, Niles found himself fascinated by the thought of one story becoming another – a piece of twist-ending science fiction based on children's toys, aimed at a discerning audience, becoming an oversexed secret agent fantasy aimed at the lowest common denominator. How had that come about? Had Hopper and Matson collaborated at all? Was Matson railing against his baby being fed to the butchers, or was it just one of many work-for-hire jobs? He rinsed his mouth out, returned to the laptop and started googling the two men, hoping for evidence of a connection, but very little came up. Sites that talked at length about *Mr Doll* would mention *Door To Nowhere* in passing, and vice versa, but nobody seemed interested in comparing the two. Niles frowned, mindful of the time. He knew how easy it was to fall down the rabbit hole of the internet, searching for that one particular piece of information you knew had to exist somewhere, while the clock ticked on and night became early morning.

Wikipedia provided some more clues. Hopper was dead – he'd been struck and killed by a snowmobile in 1992 – and his entry was too barren to be of much use, but Matson was still very much alive, at the ripe old age of seventy-four. A little more googling revealed that he had no immediate family – his wife had died some years before, and they'd had no children – and was currently living in a nursing home somewhere near Glendale. It sounded like a fairly tragic end for the man, but then from what Niles had been able to gather Fred Matson was a mostly mediocre writer. He'd had some critical successes with *Door To Nowhere* and his sketch work for *Laugh-In* was generally highly praised, but most of what he'd written during his life was plodding, low-grade hackwork. Fred Matson's star, it seemed, had only briefly burned bright before flickering down to an ember.

Still, as he went to put his pyjamas on, Niles was struck again by the urge to go and see Matson, to talk to him. It might help with the pitch – if nothing else, it would answer some of his questions. And the old man would probably be glad to see a friendly face.

"You're a good Joe," Matson said, smiling weakly from his bath chair. "A good Joe." The author felt a mixture of pity and pride, and found himself wiping away a tear.

* * *

THAT NIGHT, NILES had a dream in which he was running through the corridors of the Talisman Pictures building, searching for Jane Elson's office, but he could only find Dean's, and besides Iyla wanted to stop at the Best Buy and buy a copy of *Terrordance*. "It'll be too late tomorrow," she said, trying to keep the hen in her grip from getting away.

It's not going anywhere, Niles tried to tell her, but she shook her head. She was crying again. It's only *Terrordance*, he said. You don't even like Prince.

And then when he looked again, it was Danica Moss. "We're having *fun*," she said, softly, and he woke up with a start.

He didn't sleep again that night.

"NO, WE DON'T have anyone of that name here. Why were you calling again?"

The voice on the phone was guarded, suspicious. Niles held back a sigh and reached for his coffee. He'd spent more than a day listening to one disembodied voice after another coming out of that phone, most of them hostile, and he was on the verge of throwing it into the toilet. That or going out and buying a blender just to have the visceral satisfaction of seeing the damned thing dissolve into a blizzard of plastic dust... at least that way he'd get some sun.

"It really doesn't matter. Thank you so much. Goodbye!" he trilled, as irritatingly as possible – if he could drive one of these human-farming hags into some kind of apoplexy-related stroke, it'd be a morning well spent – then killed the call and checked the laptop screen for the next number. Why on Earth were there so many nursing homes in Glendale?

He winced. Pleasant Palms – God, they all had such insipid names. He'd have to look into some kind of suicide plan in case he ever ended up somewhere like that.

"Oh, Fred *Matson*! Oh, it'd be so *nice* for him to have a visitor!" Niles let his head flop back and gave a silent *thank you* to the ceiling, letting the woman on the other end prattle on for a second. "That'd be wonderful! Of course, we'd have to run it past him – are you a family member or a friend?"

"Neither," Niles said, allowing himself a rueful smile. "I'm a fan of his work." Of course, he'd never seen a single minute of the man's work. But he could hardly say that.

"Well, that's certainly never happened before! He'll be thrilled!" She seemed genuinely delighted, and for a moment Niles felt a stab of guilt. He should just admit that he wanted to be the latest person to pick Matson's brains about leeching off what was apparently the only decent thing he'd ever produced – but then, if he did, Matson might not agree to see him. "When are you likely to be coming? Early afternoon would be best for us."

There was a knock at the door.

"Early afternoon sounds great, if he's all right with it. I just wanted to ask him a few questions, tell him how big a fan of the show I am..." Niles made his way to the door, hoping he wasn't laying it on too strongly. "Is tomorrow all right? You'll let me know? Well, that's wonderful. You've got my number, of course – yes, this phone. Sorry, there's somebody at the door, so... yes, thanks. Bye." Ending the call, Niles pressed one eye against the peephole.

It was Bob.

"Have you seen the news?" He said, as soon as Niles opened the door. "The Sherlock Holmes case?"

Niles shook his head, turned around and walked into the small, cramped kitchenette at the back of the apartment. "You look terrible. Didn't you sleep last night?" He shot Bob a look as he put the kettle on. Bob was looking as young and handsome as ever, but there were signs – the bags under his eyes, the unwashed hair. He kept rubbing the underside of one arm, as if it itched.

"There's been another murder," Bob said, slouching in the doorway while Niles grabbed hold of the cafetiere and washed out the used grounds from earlier. "A civilian this time – at least they think it is. Poor bastard was found with no head on Van Ness Avenue. It's crazy. The police have no leads, those two other Sherlocks we saw on the news are just about running the investigation and they're still saying *another* Sherlock actually *did* it... well, they're saying it's Sexton Blake now, but, you know, same difference. Everybody's talking about it. Rush Limbaugh was on the radio saying that *'non-human freaks,'* quote, are *'running rampant.'* You ask me, things are going to get very weird over the next few days." He shook his head, watching Niles disapprovingly as he spooned new grounds into the freshly-cleaned pot. "You do know you're supposed to warm it first, right? What the hell are you doing?"

"Talking to a made-up superhero," Niles snapped, "which you'd be forgiven for thinking meant things were getting more than a little weird now."

"I'm not a made-up anything." Bob said, quietly. Niles felt his face redden.

He wasn't sure where that had come from. Irritation at Bob just walking into the apartment as if he owned the place, without even a hello – but then, he did that all the time, particularly if he was under stress. Starting a scene with *hello* and *how are you* and *what are the roads like, oh, that's awful, traffic's a nightmare here, they should really introduce a congestion charge* made for bad drama – of course Bob was going to avoid pleasantries when he could. It was no excuse for realism. For goodness' sake, Bob was his best friend.

Since the whole ugly business with Danica Moss, and the divorce – before that, even – Bob had been the one to rally round, while all Niles' other acquaintances had fallen by the wayside. Bob was the listening ear, the strong shoulder – he'd even helped Niles move in to this apartment. With his strength, he'd been the only person who could get the damned chest of drawers up the stairs. The man didn't deserve to have *'made-up'* slung in his face. What was next? The P-word?

"Sorry."

"I'm a *person*." Bob scratched his arm again, fixing Niles with a baleful glare. "It's been fifteen years since I was The Black Terror on any kind of regular basis. I'm Bob Benton. I'm a *voice actor*. There's no difference between you and me, Niles. No difference at all."

"Bob," Niles held up his hands. Bob really was too sensitive about this kind of thing. "I'm sorry. I said I was sorry –"

"No, fuck your *sorry*, let's have this out. How am I different from you? How exactly?" Bob had that steely tone to his voice that he got when he was angry. Usually it was reserved for really diabolical masterminds, like Colonel Von Claw – Tom Baker, in a guest role – or The Chuckler, and Niles found being on the receiving end of it very uncomfortable indeed. Not to mention irritating. Bob had come out of a *tube*, for God's sake. He was *imaginary*.

"Bob..." Niles sighed, trying to control the irritation and failing.. "All right, fine. Bob, you've got *super-strength*. That's one pretty big difference right there." He turned to pour the boiling water onto the grounds

"No, you don't get that one. I'm towards the edge of the bell curve – not even *at* the edge, *towards* the edge – for a man of my age and height. And I go to the gym regularly, unlike some people." Bob gave Niles another hard stare. "Nothing *super* about it."

"Come on, Bob. You know I can't go back to the gym after I threw up on the rowing machine." Niles felt hurt that he'd even bring that up.

Bob shook his head impatiently. "Bullshit. There are other gyms in the Los Angeles area, Niles. People here like to stay in shape."

"Well... I don't like the way the trainers bully you at those places. I feel like I'm on *World's Fattest Loser* or whatever that show's called." Niles turned back to the cafetiere. He'd forgotten to give the grounds a decent stir, and the coffee looked thin and watery. The hell with it – Bob could drink what he was given. "It's not like I'm fat," he muttered.

Bob rolled his eyes. "You're *all* fat. You're one of those thin fat people – well, semi-thin in your case – you've got fat squidged around every vital organ in your body, like packing peanuts. When they cremate you it'll be like cooking a goose. They'll put potatoes under the coffin, serve them to your widow. Sorry, *ex*-widow."

He looked like he was about to say something else about Iyla, but stopped himself.

"Lucky for him," the author thought, his fists bunching like twin hammers of retribution. A man could only take so much, and – while the writer had never actually been in a fight – he carried himself with the instinctive poise

of a jungle cat. He knew he could easily kill an opponent should he lose his temper and resort to violence. Even if his opponent had the unfair advantage of size and strength, like the Fictional cowering like a trapped rat in his kitchen doorway – size and strength, the author thought, which had been programmed in by a legion of modern-day Frankensteins rather than earned through hard work.

Not that the author was a realist, he reminded himself. In fact, he was the wronged party here – he was the one who deserved a full and frank apology, and the time had come to demand one or know the reason why.

"Steady on." Niles mumbled.

"Fuck you," Bob retorted angrily. "Sometimes I think the only reason you even talk to me is because you think you're somehow better than me. Like you're more real than I am."

"I am more real than you," the author bellowed. "You came out of a tube!"

"That's nonsense," Niles muttered, pushing the plunger down angrily, too quickly. What was straining up through the mesh looked like the dishwater left behind after he'd washed out the cafetiere before, or too-weak gravy. "Ralph said the same thing, and he didn't know what he was talking about either. Milk?"

"I take it black." Bob shook his head, exasperated. "Jesus, you know that, you've known me for years."

"Black. As in 'Black Terror.'" Niles smirked. "Whose idea was that?"

"You know what? Fuck you." Bob reached forward, grabbing the milk carton out of Niles' hand and all but upending it into the coffee, so it splashed over the sides of the mug. "There. Milk. Put some fucking sugar in it too, go on."

Niles frowned, taking the milk back. "What's wrong with you? You're acting..."

"Crazy? Crazy, am I?" the deranged Fictional howled. "I'll show you crazy!" With one grotesque reach, his hands locked around the author's supple throat and tore his head off like a Band-Aid.

"You're, um, you're acting up. A bit." Niles finished.

"Jesus, this coffee's fucking horrible." Bob winced, putting the mug down again. "Yes, I'm acting up. For Christ's sake, there's a guy on the radio saying I need to be rounded up –"

"Well, Rush Limbaugh says a lot of things," Niles said, pouring a little milk into his own coffee and giving it an experimental sip.

"– and now the best friend I have says I'm 'made up.' Thank you very fucking much, *asshole*." Bob turned around, stomping into the main lounge area and crashing dramatically onto the couch. Niles quietly poured his own horrible coffee into the sink and followed. He supposed it was his job to salvage this.

"Bob, come on," Niles said, weakly, as he sank into the armchair by the window. "It's not like I *meant* it. It was just... I don't know, friendly banter. Back and forth. That's the trouble with you Fictionals, you get over-dramatic."

"Jesus *fucking* Christ." Bob leaned forward, jabbing his finger at Niles. "You're not better than me, Niles. You're just as... as made-up as me, you know that? You're just as fake as I am. More so, with your goddamned pretending to be, I don't know, fucking Norman Mailer or whoever it is this week, pretending your fucking Kurt Power is some kind of immortal Joseph Campbell bullshit instead of a load of crap hacked out for a paycheck... Your personality's just as 'imaginary,' Niles. It's just as much an invention as mine is. Except you know what? I was thought up by a *good* writer."

Niles blinked.

The author stood, picked the clone up by the scruff of his neck, like a puppy, and threw him through the plate glass window to land on the parked cars four stories below. "Good riddance to bad rubbish," he quipped.

No, he wouldn't do that.

"Get out," the author snarled, livid with anger. The Fictional, seeing the blood in his eye, got to his feet and sheepishly left. He was dead to the author now. All good feeling between them had been annihilated in that moment. Their friendship was at an end.

Niles opened his mouth, then closed it again. No.

The author started to cry. Later that night, he slit his wrists with the broken shards of the mug he'd given his friend a coffee in –

No.

Bob looked back at Niles for a moment, saw the look on his face, and sighed. "Oh, God damn it... I'm sorry, Niles. I know you're sensitive about your work. Just, I don't know... chalk it up to 'friendly banter' or –"

"You can't grow."

"What?" Bob blinked.

Niles' voice was like ice. "Looking like Captain Haddock on a bad hair day doesn't count. Neither does doing your Black Terror voice for video games and cartoons and whatever pet food advert will take pity on you. You know why you can't get much voice work, Benton? Because you can only do one voice. You can only do one voice and people are bored of that voice, they're bored of you, they want someone new, someone like your replacement. And you can't be that someone, can you? Because you'll always be the same. You're like a boy who pulled a face

and then the wind changed – you're stuck like that." Bob
was staring at him now, mouth falling open, but Niles
carried on, propelled by a cold anger that sloshed in his
belly like mercury. "Do you know why you're stuck,
Benton? Because being a human being – a *human being*,
not a piece of someone else's made-up story that's been
Frankensteined into the world because we're so in love
with you fucking toys that we can't trust actors to act
anymore – being a human being means getting older.
And you're never going to do that, you're never going to
lose your hair or get wrinkles or, or not be able to get an
erection or any of the other things that are the price that
human beings pay to *change*. You can't pay that cost. You
can't get older. You'll never age, so... you can't change."
He shrugged. "That's why I'm better than you, Benton,
you fucking Pinocchio. You can't change. You can't grow."

Silence.

Niles expected Bob to stand up and storm out. Or hit
him. Or fire back with some piece of nastiness of his own,
some fresh evisceration of Niles' writing pretentions –

– *and fuck you, thought the author, fuck you fuck you
fuck you* –

– something that would confirm what they undoubtedly
both knew, that their friendship had sustained a mortal
wound, that Bob had chosen to blow it to pieces with
his vicious, unprovoked attack on Niles' work. And how
dare he? How *dare* he?

He was going to stand up, slam the door and that
would be that. That would be the end. And then Niles
would go and find some real humans to talk to and to
hell with Bob and Ralph Cutner and Dalton Doll and all
the rest of them.

Any second now.

And then Bob started crying.

* * *

"THERE YOU GO," Niles said quietly, handing Bob a fresh cup of coffee. "Careful. It's hot." Bob's hands were still shaking a little.

Bob blew on the surface of the liquid and took a sip. "It's, uh, it's much better than the last one," he said, his voice still a little thick. "Thanks."

"Well, there's no milk in it," Niles smiled, gingerly. "And I warmed the pot, like you said before. I thought that was just for tea." He padded over to the armchair and sat down again. "Bob..."

Bob shook his head. "I'm sorry."

"No –" Niles winced. "God, no. *I'm* sorry. That was... that was completely unforgivable, what I said. I want you to know –" He licked his lips, trying to find the words. "I want you to know I'm not the sort of person who goes around, who goes around using the P-word. That's not me at all. I'd never say that to someone of the, of the fictional persuasion... I mean, obviously I *did*, um, about ten minutes ago, but I never *would*, if you see what I mean –"

"It's fine." Bob said, shaking his head. "I mean, it's *not* fine, it was a shitty thing to say, but... I'd rather just get past it, okay?"

"I'm not *sensitive*, it's just – well, never mind," Niles said, fidgeting. "I just wanted to make it clear that I wasn't a realist."

Bob rolled his eyes. "Niles, you're a *huge* realist. It just doesn't fit your self-image to be a massive realist, so you write a little story in your head about how you're not –" He stopped, pinching the bridge of his nose. "Look, let's not start all this again, okay? I accept your apology, and... I don't know, I'm sorry I said you weren't Norman Mailer. Your books are okay. There's nothing wrong with them."

Niles decided not to ask why *Little Pig, Little Pig, Let Me Come In: A Kurt Power Novel* – which *Nuts* magazine had given three and a half stars and described as being "sexy with the snuff" – was just 'okay.' There was obviously something deeper going on. "Bob... are *you* okay?"

Bob stared at the carpet. Niles bit his lip for a moment, then carried on. "It's just that last time I spoke to you you seemed tired, maybe a little depressed even, and then you just turn up here this morning, and... well, I don't want to put it in terms of you starting a fight exactly, but –"

"I don't age." Bob's voice was flat. The air seemed to have gone out of him.

"Bob, don't let's get back to that –"

"No. That's the problem. You hit it." Bob looked up, and there were tears in his eyes again. "I don't age."

Suddenly, Niles craved a cup of coffee for himself. There was enough left in the cafetiere to make himself one, but he didn't dare to leave his seat. "Bob..."

"Listen." Bob sat back on the couch. "You remember when God died?"

"Um..." Niles hesitated. "I've never really been that religious myself, so..."

"God the Fictional, you ass." Bob rolled his eyes. "I wasn't around, but you were. You remember when he died?"

"Oh!" Niles nodded. "Oh, yes, vaguely. I mean, I was living in England at the time, still in my teens, but it made the news. That and *Doctor Who* being on hiatus. There was some controversy, but I remember they said he was, um..." Niles felt like he was tiptoeing through a conversational minefield. "Quite an early model. So to speak. So we needn't worry about the others."

Bob laughed mirthlessly, putting his face in his hands for a moment. "You needn't worry."

"Well..." Niles paused, wondering if he was saying the wrong thing again. "There'd been improvements made."

"Improvements. Right." Bob sat up again. "Yeah, they made improvements. How much of an improvement they made..." He shrugged. "Hard to say. I mean, God wasn't the last Fictional to die – and I'm not talking about people like Robert or the first Dracula, I mean Fictionals who died of natural causes. Or natural for us. People who just... wore out."

Niles suddenly understood. "Bob, you're not –"

"How do I know? How am I supposed to know?" He shook his head, running a hand through his thick hair. "*I don't age.* It's okay for you, you've got your damn wrinkles. You get signs, you know when your bodies are running down."

"Not always," Niles said, feeling a little flustered. "My aunt died of a stroke – out of a clear blue sky. She was forty-seven. And there are people who are, are just the picture of health and then suddenly –" He waved his hands around like a magician doing a trick. "Hit by a bus. Or heart failure. I read somewhere about someone who just collapsed in a cinema queue, a young student. Hole in her heart, never diagnosed." He looked into the distance. "Actually, it might have been a brain embolism. It was in a *Cracked* article."

Bob sighed. "Okay, fine. But you go through life thinking – even if it doesn't happen – that you'll just get older and older and everything's going to get more and more difficult until finally some important bit of your body – or maybe two or three important bits – they all stop working, one by one, and your body just can't carry on any more. And you die. And it's this slow, gradual process." He took another drink of coffee. "Do you know what a luxury that is? Thinking that's your future?"

Niles stared at him. "I... I don't, no." The way he'd put it, it sounded absolutely ghastly. It was making Niles want to check on his medical insurance.

"Think about it the other way. People like me – Fictionals – we're the students in the cinema queue. There's no warning, no aging process, just one day, *bang*" – he imitated Niles' hand-wave – "you're dead. And you know it's coming. You don't have that luxury of thinking you're going to get to run down slowly like an old watch. You just know you're going to be in the prime of your life and one day you'll go to sleep and never wake up. Or just drop dead on a crowded sidewalk, with all the tourists taking pictures on their phones as your bowels go." He grimaced. "Stealing your hair. Taking a finger. That's not paranoia, it's happened a couple of times. No family to get upset – people just think *why not*? And out come the pinking shears."

Niles shuddered. "Bob... do you seriously think you're going to die? Soon, I mean?"

Bob looked down at the carpet for a moment. "I don't know," he said at last. "Probably not. I mean, it feels like it's harder to throw off a hangover than it used to be. Or a headache. I've not been sleeping too well, I've got this itch in my arm..." He scratched, idly. "It comes and goes, it's probably nothing, but... how do I know? You get these things that are just... normal, little pangs and twitches, and you think, *is that a sign? Is that the first sign?*"

Niles nodded. "I think non-fictional people get that as well. When they pass forty, at least."

Ben rubbed his temples. "Well, I'm still thirty. I was born thirty and I'll die thirty. A young-looking thirty." He sighed. "I don't know. I've got this... this feeling of dread. All this Sherlock Holmes bullshit isn't helping."

Niles shrugged. "That doesn't matter. In six months, it'll be just another 'true story' floating around the studios." Right now he was more worried about Bob than what might or might not be happening to any Sherlocks. He wondered if this paranoia was something that descended on all Fictionals eventually. He felt a sudden, horrible chill. Maybe that was the sign. Maybe Bob was worrying himself to death.

Or maybe... God. Maybe Robert, the first Benton, had gone through the same thing. Maybe this new version of himself, this fresh-from-the-tank version, who played everything differently, who'd replaced him – maybe Bob had come along and that had triggered all these thoughts in Robert. The feeling of dread. Imagining inner processes of decay claiming him without warning. And maybe... maybe...

...maybe he'd chosen his own way out.

"Bob..." Niles paused.

"Are you going to kill yourself?" the author asked. The Fictional looked at him, visibly pleased with the thought. That night, he drank battery acid.

"Old age isn't so great." Niles said, feeling like an idiot. "Listen, I'm actually headed to an, ah, a retirement home tomorrow – you could, um... come with me? Take a look for yourself?" What was he saying? Was he really about to take his best friend on a guided tour of the horrors of the aging process? What was he going to do, point to the really big liver spots and say "Look! You don't want those, do you? They're awful!"

Bob stared at him for a moment. He seemed just as disturbed by the idea as Niles was. "Well, that sounds... um, that sounds all right. Sure, let's do that."

"Good!" Niles forced a smile, hoping he looked more convincing in his enthusiasm than Bob had.

He knew already. It wouldn't be all right.

CHAPTER EIGHT

IT WASN'T ALL right.

The drive up to the nursing home – in Niles' Ford Taurus with the broken air conditioning, on a spring morning that could have passed for midsummer – was quiet and awkward. Bob fidgeted, staring out of the window at the other cars on the freeway, while Niles pretended to be concentrating on the road. The air in the car felt like a thick, smothering blanket. Occasionally the Taurus engine made an odd rattling sound.

"Listen, about yesterday –" Bob started, then stalled.

Niles quickly interrupted. "No, no. Don't worry about it." And the blanket descended again. After another few miles, he cleared his throat and made a few humming noises, building himself up to actually speaking. "Bob..."

"Hey, there's a Denny's," Bob said. "We can get some lunch."

They ate in silence.

* * *

"HE'S IN THE day room," the nurse on duty said, scowling at Niles from behind a pair of bifocals. This wasn't the cheery, effervescent woman who'd spoken to him on the phone – her eyes were cold, sizing him up, making him feel like some shyster who'd come to worm his way into a big inheritance. Guiltily, he found himself wondering if Fred Matson had any money to speak of.

"Yep, I'm a secret billionaire," the screenwriter said, beaming magnanimously, "and I'd like to give it all to you, son, for taking my ideas into the twenty-first century and for being such a gosh-darned good Joe. Use it well."

"I will," the author said, clenching a resolute fist. Work on the Kurt Power movie began that very day.

The day room smelled of bleach and air freshener, hiding the faintest possible odour of urine. Six elderly men and women sat in a rough semicircle facing a TV that was showing *Tellytubbies* – Niles wondered queasily if that was just what happened to be on, or if the staff had selected a DVD. Nobody moved or spoke. Occasionally, one of the women made a soft cawing sound, like a bird. One of the men was drooling on his chest, eyes half-open and covered with a thin film. Niles wondered if that was Fred Matson.

Niles glanced over at Bob. He was staring at the bird-woman with a dawning look of horror on his face. The trip hadn't been a complete waste, then.

"Hey! You!"

Niles turned. A wizened old man with a white moustache and a green sun-visor was being wheeled in by an orderly. "You're Niles Golan, right?" Niles nodded, trying not to show his relief.

Matson grinned, showing his gums, and nodded to the orderly. "Put me over by the table, Clarice, I wanna play some cards with the guy."

Clarice — a largish woman of about forty — tutted. "Now, Fred, you know the rules —"

"What?" He snickered to himself. "We're playin' for matchsticks! I swear on my father's grave!"

Clarice gave Niles a look. "His father ran off with the iceman."

"Clarice!" Fred hissed, mock-outraged.

"What? You tell everybody. Listen," she said, "if you want him to tell the truth, make him swear on his ma's grave. Her, he liked. Otherwise you never know with Fred."

"Ah, my Dad was okay for an asshole." Clarice went to one of the cupboards, coming out with two packs of playing cards and a box of tiddlywinks and setting them down on the table in front of Fred's chair. "Oh, very nice, we get casino chips. Thank you, Clarice."

"I treat my man right," Clarice winked, before walking back in the direction of the bedrooms. Fred studiously watched her as she went.

"I hate to see her go," he turned, leering at Niles, "but I love to watch her walk away. Eh? Ehh-h-h?" He snickered again. Niles smiled politely. He had the feeling that he'd fallen into a Donald McGill postcard.

Bob pulled up a chair next to them, still with one eye on the woman making the bird noises. "Uh, hi," he said, looking edgily at Matson. "I'm Bob. Bob Benton."

Fred lifted his head, staring at Bob for a moment. "Sure, sure," he said, slowly, "Seen you on the TV, I think. You're one of those, uh, those clones they got now." He ran his tongue over his teeth, sizing Bob up.

"A Fictional," Niles said, helpfully.

"Right, right. Huh." Fred looked Bob over. "How's that working out for you?"

Bob pulled a face. "Honestly? Not so good."

"Oh, I'll bet." Fred shook his head. "You play cards, right?"

Bob shrugged, still staring at the bird woman. "I know Texas –"

Fred rolled his eyes. "Texas Hold 'Em! Sure you do! All anybody knows anymore is Texas Goddamned Hold 'Em! Nobody plays Chinese Bluff anymore," he grumbled. "Awright. Eights wild, dollar minimum bet." He shuffled the pack methodically and then handed it to Bob. "Deal us in, Texas."

Bob smiled weakly and started dealing the cards, his eyes still on the bird woman, who was looking away from the television now, staring at Fred and his visitors. It seemed to be making Bob nervous.

"So," Fred said slowly, as he looked over his cards. "You're a fan of my work, huh? The *Laugh-In* stuff?"

Niles felt his cheeks redden a little. "Well... not exactly..."

"Yeah, I get people asking about that every now and again. I'm in for a dollar, by the way." He tossed a tiddlywink into the middle of the table. "I had a couple of reporters up here when Dick Martin died, asking me about the Nixon thing – I told them I wasn't around for that, I didn't come in until '71."

Niles nodded politely, matching the bet. "Actually, I was more interested in *Door To Nowhere* –"

Fred blinked. "Jesus. *That* crap?" He shook his head, tossing in another chip. "That second year, we shoulda just painted *war is hell* on a bedsheet and hung it in front of the cameras for half an hour. And after that we all started dropping acid 'cause we thought that'd make the writing better – you know what they say about 'write drunk, edit sober'? Our version was 'write high, edit higher.' And then we had the gall to foist that bullshit on the public and claim we were spreading enlightenment to the masses! What the hell did I know about enlightenment? I was thirty and living in a goddamn squat. The only thing I was spreading was the clap." He glared at the small pile of tiddlywinks in front of him, then at his cards. "I check."

"Raise," Niles said, tossing in a chip. He honestly wasn't sure if what he had – a pair of nines – was good, bad or indifferent, but the worst that could happen was he lost some money. Or took money from an old man who probably couldn't afford to lose it. Or got thrown out of the place for taking said money from said old man before he'd asked any real questions. He sighed. "Bob? Your turn."

Bob was still fixated on the bird woman. "Niles? Can we talk?" He indicated the double doors to the day room. "Outside, I mean?"

Fred shot him a look. "Well," Niles said, looking between the two men, "if, uh, if it can't wait..."

Bob was already walking towards the doors, casting a last nervous glance towards the old woman as he did. Niles smiled sheepishly at Matson. "Sorry."

Matson shrugged, taking a quick look at Bob's cards. "Tell him he oughtta fold."

"I CAN'T STAY here." Bob said, rubbing the sweat off his brow with the back of his hand. "I can't go back in there."

The author smiled gently. "So, Bob, do you see now that the grass isn't always greener on the other side?" He slapped a hand on Bob's shoulder in a fatherly fashion as the foolish Fictional hung his head and admitted that yes, it wasn't as much fun to grow old as he'd thought.

"*Good man. Run along to the car.*" Smiling ruefully, Bob did as he was bid.

"*You're a good Joe, Niles,*" he said, as he left. "*You sure are a gosh-darned good Joe.*"

Niles did his best not to smile. "Well, it is a bit grim. So, um... do you see –"

"You don't get it," Bob snapped. "That woman over there. The one making those, those godawful *noises* –" He took a breath, shaking his head. "I know her. Knew her."

Niles blinked. "Sorry?"

"Yeah, you should be." Bob propped himself against a wall with his arm, staring down at the floor. He looked for a moment as if he was going to be sick. "Her name's Rose Kittering. She was a makeup artist on the show, the first couple of years. She was my makeup woman – she did the mask, glued it on, all that stuff. She was... I don't know, in her late fifties, maybe – but she looked good for it. Hell, I'd have put her ten years younger." He wet his lips, staring into the pattern of the carpet. "Christ. We used to flirt, you know that?"

"Ew." Niles couldn't hide the look of disgust at the thought.

Bob shook his head. "It was just *joking,*" he said, not looking at Niles. "She, she used to call me Bobby. She used to say I had a nice ass in the tights – 'Nice ass, Bobby.' 'Back at you, Rose.' Every day. Every day." He laughed, in a way Niles found worrying.

"Are you sure it's her?" Niles put a hand on Bob's shoulder. "Come on, let's get you some air –"

"It's her. She left the show during the second season. Health problems – wouldn't tell anyone what. We made her a cake, said we'd keep in touch... and now it's, what? Twenty years? Only fifteen? And she's in *this* fucking place, looking like, like *that*..." His voice broke, and he slumped down the wall until his was sitting on the floor. "And I still look the same. Exactly the same." He looked up at Niles, and Niles saw that he was crying again. "She keeps *looking* at me."

"Well... you keep looking at *her*... so..." Niles sucked in a breath. "Sorry, that's not much help, is it?"

"She keeps looking at me. I can't stand the idea that she'll recognise me, that she knows who I am, how I'm still the same... I *know* I should talk to her, Niles. I *know*. I just..." He buried his face in his hands as Clarice bustled down the corridor, carrying a stack of blankets.

"He okay?" she said, looking concerned. Niles nodded hastily, and she went on her way without looking back.

Niles turned back to Bob. To be honest, it hadn't really crossed his mind that the ethical thing to do in the circumstances would be to see how this Rose person was doing – he'd kind of stopped thinking of her as a person when she'd uttered her first bird-like croak – but even if it had, he didn't think it would be a good idea for Bob to go back in there. "Listen," he said quietly, "why don't you, um, go wait in the car? I won't be long."

"I'm serious. I can't stay here." Bob slowly got himself up from the floor, shaking his head over and over, looking as pale and drawn as Niles had ever seen him.

"I swear," Niles said desperately, "I'll be ten minutes. Not even that. I'll just find out what he has to say about that one episode and then we'll be out of here."

Bob stared suspiciously at Niles, then staggered towards the exit, still looking as if he might throw up at any moment.

"Ten minutes!" Niles called after him.

* * *

HALF AN HOUR later, Niles had lost nearly sixty dollars to Fred, and Fred had slowly loosened up about how *Door To Nowhere* had been turned into *The Delicious Mr Doll*. Niles couldn't help wondering if those two facts were connected.

"Hutton Hopper was a guy who lived in the squat for a while – this was in New York, down on the Lower East Side," he said, flipping another tiddlywink into the ever-increasing pile, "and then later after that all fell apart, which was about the time the ratings for *Door To Nowhere* collapsed and I realised I was out of work, he comes at me with this idea to move to LA and split the rent on a place – me, him, his old lady and this guy Johnny Garfield. He took a lot of bennies. So anyway, I figured, *hey, why not?*" Niles saw the bet, and Fred turned over his cards – an eight and a Queen, joining the Queen, two Jacks, King and seven already in play. "Ladies on top, Jacks underneath – story of my life. What you got?"

Niles sighed gently, turning over a two and a four. "Mind if we stop playing for a while? It's a little distracting." Not to mention potentially expensive.

"What, you don't wanna to win this back?" Fred flashed his gummy, cocksure grin, doing another of his little snickers. "Could be lucky."

Niles shook his head. He was fairly certain Fred was cheating, but he didn't want to make any accusations just when the story was getting interesting. "So were you living with Hutton Hopper when he started work on *Mr Doll?*"

Fred nodded. "Yeah, yeah. I was trying to get some short stories published in between working at a deli counter – I wasn't doing so well at that. The stories, not the deli – you would not *believe* the kind of pussy you can score working behind a deli counter! I could tell you stories that'd curl your damn hair. This one dame, I swear – titties you could bounce a quarter off – she just comes in the door and asks for –"

Niles started coughing loudly. He'd somehow managed to swallow his own saliva down the wrong pipe when Fred had mentioned the bouncing quarter. He tried to remember what the website had said about "The Doll House" and its exploration of gender roles, but it wasn't coming to mind.

Fred paused, made an apologetic face, and changed tack. "Well, never mind about that. I was doin' okay in that department, that's all I need to say. But those stories – it was the damn *Door To Nowhere* all over again. I'd take a hit of blotting paper, start banging on the keys, send whatever bullshit poured out to *Collier's* and then act surprised when they didn't take it. Took me a while to get outta that rut." He sighed. "Did better than Garfield, though – he got shot pulling a liquor store robbery, did ten years in San Quentin. Hell of a waste, plus it left us in the hole with the rent." He began to pack the cards away, sorting them into numbered and suited order before they went in the pack. Niles looked at the pile of tiddlywinks sitting in front of him – sorted as meticulously as the cards – and made a mental note never to play poker again. At least not with anyone over seventy.

"Hopper, though... he was doing just fine." Matson chuckled dryly. "He was knocking out these cheap sex novels every month for different publishers – *Sorority Sinners, Harlot In Heat, The Man Stealers*, that kinda thing. All different names – Tony Trellis was one he used a lot, and Eva Von Vance, that was for the lesbian stuff. Occasionally he'd do 'em as these serious scientific exposés, slap some fake degrees on the names – *The Lust Equation,* that was the big seller there, he did six more off the back of that one." Matson grinned, nodding at Clarice as she walked by again.

Niles' voice was still a little hoarse from the coughing fit. "Didn't you – sorry – didn't you have a problem with the ethics of that? The, um, the exploitation factor?"

"What are you talking about?" Matson looked confused. "Hopper groused about it occasionally, sure – even said he was trying to *subvert the genre* a couple times, like an asshole – but hell, it was easy money. Kept us in booze and pills. Anyway, you're wondering how *Door To Nowhere* comes into all this, right?"

"Right." Niles leant forward, straining to hear. This was what he'd come to hear – the why of *Mr Doll,* and the how.

"Hopper did these Private Eye novels too – under his own name. He used to do 'em when he got bored of the other stuff, and he'd pack 'em full of blood and guts, y'know, pushing the envelope – I remember the first one was *Man In A Woodchipper,* and then... aw, man, what was the one they almost couldn't print?" He gave his unpleasant little snicker again. "*A Cleaver For Clara.* He had to cut about ten thousand words out of that one, most of the cleaver action – I remember he got a letter from his editor saying how he nearly called the cops when he read it. He said he was just giving the people who read that bullshit what they really wanted." Matson closed his eyes for a second, chuckling at the memory. "Anyway, one of these things – and this one's a little more us-against-the-commies than usual, I think it was called *Sickle Where The Sun Don't Shine* – one of these things gets to a big shot at Talisman Pictures, and they love it. What's not to love, right?"

Niles smiled hollowly. Quite a lot, by the sound of it.

"So this bigwig, he gets Hopper's number and asks if he's available to work up a screenplay." His eyes twinkled. "Guess what they wanted?"

Niles wet his lips. "A Bond knockoff."

Matson nodded, grinning. "Right. Secret agent stuff. And they wanted it hard-boiled, see? But not quite *fella-goes-into-a-woodchipper-on-page-one* hard-boiled. Not *sickle-up-the-ass* hard-boiled either. And they definitely don't want it too sexy."

"They don't?"

"Not yet." Matson snickered, shaking his head. "So they want Hopper, but they don't want Hopper to be Hopper. That's Hollywood, right?"

Niles remembered his meeting with Dean. "...Right."

"So Hopper, he's bored right away – like before he even gets started – so he's putting it off, putting it off... but on the other hand this is the big time, you know? So he's kind of looking around for something, some idea that's gonna make it interesting enough for him to start on. And that's when he finds a bunch of old *Door To Nowhere* stuff. We were" – he was snickering again – "we were using that crap as the lining for a parakeet cage, can you believe it? So he goes to change the parakeet and he starts reading this script all covered in parrot shit... he's saying, *'this is blowing my mind, man!'*" He started chuckling, then laughing loudly, a harsh, raucous sound that echoed around the room. Clarice was walking through with a fresh towel and some talcum powder, and she gave him a worried look. "*'This is blowing my goddamn mind!'* Ha!"

"That was 'The Doll House'?"

"Right. The one Shatner butchered. Jesus, *that's* a story for another day." Matson's laughter faded, and he gave Niles a long, speculative look, still smiling his gummy smile. "That's the one you came here to talk to me about?"

"Yes," *the author smiled,* "*you see, I was wanting to re-adapt it, if you will, for a remake of* The Delicious Mister —"

"*You mean steal it,*" *the screenwriter hissed.* "*Like Hopper did. After I used my golden words to clean up after his parakeet!*" *He drew himself out of the chair, rising to his full height, and pointed an imperious finger.* "*Get thee hence!*"

Niles paused. "...yes."

Matson raised an eyebrow. "You a reporter? I heard there was a remake in the works."

"I'm... um." Niles swallowed hard, staring down at his hands. "I'm a writer."

"Huh." Matson grinned. "Well, here's what happened. Hopper reads the thing, and he tells me it's perfect for what he wants to do. Apparently it's full of all this gender-bender stuff, all this queer David Bowie crap – anyway, Hopper wants to... Jesus, how did he say it... he wants to '*smuggle a conversation*' past the studio people." Matson rolled his eyes. "I don't know. So he sits down and does this way-over-the-top take on 'Doll House' as this secret agent fantasy, and he's highlighting all the gender stuff he said was in there – which was all news to me, let me tell you –"

"But..." Niles started, then stopped. Matson waved the objection aside.

"Anyway. Susan Sontag had just written that piece on camp, so I kind of knew what he was going for, but... man, this was *vicious*. Like those movies he made. Vicious camp. He had hate in his eyes for James Bond, you know? Anyway, the studio *loved* it – I could have told him they would – and then they put this crazy French guy on it, or maybe he was Italian, and he put all the sex back in and then a little bit more – I figure he'd read plenty of Tony Trellis – and Hopper got so royally pissed off about what they did to it, he moved to the goddamn desert and started churning out the gore films. He said that's what the culture wanted, so that's what the culture deserved." Matson shrugged, shaking his head with a smile. "Hutton Hopper, God rest his soul. Craziest son of a bitch I ever knew."

"Wait." Niles shook his head, feeling completely out of his depth. "You're saying that you... you never intended 'The Doll House' to be about masculinity? About, about war, and the male, um, drive to..." He tailed off. Matson was snickering again. Niles was starting to hate that sound.

"Ah, it was anti-war, sure." He nodded. "Everything we did then was anti-war. We were seriously considering changing the title to *War Is Nowhere* until management told us we were being assholes. But all that masculinity stuff... ah, who knows where that came from. It's in there if you want to look for it, I guess." He shrugged again, looking apologetic, as if he was sorry he couldn't do more.

"Well..." Niles blinked, looking down at the pile of tiddlywinks, representing the sixty dollars he'd paid for these answers. He wondered if he could just leave without paying, or if Matson would kick up a fuss. He'd certainly tell Clarice about it, and Niles wasn't sure he could take a dressing-down right now. "Well, what *was* it about? If you don't mind me asking?"

Matson was silent for a few moments, mulling the question over in his mind. "Toys," he said at last. "Barbies, toy soldiers, stuff like that. Things children play with, things they make up stories for. I guess I just wondered how a toy soldier might feel if he was taken out of his box and taken to tea with some dollies."

"And that's it?" Niles felt intensely disappointed. He'd assumed there was some deep meaning to be found in the original story, but Matson was just a mediocre writer who'd wasted his life after all. And worse, his 'bold take' on the *Mr Doll* material was just a pale, toothless imitation of Hutton Hopper's savage original critique of Bond – of course, Niles had seen the irony in it all along – and it'd probably be dealt with in much the same way. Some music director would sweep in, fill the screen with explosions and lingerie, and render any statement he tried to make worthless. He was back at a dead end.

"That's it," Matson sighed. "I guess I was just ahead of my time."

Niles narrowed his eyes. "How so?"

"Ah, how things are now." He indicated the direction Bob had left in. "People like your friend. Not much different to a G.I. Joe, if you think about it. Make up a story for him, set him loose, and if he doesn't like it... tough shit, right?" Matson chuckled again, but this time it was bitter, as if he wasn't much liking the story that had been drawn up for him, either.

Niles wasn't paying attention.

He'd had a wonderful idea. A perfect, stupendous idea.

The new *Mr Doll* would be about Fictionals.

It had been staring him in the face the whole time – ever since he'd seen the review for 'The Doll House' – but it had taken him until now to really see it. The one subject that cinema hadn't yet made its definitive statement on. The one subject that was right in front of their noses and nobody had tackled. The elephant in the room, the taboo, the festering wound nobody dared to cut open. Fictionals. Their feelings, their hopes and dreams.

Dalton Doll would be the first Fictional *to portray a Fictional*. It would be a brilliant meta-narrative about the making of a secret agent movie – and of course, the Fictional playing the secret agent would get caught up in some real secret agent shenanigans. Girls in lingerie. Magnificent explosions.

It'd win an Oscar.

Niles reached into his pocket, drawing out his wallet, and Matson stopped him with a rueful smile. "Ah, I was just joking about the money, kid. How about we call it a tab? Maybe next time you come by we could –"

"Mr Matson," Niles ignored him, putting six ten-dollar bills on the table, "could I get permission from you to use that idea? It's just that there's something I'm writing at the moment which –"

Matson shook his head, showing his gums again. "Oh, I don't think I can sell you that idea, Mr Golan."

Niles flushed. "Well, I wasn't actually... ah..."

"It's not mine to sell." He shrugged, grinning wider. "Got it out of a children's book."

Niles stared at the old man. "I'm sorry?"

He burst into laughter. "What, you thought I ever had an original idea in my life? No, *The Doll's Delight*, that's what it was called. Saw it in some girl's apartment I was crashing in, had to have it. Strangest damn book I ever saw. Ended up selling it for windowpane. Anyway, there was this verse in it about toy soldiers running away from the war and going to play with the dolls – I pretty much wrote the whole script that night. Sat in a drawer until I had a place to sell it."

"So... who wrote that? The children's book?" Niles felt like he was on a ship at sea. Every five minutes ground he thought was perfectly solid would shift beneath his feet. He hadn't felt so uprooted from reality since... well, since what had happened with Danica Moss.

Matson stared into the distance. "Let me see... it was D-somebody... Dalton? No, that was something else. Sounded like it, though. And I'm pretty sure there was an H in there some –"

At that moment, Clarice reached down from seemingly nowhere and grabbed the sixty dollars off the table, waving them in Niles' face.

"What the *hell*," she screamed, "is *this?*"

"ALL RIGHT, ALL right, I'm on my way out..." Niles marched briskly through the lobby, past the mortifying gaze of the nurse on duty, who had presumably had her every suspicion about Niles confirmed.

Considering the humiliation of the situation, Niles was in remarkably good spirits. For one thing, he definitely wouldn't feel any obligation to go back and talk to Matson again now, so he was off the hook there. For another thing, he had the perfect idea for *Mr Doll* – he could even work Bob's problems into it, give the thing some dramatic depth. A Fictional playing a Fictional – it was a fantastic idea, and it'd probably produce the most emotionally stable Fictional yet. He'd bounce the idea off Bob on the way back, see what he made of it...

But when Niles reached the Ford Taurus, Bob was nowhere to be found.

CHAPTER NINE

"BOB? LISTEN, CAN you give me a call back as soon as you get this? I'm waiting by the car, but I've been waiting here about twenty minutes and I'm going to have to get moving soon. It's, um, it's Niles. Bye."

Voicemail again. Niles ended the call and looked around, hoping to see some sort of sign that might show him where Bob had run off to, willing a mall or a Denny's or a park to pop into existence – anything apart from the nursing home and the barren stretch of sidewalk it was situated on. There was literally nothing here but concrete, a few spare blades of grass, some shuttered buildings that could have been offices or apartments – or squats, he thought bitterly, thinking of Matson – and a closed-up gas station. He couldn't see that Bob would have wandered into any of those, unless he'd discovered a sudden taste for urban exploration.

He could just about make out a bus stop a few hundred yards away, but the idea seemed absurd. Why would Bob just hop on a bus home? He'd have known Niles would be coming out to drive him home any minute. All right, Niles had been a little late, maybe, and it was an unseasonably hot day, even for California, but still. Surely Bob wouldn't have just deserted him here?

He turned around and marched up to the glass doors of the nursing home – then marched back again as he saw the head nurse staring out at him like a basilisk. He'd thought he could pop in and have a look around – made sure he and Bob hadn't just missed each other somehow, and he wasn't still wandering around in there – but to be honest, they'd have thrown him out by now as well.

Niles checked his phone for the time, made sure it wasn't on silent, and then looked in the direction of the empty car. It had been almost twenty-five minutes now. There wasn't anything else for it.

He unlocked the door and slid in behind the wheel, mentally willing Bob to appear at the last possible second. But Bob didn't show.

"BOB? LISTEN, I NEED you to give me a call back. If you're still at the home, I can come back and get you, I won't be upset, just give me a call, all right? I'm on the freeway at the moment, so I can easily – hang on, a police car just pulled out behind me. He's signalling me to pull over. Hang on. Look, as soon as you get this, give me a call and I'll come find you wherever you – shit, he's tapping on the window. I'll try again later. It's Niles. Bye."

"BOB? LISTEN, PLEASE give me a call back. I just got a ticket for $150. I'm at home now. Look, I'll be here for a while, if you need me to come pick you up – well, let me know if you're okay. Um. It's Niles. Bye."

Niles flopped into his couch, staring up at the ceiling. He supposed he should be working on the pitch, but he was too worried about where Bob might be to really think about that. It wasn't that he thought Bob was in trouble – with his build, there wasn't realistically that much trouble he could get in. Well, unless he was shot. Or someone cut off his finger with pinking shears. Or something else.

"Yes, that's his head," the author said mournfully, as the police opened the box to show him the carefully stuffed and lacquered object. "You say you found it on eBay?"

"The secret eBay," the officer said, grimly. "There are quite a number of his bits on there now. We'll never recover them all. Of course," he said, looking the author over admiringly, "your dismembered corpse would fetch far more. The brain that penned The Moon Comes Out As Bright As Day: A Kurt Power Novel *is probably worth several million dollars."*

The author nodded soberly. He knew criminals would stop at nothing to procure his precious organs.

Niles shuddered. "What is *wrong* with you?" he muttered to himself, reaching for his laptop. At least he could do a bit of research while he waited for Bob to call.

Typing *'The Doll's Delight'* into a search engine brought back about eight pages of results – it was the name of a small British chain of dollhouse furniture shops, each with their own poorly-crafted website, two club nights for BDSM groups, an indie band, several dozen slash fiction stories about an old Joss Whedon series, and a porno movie from the early 'nineties involving women in very tight rubber clothing pouring cold tea on each other and rolling around in cream cakes, which Niles watched for several minutes, trying to decide if he felt aroused or just mystified. He settled on mystified.

Buried somewhere in the middle of it all was one blog post from a collector of 'fifties ephemera and one eBay listing, both of which referred to *"The Doll's Delight, by Henry R Dalrymple, Illustrations by Mervyn Burroughs."* Niles – still a little spooked by his daydream of the 'secret eBay' – checked the blog first. It was a sparse entry. A tiny, blurry photo of the cover – involving what looked like a number of glassy-eyed homunculi playing in the moonlight next to a dead child – and some meagre publishing information (Aspidistra Press, 1951), and the single word *"Weird!!!!"* sandwiched between a dangerous-looking Atomic Energy Lab play set and a Schwinn bike, both of which got several paragraphs and a crystal-clear Instagram.

Warily, Niles turned to the eBay site, which informed him tersely that there was a *'rare children's book'* – no photo – which he could BUY NOW for $120 from an entity named *needleblissss74*. Apparently, for an extra postage fee of ten dollars, he could have the book in his hands in a mere two to four days' time.

Although couldn't he do without *The Doll's Delight?* He had everything he needed – a starting point, an idea that was bound to win him an Oscar, and *Mr Doll* on his hard drive for reference. Why should he spend over a hundred dollars on a children's book from more than sixty years ago?

At the premiere, the author tried to relax in his seat, but he couldn't help fidgeting. Liz, sat next to him in her McCartney evening gown, gave him a curious look, as if to ask what might be wrong, but the author only shook his head. He couldn't burden her with it, not only ten minutes into the film. And yet, he could already see what was wrong.

It wasn't the direction – that was marvellous, meticulous, Nolan at his very best. The score pulsed threateningly over the speakers in a tone of existential dread, the acting was superb, particularly Mr Dalton Doll himself... and yet, there was something about that central performance, something that didn't quite work. Some subtle quality that the author had failed to include in the screenplay, leaving the persona of the leading man missing a tiny, yet vital spark.

It was the want of a nail, the author thought, burying his head in his hands. Slowly, the others in the audience began to notice the subtle flatness of it, and began to grumble, rest their feet on the seat backs, throw popcorn. Eventually, they walked out, first one or two, then a trickle, then a flood. Even Nolan became visibly disinterested, shrugged, and walked out with the rest. The author looked around for Liz, but she too was gone. Only Dalton Doll was left, sat in the front row, clapping like a small boy.

The author was left alone, staring at the empty, hollow spectacle unfolding before him, the idiot man-child applauding it all. He felt a great weariness come over him – the understanding that all this, his greatest failure, the end of all his hopes, stemmed simply from a lack of proper research at the pitch level, from failing to glean every last glimmer of insight possible.

But then, he hadn't wanted to spend the $120...

"$130," muttered Niles, "including postage." He fumbled for his wallet.

* * *

"Bob? Listen... you haven't called. I'm going to assume you've got this and you're not dead in a ditch somewhere, but... look, please call, okay? I'm sorry if I was... I don't know, late coming out or rude to you or whatever. I'm sorry I took you to see your old make-up woman. Just call me, all right? Anyway, I'm going to the Victoria, so... so that's where I am. It's Niles. Bye."

The sun was just starting to dip below the buildings when Niles walked into the bar. This time, there was a reasonable crowd, enough that Niles didn't see Liz until she touched him lightly on the shoulder while he waited for his drink.

"Hello, author," she said, smiling prettily. This time she was dressed in 'fifties fashions – a polka-dot halter neck dress with a raincoat over the top and white gloves, her hair stiffly lacquered in place under a dotted shawl and a pair of shades. Her accent had warped into some approximation of Marilyn's best Betty Boop, and Niles had to stare at her for a moment before he recognised her.

"It's Niles," he said with a tight smile, before turning back to the barman. "And can I have a pink gin for the lady as well? Thank you."

Liz leaned forward, smirking, to get the barman's attention. "Make that a Manhattan, honey." She grinned at him, showing those white teeth – too white, thought Niles, feeling suddenly very conscious of his own. He'd had a little bit of work done since arriving in LA – you couldn't not do, not in this town – but nothing like that. If someone shone a UV light, he had a feeling her teeth would start glowing. And her eyes were still the same dazzling shade of clear, perfect green.

He paid for his pint and her Manhattan with a twenty, telling the barman to keep the change. He didn't know quite why he was trying to impress her, or if she was impressed by that kind of thing. Bobbi had been impressed by things like that – he'd spent money like water around her – but then that was the trouble in the end, wasn't it? She'd been impressed by everything. He didn't want that again.

"Aren't you being a little presumptuous?" the girl asked the author, lifting an eyebrow. "How do you know I'm even interested in you? Your hairline's getting higher, you're starting to carry a spare tyre around your middle. You don't exercise properly. You're a not-so-thin fat person, and a closet realist. Maybe what this is is me feeling sorry for you. Or maybe you don't have the first clue about me or what I'm thinking." She tilted her head. "How long is it since anyone actually wanted you, Niles? And don't say Iyla, you killed that long before the marriage ended. Perfunctory, last-ditch fucking that ends in tears doesn't really count, does it? Who was the last person who really seemed to want to have sex with Niles Golan?"

"Let's not talk about her." The author's voice sounded thin and reedy in his own ears, like someone talking on a bad phone connection.

Danica smiled at him, toying with her red hair.

Niles shook himself, grimacing. It seemed like he spent more and more time zoning out, filling his head with these strange, ghoulish fantasies. He'd have to talk to Ralph about it at their next session.

Or maybe Iyla had been right and he needed to see a real therapist. Either way, something had to be done. He couldn't function like this.

"Oh, look!" cooed Liz, "There's a table free!" She immediately sashayed over to it, doing her best to copy the 'jello on springs' movement of Marilyn – or Betty. To Niles' eyes, it was an odd, jerky little walk, like a wind-up toy, but he noticed the eyes of a couple of the older men in the bar following Liz and felt a brief surge of something like pride as he sat down next to her.

"Here's to you," she grinned, raising her glass. "My author." That, Niles decided, was definitely some sort of green light. He raised his own glass and clinked.

"There's something I've got to ask," he said, flashing her what he hoped was a winning smile. "All..." – he indicated her dress, the shawl and shades – "all this. Every time I see you, you're – well, you're dressed so oddly. You never seem to use your real voice. It's disconcerting. Is it, er, some kind of... " He took a judicious sip of his beer. He didn't want to use the word *hipster*. Or, he decided, *Fictional*. "Some kind of fashion thing?"

She laughed, loud enough to turn heads. "Do I seem like a *character* to you, Niles?" There was a look in her eyes he couldn't quite place. "Well, maybe I am. Maybe I'm one of your characters." She giggled, leaning in.

Niles forced a smile. "Let's not start that again," he mumbled. He wondered, again, if he should just come right out and ask her the question.

"Are you a Fictional?" The author asked, quietly.

"Yes," she said, "and I want to go to bed with you. I, a Fictional, want to sleep with you, a human. I want you to put your penis in my made-up vagina. I want to be your body pillow. Your cartoon horse. Your little wooden girl. Tell me, Niles, how does that make you feel?"

The author threw up.

As he vomited onto the carpet, spewing continuously until he was coughing up chunks of meat and blood, she fixed him with a simmering green gaze. "Let's tell the world, Niles. Obviously, they'll burn your books in huge piles and we'll have to move to Sweden, but what does that matter in the face of love?"

He swallowed. "Are you... um...?" He paused, hoping she'd finish the sentence for him.

Instead, she smiled, leaning back, and moved her sunglasses down over her eyes so she was looking at him through a pair of opaque walls. "I don't know. Do you *want* me to be, Niles?" She smiled, in such a way that Niles couldn't decide whether it was flirtatious or mocking. "You're the author, after all."

Niles frowned and shook his head. He should really make that his cue to stand up and walk away – find another part of the bar, or just go home if sticking around was too socially awkward. Liz Lavenza, whoever she was, was definitely not his type. She was... well, a little too manic and pixie-ish for his liking, and he had the uncomfortable feeling that she was playing a game with him, and that was something that brought back unpleasant memories.

On the other hand, he mused, there was *something* about her – her artificiality, her mystery. Maybe just her green eyes. He took another long sip of his drink and changed the subject. "Have you seen Bob in here at all?"

"Bob?" She looked blank.

"My friend with the beard. Black shaggy hair. He was with me in here the other day – you said you overheard our conversation." He craned his neck, looking around the bar. He hadn't seen Bob on the way in – but then again, the Victoria was full of all sorts of nooks and crannies, especially when it was this crowded. Niles took out his phone again, checking to make sure Bob hadn't called.

"The Fictional," she said, with another secret little smile. "Do you spend a lot of time with Fictionals?"

Niles could feel her eyes on him, through the black lenses. He took another gulp of beer. "No more than most people in the industry," he said, guardedly, neglecting to mention that he'd been 'in the industry' for less than a week.

"He's a friend, then? A close friend?" She cocked her head, taking the dark glasses off, and a strand of red hair fell out of the heavily-lacquered do and over her forehead. Niles felt something stir. "How did you two meet?" she asked.

"It's a long story," Niles shrugged.

Liz smirked. "I like long stories."

It had been at a New Year's party ten years before – soon after Niles had moved to Los Angeles. A friend of Iyla's had brought him, someone who'd worked with him on one of the *Toy Story* cartoons – he'd had a brief cameo role as a Black Terror action figure. It had seemed like a pity gesture on behalf of Iyla's friend – what was his name? Toby? Tony? – and one he had evidently regretted, as he'd left Bob alone the whole evening, in a house full of people he barely knew.

Iyla had been the first to go over and talk to him, Niles remembered. Now that he looked back, that seemed odd, given her realist streak – but then she didn't really start acting coolly towards him until later, during the aftermath of the business with Justine. Maybe that was when she found out he was a Fictional?

Could that be right? He remembered standing politely on the edge of their conversation – as they talked about voice work, the hierarchies of Hollywood, the impossibility of living in LA without a car, a dozen other subjects – and waiting for his turn to speak. Eventually, he'd drifted over to the canapés, buttonholing the hostess about the plot he was working on for *Eye Of*

The Scimitar: A Kurt Power Novel. They hadn't been invited back the next year.

He'd seen Bob after that, albeit infrequently. Occasionally they ran into each other at dinner parties or social gatherings, and over time Niles had grown to appreciate Bob's quiet demeanour, his ability to be a good listener. Still, they were acquaintances, not friends – at least until that business with Justine, when his marriage had almost, but not quite, fallen apart.

After that, Bob had started showing up at the apartment occasionally – to be greeted with strained, feigned politeness by Iyla, who must surely have twigged what he was by then – and making a special effort to see how Niles was doing. They began drinking together socially, and as more and more of his friends turned out to have been Iyla's friends all along – making little excuses not to see him or talk to him, avoiding him in the street – Bob had been there, always making sure he was all right.

Even during the whole sordid, sorry mess with Danica, he'd been there, offering no judgements, no recriminations, just an understanding shoulder. "Some things just don't work out," Niles remembered him saying. "Nothing you can do. It's the way we're made."

Niles found himself relating a sanitised version of the events to Liz – drawing a veil over the worst parts, making his indiscretions seem like the unavoidable consequence of a marriage in decline, not mentioning Danica at all. "To be honest," he said at the end, "Bob's just about the best friend I've got." He laughed, humourlessly. Bob was the only friend he had left. "In fact, it's down to him and my agent."

"And me?" Liz said, resting her chin on one gloved hand, smiling mischievously.

Niles studied her for a moment, finishing his beer. Now that he had a pint in him, his paranoia about her being a Fictional seemed ridiculous. She was just a lively girl with a sense of fun, that was all. He smiled. "Are we friends?" he said, attempting a playful tone.

She smiled. "I don't know. You tell me."

"I'll get you another drink," he said, and went to the bar.

HER APARTMENT WAS five minutes away by cab – a dusty, musty place, filled with old books, VHS tapes, cassettes. The ephemera of the past. Even the bed was old, creaking and groaning under them as if it might collapse at any moment.

At first, Niles was aroused by the adventure, by the strangeness of her, the 'fifties clothes, the vintage underwear, the gloves she never took off. Messing up her immaculately lacquered hair felt like breaking some primal taboo.

But at the same time, she didn't seem to be present. He found himself taking the lead, telling her what to do, how to position herself, moving her like a showroom dummy as she lay back on the bed, the dreamy smile on her face unchanging even as his erection started to wilt and grow soft inside her, and he grew conscious of the flab of his belly slapping against her, the churn of the alcohol in his gut, the fullness growing in his bladder and bowels.

Five minutes later, he gave up, and she stopped smiling.

SHE'D LISTENED TO his excuses – his faltering speech about how long it had been, how he'd been through a terrible emotional trauma, how he was so worried about Bob he couldn't concentrate – in silence, expressionless. When he found himself saying that perhaps they could try again later, she rolled her eyes almost imperceptibly, turned over and went immediately to sleep.

Now he lay on the bed, staring up at the ceiling, as the sweat dried on his skin. An old air-conditioner chugged slowly in the corner of the room, pushing the air around, but it didn't seem to be doing much about the oppressive heat. He found himself wondering why he'd gone home with her, this strange girl who he didn't even really know – why now, after three years of celibacy? And why her? There'd been other women in that time he could have made a play for, surely? What was so special about Liz Lavenza?

Niles realised that he couldn't put his bladder off any longer. He looked over at her, coiled in the foetal position, and decided against waking her – he could find his way on his own.

The bathroom was behind the second door he tried – a small, cramped-looking space with a shower, sink and toilet, and dozens of hair and beauty products, all seemingly to recreate different eras of the past. The tiny room still stank of hairspray – she must have used up a whole can of the stuff before going to the Victoria. Perched on top of the cistern was a small stack of books – *Breakfast At Tiffany's*. *The Maltese Falcon*. *Ubik*. *Frankenstein*. Bath time reading, he supposed, although she didn't have a bath.

He unbuttoned his trousers, pulled them down to his ankles, then reached, on a whim, for *Frankenstein*, opening it near the beginning.

Her presence had seemed a blessing to them, but it would be unfair to her to keep her in poverty and want when Providence afforded her such powerful protection.

They consulted their village priest, and the result was that Elizabeth Lavenza became the inmate of my parents' house—my more than sister—the beautiful and adored companion of all my occupations and my pleasures.

Niles blinked.

the result was that **Elizabeth Lavenza**

Underneath him, the contents of his bowels hit the water with a splash. He swallowed hard, fighting the urge to vomit.

Liz Lavenza.

Was a *Fictional*.

Next day, the papers were full of the story. LITERARY LOTHARIO LUSTED FOR TORRID TRYST WITH TRANSLATED TART. Sources had it that the author had been spending increasing time with Fictionals, to the detriment of his human friends. "I'm just glad he didn't try any of that disgusting stuff with me," his Life Coach, Ralph Cutner, was quoted as saying. "When I think of how he rubbed himself against my chair – well, now that I know the truth about his depravity, I have recommended that the man be sectioned immediately, for an imminent lobotomy to cure his perversions."

"He had a Fictional therapist," the author's ex-wife said in a prepared statement, "which I thought was disturbing. When I voiced my concerns, he called me a realist. That's when I knew he was a filthy little deviant."

"He seemed very keen to have Kurt Power translated," said Maurice Zuckerbroth, winking at the waiting television cameras. "A little too keen, if you get my meaning, and I think you do. And I'm betting it turns

your stomach, buddy – if you're not a Pinocchio-lover, that is."

The author was murdered later that day by an angry mob armed with pitchforks and fire. "I'm glad this happened," said the Mayor of Los Angeles to reporters. "Now we can forget Niles Golan ever existed. When we're not burning his filthy books in vast piles in the middle of the street, something I plan to organise immediately."

He had to get out of there.

"Niles?" He heard her voice in the corridor. Not bothering to wipe or flush, he yanked his trousers back up, running towards the bathroom door just as she knocked on it. He pushed the wooden door back against her, sending her naked body – *her clone-body, her Fictional body, the body he'd been inside, and of course he must have known what she was, that was why he hadn't been able to keep it up* – sending her naked body tumbling backwards, banging her head against one of the dusty bookshelves.

Then she was on the carpet, clutching her head and crying, and he was screaming at her, red-faced and terrified, a high-pitched squeal: "I was never here! I never touched you, you understand? *I was never here!*"

Then he was racing down the stairs of the apartment, his hands tugging at the waistband of his trousers, a clinging lump of faecal matter slowly making its way down his leg as he ran.

CHAPTER TEN

NILES SAT ON the couch, staring at the dead black eye of the television. In the kitchenette, his clothes tumbled and sloshed in the washing machine. He'd tipped in too much powder, he knew. Too high a setting. He'd probably ruined them. After this, he'd send them round again, just to be sure.

He felt sick.

"It was an accident. I didn't *mean* to," he said aloud. His voice sounded strange and cracked in the empty room. "She tricked me."

But she'd done nothing of the sort, of course. She'd been hinting at her Fictional status from the moment they'd met. He was the one who'd ignored all the signals. He sighed, leaning forward and putting his head in his hands. She'd been looking for someone human, someone sick enough to want to sleep with a Fictional – the Victoria was one of the places people like that hung out, for all he knew, maybe *that* would be used against him – and he'd led her on, unwittingly made her think she'd found what she wanted in him. He'd been the one to trick her.

He wondered why she wanted to sleep with real people anyway. Some basic fault in her makeup, he supposed. A kink in the personality data some witless screenwriter or technician had programmed in.

"Bad writing," he said, humourlessly. He wished Bob would call – he, of all people, might understand.

Who else could he talk to? Did he have any real friends left, apart from Bob? Surely they hadn't all been his wife's? But he couldn't think of a single person who hadn't made some excuse or other and drifted away over the last three years. He was completely alone.

There was always Maurice – no, not Maurice. Maurice would cut his ties the moment Niles told him what he'd done. Would he keep the secret? Probably not, Niles thought glumly. He imagined there was some kind of reward or career advancement in telling the world about it, which meant Maurice would do it without even thinking about it.

He wondered if Liz would keep quiet – again, probably not, not after the way he'd left her. He shuddered, feeling his cheeks burn. He'd panicked, acted like an animal caught in a trap, a thug. Next to him, Dalton Doll was the model of chivalry.

And now Liz Lavenza, from Geneva – he should have seen it then, why hadn't he *seen* it – was going to tell the world. Why shouldn't she? What did *she* have to lose? Maybe she'd blackmail him first, he thought. A brown envelope through the letterbox. Monthly demands. He'd seen how she lived, she could use the money. Maybe if he got out ahead of it, paid her shut-up money... no. He could never see her again.

He dug the heel of his hand into his eye, wiping away

the tears. Where was *Bob*? He stared at his phone, looking through the recent calls, checking to see if Bob had somehow called. Iyla's name sprang up.

Iyla.

She wouldn't sympathise, of course, or even want to hear it – not after the way she'd ended things last time. But even if she was disgusted with him, screamed at him, hated him forever, it was no more than he deserved. And she'd keep his secrets, he knew – she'd never told anyone about Danica.

And he had to tell *someone*.

He tapped his thumb on her name, before he could think better of it, and heard the tinny sound of the phone on the other end ringing. He was committed now.

The phone stopped ringing. "– probably worried. Look, just keep quiet," he heard her say, before she lifted the phone to her ear and answered him properly. "I don't really want to talk to you right now, Niles."

"I know," he said, "I'm sorry, it's just something's –" In the background, he could hear someone moving around, the slight creak of a heavy body settling into her Noguchi chair, the one she'd taken from the old place. "Who's that?"

"None of your business. If I have a – a – a *gentleman caller*" – she sounded tense, flustered – "then I don't think you get to say a damn thing about it, do you? Not with *your* history."

She was right, of course. "Sorry," he sighed, rubbing his forehead. "It's just that I had... I had a very ugly encounter last night, and I needed someone to..." To confess to, he thought. Perhaps it was time he got a religion. He was seeing Cutner tomorrow – he could pay him extra to dress up as a priest. It made about as much sense as paying him to dress up as a therapist.

The man in the background coughed.

"Who *is* that?" Niles said, eyes narrowing.

"I told you," Iyla said angrily, "it's none of your business. Look, I don't have time for any of your –" Niles heard the man mutter something about her just getting off the phone. He knew that voice – that sullen, childish grumble.

He could feel his blood starting to boil. What was *he* doing there? "I'm coming over," he heard himself say.

"Niles, for goodness' sake –" Iyla said, but by then she was talking into a dead phone.

"IYLA! OPEN THE door!"

She'd got the house, of course. He hadn't contested that – although then again, he hadn't had a clear understanding of how much the value had risen since they'd bought it. Between that and landing a prestigious job at Fantasia's animation department in the year of the divorce, the kind that came with large bonuses and performance incentives, she'd had enough to buy some Malibu property – not on the beach, but still very nice indeed, especially compared with his own cramped one-bedroom duplex. When he went there, it always felt like a subtle slap in the face – not from her, exactly, but from whatever part of his nature had destroyed things so completely between them. *Look at what you could have won.*

She'd replaced her old Audi with a Mercedes. He'd helpfully blocked it in the driveway by parking his car on the sidewalk directly in front. Now he was banging on the front door with one hand, furiously pressing the doorbell with the other and yelling at the top of his lungs – the full Stanley Kowalski. Part of him was hoping she'd call the cops on him, create a terrible scene in her driveway, lower house prices in the area for years – instead, she opened the door, letting him storm into her hallway and come face to face with Bob.

The author's gnarled fist slammed into the Fictional's face, flattening his nose like putty. "You owe me $150 for the traffic ticket," he snarled, snapping the man's ribs with powerful, focussed kicks as he lay howling and bleeding on the ground, "and an apology for not calling." He aimed the heel of his shoe at the clone's skull, the powerful blow cracking it like porcelain. Brain matter leaked out onto the expensive hardwood flooring. "Don't you know how worried I was about you?" the author screamed.

Niles marched up to Bob, realised that Bob was taller and quite a lot stronger, and took a step back. "Where have you *been*?" He hissed.

Bob had the decency to look embarrassed, at least. "You didn't come out. It was getting on for forty minutes, and then a bus came, so I got on and rode it back to the city. I, uh, I sent you a text about it, but..." He glanced down at the floor. "It, uh, it didn't send. And then I switched my phone off for a while." He shrugged. "I just couldn't deal with you."

Niles stared at him. "What?" Why wouldn't Bob want to deal with *him*?

"Let's sit down," Iyla said briskly, walking past them and into the lounge.

Bob turned and went with her, leaving Niles standing in the hallway. On the drive over, and during the process of hammering on her door and screaming the street down, he'd been boiling with anger; but now all that had drained out of him, and he was left feeling suddenly deflated. Then he remembered that it was because of

Bob not returning his calls that he'd met up with Liz last night. That was Bob's responsibility. He was the one to blame.

And what was he doing *here,* of all places? He accused Niles of being a realist one minute, and the next minute he was off taking morning coffee with the biggest realist either of them knew?

After a moment, he followed them into the lounge, mutely flopping into one of the larger rattan chairs – a Kenmochi. "I always liked this one," he muttered bitterly.

Iyla flashed him an exasperated look, then turned to Bob. "Could you get us some coffee? It should be brewed by now, there's enough for three." Her voice was brisk, business-like, as it had been when they'd sat with their solicitors and finalised things. Niles shifted on his chair, rocking it slightly. He had the disconcerting feeling that this was going even less well than it appeared.

"Iyla –"

She cut him off. "You don't get to just barge into my house whenever you want to, Niles."

He scowled. "I was hardly *barging* –"

"You were banging on the door like a madman. I actually thought twice about opening it – I was about half a second away from calling the police, but... well, Bob said it wasn't a good idea." She looked away, at one of the prints on the wall, avoiding his eyes for a moment.

"Nice to know I can rely on him," Niles said, acid in his voice. "What's he doing here, anyway? You always hated him."

Iyla looked at him like he'd gone mad. "What?"

"Oh, please." Niles rolled his eyes. "Don't pretend I never noticed. You've acted off around him ever since you found out he was a –"

"Coffee," Bob said, placing one down on a coaster next to Niles, then going back for the other two. He sat down next to Iyla on the couch, and she flashed him a nervous smile. Niles wondered for a moment if he'd been wrong about Iyla and Bob, but that didn't make sense. There'd always been that tension between –

He blinked.

"Look," Bob said, with the air of a hostage negotiator, "I'm sorry I had my phone off. That was just wrong. I just couldn't deal with seeing Rose again, and I needed some space to clear my head, and..." He shrugged. "I'm sorry."

"Don't enable him," muttered Iyla, looking irritated. Niles ignored her.

"Bob –" he said, and paused. He felt like there was an elephant in the room, something he was unable or unwilling to see. He forged ahead anyway. "Did you listen to my voicemails?"

He looked sheepish. "Uh, yeah. I listened while you were coming over here. Look, I'm sorry about the traffic ticket, I could, uh... well, I can't pay you back, but I could give you maybe forty dollars now and –"

"Don't even think about it," Iyla snapped. She fixed him with a contemptuous stare. "Honestly, Niles, is that what you came storming over here for? To extort money?"

Niles scowled, tight-lipped. "Did you hear the message about going down to the bar?" Bob nodded. "Well, something happened while I was there. Something that... I don't really want to go into details, but it was awful, and it happened because I went looking for you. How could you just – just go off the grid like that? When you *knew* I'd be worried about you?" He shook his head, honestly perplexed. "What are you doing *here*?"

Bob and Iyla looked at each other nervously. His hand made the slightest motion towards hers.

Niles felt the floor drop out from underneath him, and his stomach did a slow, lazy flip. His skin felt cold and clammy. He shook his head. "What? No."

Iyla's hand moved closer to Bob's, and he took hold of it briefly, giving it a small squeeze. Then they returned their hands to their laps, looking guilty. Niles' stomach flipped again, in free fall. "How long?" he croaked.

Iyla sighed. "Niles..."

"How long have... you *haven't*, have you?" He was going to be sick. He was actually going to be sick right where he was sitting, all over the Kenmochi, the Mostböck rug, the Fran Taubman coffee table. Be sick on it all.

"Niles, just..." Iyla sighed. "Just shut up and listen for a minute, will you?"

Niles nodded. Iyla took a long, fortifying sip of the coffee, and told Niles about Justine, and after.

SHE'D ACTUALLY SEEN them, that had been the worst thing. It wasn't just a receipt in his pocket, it wasn't just a text message that he'd forgotten to delete from his phone or the smell of her perfume or anything that she could ignore or rationalise, like she'd ignored or rationalised everything for three months – including the two weeks her parents had visited and he'd got bored and gone to hers for a quickie. By then, she'd known exactly what he was doing. But she hadn't seen it.

What happened was: she'd heard noises from Justine's office and thought she might have been having an asthma attack. So she'd pushed Justine's door open, only a crack, just to see if she needed help. And that was just enough

to see Justine bent over her desk, skirt hitched up over her waist, and Niles buried in her with his game face on.

"I suppose I must have known on some level," Iyla said, sipping her coffee. "Otherwise I'd have knocked. I suppose there was some part of me that just had to catch you red-handed before I could really do anything."

She walked away and carried on with her working day, telling nobody what she'd stumbled on. Midway through the afternoon, she took a twenty-minute break to cry helplessly on the toilet, but aside from that she completed all her tasks with almost robotic efficiency. "Great work today, Iyla," Justine had told her on the way out.

She drove home to find her husband in his study, telling her what a productive day he'd had, how he'd put the third chapter of *One, Two, Buckle My Shoe: A Kurt Power Novel* to bed. She decided she wasn't going to get a better opening line than that.

"You kept changing your story. I remember that. First you said there was nothing going on, then that it had happened only the once, that that was the first and last time... then that she'd forced you, tricked you somehow..." Iyla made a face. "And every time it was like you really believed it. Like this was the new reality for you. It felt like all you were was just a – a collection of stories you told yourself."

Eventually, after arguing and crying and shouting their way through most of the night, they'd arrived at a version of the truth they could live with – that Justine was needy, clingy, a stalker who'd inveigled her way into Niles' life, who he was sick of, who he never wanted to see again. It wasn't much of a story, but by that stage Iyla was too tired and heartsick for further revisions. It would have to do.

Iyla asked Niles to end it, but he procrastinated. He'd end it the next day. Or the one after that. *Jam tomorrow,* as her father would say.

It turned out Iyla couldn't get through many more days with Justine telling her what good work she was doing, and asking how her husband was, so she ended up pulling the pin out of the grenade herself and then walking away. Freshly unemployed, with Justine's insults and half-baked justifications ringing in her ears and her belongings in a cardboard box on the seat behind her, she'd driven the car round to Bob Benton's place.

"WHY?" NILES ASKED, numb.

Iyla looked at him for a moment. "What do you want me to say? I couldn't go home. I couldn't stand seeing your face again. And most of the people I'd have trusted to cry on in a situation like that were back in San Francisco. Everyone else was either a work friend or the kind of person who'd have..." She made another face. "'Of course he was going to cheat again, you're an idiot.' That kind of thing. I needed someone who wasn't going to judge, someone who was going to be..."

She stared into space for a moment, then finished her coffee. Niles stared stonily at her. He hadn't touched his.

"I needed a good person, essentially." She put her mug down carefully on the coaster in front of her. "And Bob – you've got to admit – is a very good person." She smiled wanly. "It's how he's made."

Niles said nothing. He remembered how he'd spent most of that evening talking to Justine on the phone, trying to talk her down. He'd been too busy with that to call Iyla, and then when she'd finally got home, at close to midnight, shaking and staring into space, he hadn't

bothered asking where she'd been or what she'd been doing. He remembered that all he'd wanted to know was what he could do to make everything like it was. Before she'd found out. He wished he hadn't bothered with that, now.

He considered standing up, walking out of there, leaving them to it. Instead, he just sat.

IYLA AND BOB had got on like a house on fire since the moment they'd met, at that New Year's party. When she found out he was a Fictional – he'd mentioned the episode of *CSI* in passing and she'd ended up googling it, and him – it was actually a surprise. Most Fictionals seemed to cling doggedly to the personalities they'd stepped out of the tube with, but Bob had always seemed more vibrant, more willing to embrace and accept change. He was the only Fictional she knew of who'd quit of his own accord rather than being cancelled, for example – there was easily another season or two in *The New Adventures*, but he'd sided with the writing team in stopping while they were ahead. Then there was the beard, the attempts to find a career for himself – to define himself – rather than just grubbing a living on the convention circuit. Little things, like learning to cook or dance salsa. Things that weren't in his 'character.'

It wasn't that Bob wanted to be a human being. It's that he already felt he was human. And he didn't see why he had to limit himself to what he'd been born with.

Bob listened to this with a blush, looking away. "Good writing," he muttered to himself.

When Iyla had gone to see him – after nearly crashing on the freeway from crying and driving – he'd made her coffee and listened to her story, offering her tissues and

reassurances and no judgements. She'd confided her fear of confessing to her friends, of their rolled eyes and I-told-you-sos. "It's not on you," he'd said, and held onto her, without it being any more than that... and she honestly forgot that he wasn't real.

"He wasn't making up a story he could live in," she said, "that was the thing. He didn't have a little version of the moment playing in his head where he was the hero. He didn't need to. He was just *there*." She shook her head. "For me, in that moment, he wasn't imaginary. He was less fictional than you were."

She'd kissed him, on impulse, a mixture of petty revenge – *I can cheat too,* she wasn't above that – and a deeper attraction. And he'd kissed her back. And a few minutes later they were on his couch. And neither of them were thinking of body pillows or cartoon horses or social taboos or anything else. Neither of them cared.

It was only later, when she was lying in his arms and she suddenly realised that those arms had been grown in a *tank* – that the man she'd just slept with wasn't even real or human, that he'd been grown for a TV show, and what would her parents think, and what if someone found out, and what about the papers, and all the rest of it – that she'd got up, pulled her clothes on, made her excuses and gotten the fuck out of there. She could tell he was just as freaked out, just as terrified of himself, she could see it in his eyes, but all it had meant to her then was that he wouldn't tell anyone about the awful thing they'd just done. All she felt was a sick sense of relief.

A couple of days later, after she'd thrown up a couple of times, after she'd agreed with Niles that of *course* they'd try to save the marriage – it wasn't like she had a leg to stand on any more, was it? – she'd risked calling Bob on the phone, arranging to meet in a downtown

coffee shop like a pair of Russian spies, so they could talk about what had happened. Iyla had been planning to tell him that the best thing would be for them to never see or speak to each other again – she expected he'd agree to that readily enough – but when he'd walked in, with his hang-dog face and his gentle eyes, she hadn't seen a Fictional, some imaginary thing that had been grown in a lab.

She just saw... Bob.

The second time, neither of them had forgotten anything. They knew exactly what they were doing. They knew it was wrong.

But it was a right kind of wrong.

"You don't have to go into details," Niles said, icily. "I'm feeling ill enough as it is."

Iyla raised an eyebrow. "Oh, really? Do you feel like you're at work and you just walked in on me fucking your boss? That kind of ill?"

Bob winced. "Iyla –"

"No, don't you dare, Bob. Don't you dare take his fucking side." She scowled angrily at Bob. "He's not 'a nice enough guy deep down,' he's a fucking asshole and I shouldn't ever have had anything to do with him."

It hung in the air. Bob looked at Niles with a pained expression. Niles stared daggers back at him.

"So," he said sarcastically, "I'm a nice *enough* guy. But you have to go deep down. Those really are the kind of sentiments you want from your best friend. That and fucking your wife."

"I'm not your wife." Iyla stared him down. "I never should have been your wife. From the way you were carrying on, I never *was* your wife. All I ever was to you was the closest thing to hand, the thing for you when you couldn't find anything newer, or younger, or just different."

"That's not true," Niles muttered, flushing red. "I loved you. I *married* you, for God's sake."

"Right," Iyla said. "And then you got bored."

Bob fidgeted, staring at the carpet, his hands in his lap. Niles couldn't stand to look at him. "So how long were you and him... he and you..."

He couldn't even finish the sentence.

IT HAD LASTED three months. The sneaking around was what killed it, in the end.

It wasn't just that they had to hide it from Niles. If that had been the end of it, she'd have just come out and told him – she'd have had a party, with cake and a band. HAPPY ADULTERY, NILES.

But it wasn't just him. It was everyone.

Iyla wasn't stupid, and neither was Bob. She knew that if anything came out about what they were doing – once, twice a week, during the stolen moments when they were absolutely sure they were safe – it was over for them. She'd seen it happen in 2000, when Ethan Hunt had had that fling with his co-star and they'd been all but hounded off the face of the Earth. Where were they living now? Somewhere in Argentina?

She'd never be able to get another job – any employer, in any city, any *country,* would be one Google search away from all the sordid details. They'd have reporters stalking them day and night, wanting salacious quotes and photos, making up their own when they didn't get them.

And for the rest of their lives, they'd never really know if it wasn't all about to come crashing down. If

something turned up on the internet in 2030 it would –
unless public attitudes had changed completely by then
– be just as damaging as if it appeared the next day. Their
relationship wasn't just a bomb waiting to go off – it was
one with a half-life of fifty or sixty years.

After three months, the stress of it all was too much –
they were both tired of living with the constant tension.
It was time to do what they should have done from the
start and get out of each other's lives for good. And they
nearly did.

During all the sneaking around, Bob had been at the
house a couple of times when Niles had come home
unexpectedly – thankfully while they were both still
clothed. They'd played it off as Iyla teaching Bob to cook
Indian food – the kind of lie Niles would readily believe
– and the three of them had ended up sitting down for
dinner and trying what Bob had made. The dinners
had been full of little overcompensations – Iyla acting
withdrawn, not speaking to Bob or looking at him, while
Bob engaged Niles in endless conversation, letting him
run his mouth off about Kurt Power or the *London
Review* or anything else. When Niles had started calling
Bob on the phone, asking if he fancied a pint, Bob hadn't
felt able to refuse without it looking suspicious – even
after the affair with Iyla was long over.

After a while, though, Bob had begun to honestly
warm to Niles. He seemed to be making an honest effort
to improve himself, to save his relationship, to be a
better person. He had a hell of a blind spot when it came
to self-criticism, Bob would be the first to admit, but...
there was something there. You had to dig for it a little,
but underneath it all he felt sure there was a good person
waiting to get out.

Bob didn't want to abandon him.

* * *

"How nice of you," Niles said, coldly.

"Niles..." Bob sighed, shaking his head. "This doesn't change anything. You're still my best friend. I... I *like* you. I mean, I had to kind of... *grow* to like you... but..." He started again. "Look, I honestly never meant for you to find out about Iyla like this. I never meant for you to find out at *all*. I just... I just needed someone to talk to, that's all. Someone else."

Niles stared at Bob for a long moment. Then he stood up. He couldn't take this anymore. He had to get out before he threw up.

Bob looked nervous, he noticed. Almost afraid. "Niles?"

The author paused on the way to the door, then turned and stared down the trembling clone sitting in front of him, the inhuman thing his wife had whored herself out to while they still slept in the same bed. Slowly, he clenched his fist. Then he drew it back and – no.

No, don't narrate it.

Do it.

Niles leaned forward and punched Bob as hard as he could in the face.

He felt the nose bone crack, and his knuckle shift painfully, and he saw a gush of blood spurt from Bob's nose and into his thick moustache and beard, and then Bob was clutching his face and Iyla was on her feet and screaming at him to get out, to get out of her house now – telling him she'd call the police.

"No you won't, because then everyone'll know *you fucked a Pinocchio –*" That was as far as he got before Bob's fist hit him in the belly hard enough to drive the wind from him. As he went down, Niles found himself oddly thankful Bob hadn't reverted to type and given him a sock on the jaw. It would have cracked in two like a stick of rock.

"You've got a lot of fucking nerve, you piece of shit!" Iyla screamed at him. She was crying again, angry tears rolling down her face. "You're accusing *me* of fucking someone imaginary? *After what you did?*" She lashed out at him with a foot as he scrambled away, getting to his feet, trying to run for the door as best he could. She knew. Somehow, she knew about Liz. She knew he was just as bad as she was. Two Pinocchio-lovers together.

Out of the corner of his eye he saw Bob holding her back, stopping her from kicking him again. Good old Bob, he thought bitterly. What a friend. Then he was out of the door and scrabbling in his pocket for his car keys.

It was only once he'd pulled onto the freeway – while he was thinking desperately about whether she'd hold off on exposing him because of her own position, or whether she'd simply bring the fires of mutually assured destruction down upon them all – he realised that she couldn't possibly have meant Liz when she'd said that.

She'd meant Danica, of course.

He realised that he'd been shaking for the last two miles, and pulled over. Then he started to cry.

He definitely needed to have a chat with Ralph.

CHAPTER ELEVEN

RALPH POURED ANOTHER apple juice. "And then you hit him?"

Niles nodded. "I hit him. And then he hit me. There were also some kicks – from Iyla, I mean. Bob wouldn't ever kick a man while he was down. She was saying something about how I had a lot of nerve after I'd fallen for someone imaginary myself." He gnawed his lip, eyeing Ralph's fake whiskey. "And then... then I came straight here. Pretty much."

Ralph took a sip. "You didn't leave anything out of that at all? You didn't steal a cop's gun and shoot him with it, maybe? You could have fit that in between getting thrown out of the nursing home and hitting a woman you'd just slept with in the face with a door, I really wouldn't put it past you..."

Niles tried to ignore his tone. "This is all completely confidential?" It was the sixth time he'd asked the question.

Ralph nodded, seemingly not minding the repetition. "I keep telling you. It's my first rule – never betray a patient's confidence. Remember that episode with the mafia hit man?" He smiled ruefully. "Great television, they tell me. Personally, all I remember is being absolutely wracked with guilt – honest to God. For as long as the cameras were rolling, as far as I was concerned, I *was* protecting a killer. And, as you'll recall, I didn't breathe a word."

"Actually, I never saw that episode," Niles frowned.

It made some sense, though. He'd heard stories about how deeply some Fictionals got into the 'method' – there was the apocryphal story of how Indiana Jones had donated half his props to a local museum, claiming that they "belonged there," and the props department had had to shamefacedly beg for them back from the bemused museum staff. More recently, there was that ugly business with Dexter, which was fortunately nipped in the bud before anyone was badly hurt. And, of course, there was Sherlock Holmes – the one helping the police with their enquiries – who didn't seem to see a difference between onscreen and off.

It just made Bob's behaviour all the more puzzling to him.

"Ralph... do *you* mind not being real?"

Ralph raised his eyebrows. "Wow."

"I know."

"I see someone's closet realism is no longer very closet."

Niles sighed heavily. "I *know*. I called a Fictional a... a P-word. I don't think I get a closet now." He rubbed his temples, feeling a headache coming on. "Feel free to hit me in the stomach if you want."

Ralph looked at him for a moment, then sat down in the *Cutner's Chair* chair. Since he'd made that little confession about it at their last session, Niles had refused to sit in the thing, and was now perched on the wooden chair opposite where Ralph usually sat. "Do I mind not being *real*..." He seemed to be mulling the question over.

"Am I analysing you now?" Niles groaned. He looked at the clock on Ralph's wall – he had another thirty-five minutes of the session to go and then he'd have to pay for an extra hour on top of his usual time, assuming Ralph didn't have that hour booked for another client. Either way, he wasn't in the mood for Ralph to waste time with games.

Ralph smiled one of his enigmatic smiles. "Maybe. We used to do that occasionally on *Cutner's Chair* – we'd use it for bottle episodes. I'd sit in the chair for a few hours, do some improv – well, it was improv for the actors, but for me it was serious therapy, and therapy I badly needed considering all the crap that got laid on me in the show. They'd edit it down, we'd have an hour of electrifying emotional drama for not very much money, and I'd feel a little better." He paused, looking at Niles. "So, are *you* real?"

Niles looked at him, unable to fathom what he meant. "What do you mean? Metaphorically? Am I authentic? Because a lot of people would say that the Kurt Power novels set in the Middle East –"

"Yeah, yeah," Ralph said, waving it aside. "Think about it from my perspective. When I came out of the tube, I knew who I was. I had a full set of – not *memories*, exactly, but a clear understanding of who I was and the course of my life so far. I was pretty well written in that way – I came with a lot of background." He took another sip from his drink. "But I stepped out of the tube into a world where my life was fiction, a TV show. The closest I could get to it was when that show was being filmed. To me, those times, those takes, were what was real – as real as anything got. The rest... this..." He waved his hand again, dismissively. "*Are* you real? I mean, why should I believe you are?"

"Well..." Niles blinked, confused. "Because I *am* real. You're imaginary."

"To *you*." Ralph grinned. "I'm pretty sure I'm not the only 'Fictional,'" he did 'air quotes,' which for some reason infuriated Niles, "to think about it that way, either. So, do *you* mind not being real?"

Niles shook his head, annoyed. The whole discussion was completely absurd. "Of course not," he snapped. "Don't be stupid."

"Well, there you go. That's my answer too. You've got your reality, I've got mine, I'm perfectly content if never the twain shall meet. In fact, I'm a lot happier that way." He grinned. "And most Fictionals are the same. We've all got our own internal reality, and mixing those realities up feels..." He hesitated.

"Wrong," supplied Niles.

"Right." Ralph nodded. "And maybe it does feel right to some people – mixing reality and fiction like that. A lot of social taboos are made to be broken, right?"

"Eww," Niles grimaced, reacting instinctively. "You're not saying it's all right to –"

"Why not? This taboo's very strong and fresh, and the media love to demonise people over it, but... what's actually wrong with real people and imaginary people doing it? In a hundred years, people are going to wonder what all the fuss was about. Then again" – Ralph smiled, a little sheepishly – "I've got a theory that in a hundred years most people are going to be coming out of tubes anyway. It'll be the only way to beat all the shit the planet's starting to throw at us – mass genetic modification."

"You should be a writer," Niles said, sardonically.

"Look, I'll let you in on a secret," Ralph smiled. "When two Fictionals get together? You 'real' people" – finger quotes – "you people love it. But for the rest of us, it's that taboo again. It's wrong. Like... worlds colliding. That's why Fictional weddings are usually the bride, the groom, and a bunch of non-fictionals hooting at them like they're the last two giant pandas, and none of the rest of us to be seen –"

"Can we change the subject back to me?" Niles said, pointing a finger at the clock. "I mean, much as I'm fascinated by the lives of imaginary people – and you *are* imaginary, you're just delusional with it – I'm not paying extra for this session because you decided to run off on a tangent."

"Not running off, circling round." Ralph grinned, finished his apple juice and put the glass down on the floor. "You've got your reality, I've got mine. We're both fine with them giving each other a wide berth in the bedroom. But from the sound of it, your reality is Bob Benton's reality too. Now, maybe that's just bad writing at the tube stage. Who knows? But as far as he's concerned, he's on your side of the line. He's *real*."

Niles scowled. "That's ridiculous."

"What?" Ralph burst out laughing. "That the Pinocchio wants to be a real boy? That you'd ever let him use your golf course? What?"

"It's just nonsense." Niles muttered, but of course it wasn't. It made all the sense in the world. It was why Bob was Bob, telling everyone that he was a voice actor, growing that damned beard, drinking real alcohol, and yes, yes, *say it* – sleeping with Iyla. Sleeping with his *wife*.

Ralph read the look of disgust on his face and drew the obvious conclusion. "So why shouldn't he sleep with her?"

"What?" Niles' mind boggled. Was he *honestly* suggesting –

Ralph shrugged. "Why not? What's the problem?"

"He's a *Fictional* –" Niles spat the word, surprised as his own vehemence.

"Is he?" Ralph asked. "He doesn't act like one. Hell, he's the least fictional Fictional I ever heard of. In fact, as far as I'm concerned, he's one of you people. You should just accept it."

Niles knew it made sense, but he wasn't about to accept it. If he started deciding who was Fictional and who wasn't on *that* basis, where would it end? There had to be some kind of objective demarcations, otherwise it'd all be chaos. Anybody could just be anything they wanted to be. What sort of world was *that*? "Anyway, she's still my wife," he muttered. "At least, she was then. He had no right."

Ralph got up, wandering back towards the decanter. Niles wished he'd cut back on that stuff, especially after all that gibberish about different realities. If the apple juice really was whiskey in Ralph's reality, it actually explained an awful lot.

"Some might say," Ralph said, pouring himself a double, "that you gave him that right when you had sex with her boss. Or even before then, when you cheated on her with that teenage barista –"

"She was twenty, and it was a smart drink café," Niles mumbled.

"– and some other people, including me, might say that it's not about 'rights' but about freedoms, and Iyla had the freedom to do whatever the hell she wanted with whoever the hell she wanted, womb-born or otherwise. You didn't own her. She was your wife, not your property – if she didn't like being tied to a philandering egomaniac, there was no reason on earth she had to be." Ralph shrugged. "If you think there was, that just makes you a hypocrite as well as a cheat."

Niles stared in disbelief. "Good God, Ralph, tell me what you really think, why don't you –"

Ralph rolled his eyes. "Ah, you were quitting anyway. You never paid much attention to me – now you've finally realised you might actually need some help, you're probably looking around for a real therapist. Someone with a real degree in what the hell's going on with you." He took a slug of the apple juice. "And good luck to 'em. You're the case of a lifetime."

Niles fidgeted in his chair, looking sour. "Thanks," he said, bitterly. He stared at the fake degrees on the wall for a moment, then sighed heavily. "Look, I still need help with this whole Bob and Iyla situation – I can't go to a new therapist with that."

"Oh?" Ralph smirked. "Not going to bring the wrath of polite society down on the star-crossed lovers?"

Niles shook his head, his mouth an angry line. "No. No, I'm not."

"Because you've realised I'm right?" Niles didn't say anything. Ralph chuckled. "No, of course not. It's because if you tell everyone you know about them, you might end up having to talk about this Liz Lavenza – that whole little adventure. I like the way you didn't mention *her* at all during your little tirade against the evils of real-on-imaginary love, by the way..."

"It's not the same thing at all," Niles fumed. "She tricked me – I mean, she didn't disclose. She was giving all kinds of mixed signals –"

"Jesus," Ralph said, shaking his head sadly. "You're a real mess, Niles. Well, we can stick a pin in that – get back to it later. Right now there's something else I'm more interested in." He leaned against the wall, studying Niles carefully. "You said your wife accused you of falling for someone imaginary, but you didn't tell her about Ms Lavenza, did you?"

"No, I didn't," Niles admitted. "I worked out that couldn't have been who she meant on the way home."

"Well, I'll bite." Ralph smiled, returning to the warm embrace of the chair and sitting himself down. "This was the mysterious event that finally triggered the divorce, am I right? The one you've consistently managed to avoid talking about in all the time you've been coming to see me?"

"Yes," Niles said, guardedly.

Ralph nodded. "So. What was her name?"

"Danica," said Niles. "Danica Moss."

THINGS HAD SLOWED between them since the Justine debacle, but not stopped. Not completely.

Sex had gone from a weekly event, to fortnightly, to monthly, and now Niles was noticing the periods between their perfunctory coitus creeping up to five or six weeks. At first he'd been annoyed about it, feeling like he was being punished, but now there seemed little point in kicking up a fuss. He was saving the marriage, that was the important thing.

He felt like a definite corner was being turned there – Iyla had started to lean on him on the couch again, relaxing in a way she hadn't seemed able to for months. Sunday lunch had become a regular culinary adventure as they tried to cook a dish from a different country every week – her idea. They'd joined a book group together, and he was managing not to point out how wrong the various opinions on display were. People who'd wandered away from him in disgust during the worst of it were starting to drift back into his life, though they still eyed him with a wary suspicion at dinner parties, and the look in their eyes as they asked him how the latest book was going – *"oh, it's going,"* he'd say, followed by a lengthy description of the minutiae of every single plot twist and character arc – suggested they'd rather be literally anywhere else.

Occasionally, Iyla would still dig into the wound – bitter, tearful arguments at three in the morning. Niles took these infrequent eruptions stoically, and after the Justine situation he'd become much more discreet, confining himself to very occasional one-night stands with publishing reps, PR assistants and barflies – usually, like him, just looking for a warm body – which he always dutifully regretted the next morning. Generally speaking, life was good, and Niles had felt that he could easily move forward into his sunset years at this steady pace.

He met Danica Moss at the Century City mall.

He'd been browsing laptops, wondering if he could afford to replace the old Dell he was using – it was wheezing and groaning, occasionally overheating, barely ticking over, and although he backed up regularly he was still paranoid about the whole thing just keeling over and dying, leaving him stranded in the middle of a deadline. It was past time to trade up. He was absorbed in these thoughts, idly heading in the direction of the food court, when he noticed the woman with the red hair.

She was sitting on one of the benches in a green coat, a couple of shopping bags at her feet, people-watching – her eyes flitting from one shopper to another, idly taking in the families out for the January sales. He stopped for a moment to take her in – bored, early-to-mid-thirties (possibly a very good forty), well put together, especially her top half – and then looked away hurriedly when she turned her eyes on him. He had business with a bagel in the food court, anyway.

Ten minutes later, while he was eating, she sat down at his plastic table and flashed him a disarming smile. "Hi," she said, "I was wondering if you could help me out with something?"

Her eyes were a very clear, piercing shade of emerald. "Sure," he mumbled through a mouthful of salmon and cream cheese.

She rummaged in her bags for a moment before pulling out a pair of bikini tops. "I'm planning a vacation in Aruba this summer," she said blithely, "and I was wondering which of these you thought would look better? I can't decide."

He blinked. "I'm sorry?" He wondered for a moment if she was serious. It seemed too clumsy not to be a real question.

"You look like a man with good taste," she said, reaching out and patting his arm. The suit jacket had been Iyla's Christmas present to him – he'd asked for something smart he could wear to launches. He found himself oddly glad that he'd worn it.

"It's Armani," he lied, and she smiled warmly. He felt like he'd given a countersign.

"So, what do you think? I like this one, but this one shows off more." Another winning smile. He relaxed, feeling the old urges stirring again – he was enjoying her confidence, the corniness of the routine. And it was nice to feel desired again – to feel like he'd been chosen out of many, not simply because he was the last turkey in the shop.

"Well," he laughed, "I'd have to see you without the coat," and thirty minutes later they were clawing at each other in a motel.

The sex was exciting, energetic, something he'd almost forgotten. Between bouts, they cracked open the minibar and found out more about each other, and he learned that her name was Danica Moss and she was a divorcee living and working in Santa Monica as a fashion buyer. He told her a sanitised version of his marriage, mentioning that Iyla didn't really understand him anymore, and he told her about his novels, about Kurt Power and his dream of eventually getting a movie made. For the most part, she seemed interested – when she was bored, she'd shut him up with her mouth or her fingers and they'd tumble back onto the sheets. He was amazed by his own stamina.

The only sour note was that she never let him touch her hair.

He felt full of beans when he finally returned to the house that evening. Iyla remarked on the change in him, but he'd made sure he wasn't smelling of Danica's perfume or any of the other signifiers, and the motel receipt had been safely disposed of. Iyla really had no reason to suspect anything.

Danica had enjoyed the afternoon enough to give him her number – "I don't usually do this," she'd said, "but what the hell" – and it wasn't long before he called her and arranged to meet again. He felt like some shrunken, vestigial piece of him was coming to life again. The old adrenaline buzz was there, the thrill of hiding a secret, but where Bobbi had felt immature to him, and Justine had been clingy and abrasive, Danica was witty, effervescent, intellectual – she seemed like the perfect match for him, in bed and increasingly out of it. More than once, he found himself wondering what it would be like to spend the evening with her instead of Iyla, to have her head rest on his shoulder while they watched

TV. What it would be like to wake up in the morning to her knowing eyes, her amused smile.

He could tell she felt the same way – she insisted that their regular get-togethers were 'fun,' that she 'had a good time with him.' He'd drive home in a pink fog, bringing his good mood home to Iyla – increasingly he noticed that she was getting short with him, irritable, snapping when he asked her simple questions. As far as he knew, he was still being discreet – destroying the receipts, showering after every time.

He began to think about leaving her.

It was a couple of days before Valentine's Day when he casually suggested that February 14th wasn't so important, that it was just a greeting-card holiday, that maybe he'd take a drive to Burbank, see how it would work as a setting for the new Kurt Power – Danica had already agreed to an afternoon on the most romantic day of the year, which was confirmation that she was falling in love with him, too. Iyla had blown up at him. She'd suspected the affair for weeks, known conclusively for days – one of the motel visits had gone onto his credit card, and she'd opened the bill. This time, he didn't feel like protesting. He told her bluntly that he'd met someone else, someone better, that it was over. Saying it felt like hearing a parole board say he was free to go.

He went out and bought a ring.

On Valentine's Day, they had their usual meeting – he brought chocolates and champagne, she thanked him with fellatio, which felt strangely depressing to him – and he tried to broach the subject of him leaving his wife, of them turning what they had into something concrete, legitimate. But she didn't seem to hear him – every time he got close to talking about real feelings she smiled tightly and changed the subject to anal or scarf bondage or the cubes in the ice machine. "Come on, this is *fun*," she said at one point, laughing. "God, you're so *tense* today!"

Eventually, she said she had to be getting home – tomorrow was a big day at work – and he'd glanced at the ring in the box in the jacket on the chair, unopened, unmentioned. He opened his mouth, trying to find a way into the speech he'd prepared, but the timing was all wrong. As she dressed, she idly tossed off a line about taking a break for a while – "we can pick it up again when it's fresh," she said, and grinned as if that was no major issue. "You've got my number. Call me in a month or two." And then she was out the door, leaving him sitting on the bed, unable to speak. He felt like she'd taken an ice-cream scoop out of her handbag and hollowed out everything he was in one quick motion.

Suddenly, a mad idea came to him. He'd prove to her how he felt.

He reached the lobby in time to see her walking out to her car, calling someone on the phone – *her work*, he thought – and quietly tailed her in his own car, making sure he wasn't spotted. He was surprised at how easy it was to follow someone in a car – the research he'd done had made it seem more of a difficult operation – and fairly soon he'd followed her onto the San Bernardino freeway, driving far away from Santa Monica, towards San Dimas. By the time he reached her place – a modest suburban house with a large front window and a couple of sturdy plastic toys strewn about the yard – the sun had gone down. It made it easier for him to park across the street without being noticed after she'd gone in.

His plan had been to knock on her door, and then – when she opened it – to be kneeling down with the ring, using the shock to launch into his speech, which would have obviously won her over. He couldn't see how a gesture like that couldn't be construed as romantic. But he found himself waiting in the car, staring into that front window at the empty living room. The lights were on, and the curtains were open – it felt like watching a television set.

A blond, well-built man of about forty-five walked into the room, taking a seat on a leather sofa, and Danica followed him in. She was spraying her hairline with something from a can – some sort of solvent, he figured out later – and talking energetically about something. The man listened, leaning forward, one hand straying over an obvious erection as Danica continued describing how she'd spent her afternoon. Occasionally, she looked rueful, and the man would nod sympathetically, but then he'd ask something else and her expression would shift back to the flushed, aroused grin he'd seen up close so many times.

After a couple of minutes, she began to peel the lace wig off her head. Underneath, her hair was short and dark. As the man began unzipping his fly, she moved briskly to the curtains and hurriedly closed them.

He waited a moment, and then – very quietly – he walked towards their front door, summoning the courage to knock. Before he got there, he noticed what was written on their mailbox: DAN & MONICA BEAUFORT.

He threw the ring away on the drive home.

"SO THERE NEVER was a Danica Moss."

"No." Niles' fingers were clenched, and he was hunched over in the chair. The time limit for the session had passed by halfway through the story, but neither man had mentioned it. Instead Ralph had simply listened, cocking his head, taking the occasional note.

"Did you meet her when she was Monica Beaufort?" Ralph sounded genuinely curious. "I'm wondering if she had a different personality when she was, uh, at home. The way you describe her..." He looked apologetic. "It's a little... too good to be true, if you see what I mean."

Niles nodded. "I never saw her again, no." He didn't respond to Ralph's other point, but he'd thought the same thing in his darker moments – that he'd been the victim of a terrible, sick joke, a sexual prank played by two horrible perverts. How many others had they played that game with? Who else had they used as fuel?

"So she was imaginary. Fictional."

"No. I mean, in the most technical sense..."

"She was a made-up character," Ralph shrugged, "playing a show for an audience of three – you, Monica Beaufort, and her husband Dan. Audience response was very positive. All three of you got off on it."

"She didn't come out of a *tube* –" Niles snarled, then tailed off, seeing Ralph's expression. "Sorry."

"Oh no, don't worry about it," Ralph said, curling his lip. "I'm really enjoying draining all the pus out of this mental cyst of yours. No, she didn't come out of a tube, but that's just a matter of technology. The fact is that you slept with a fictional character and it destroyed your life and put you off any kind of intimacy for years. Apart from Iyla and Maurice – who you *have* to talk to – do you ever actually see any human beings? Socially? At all, if you can help it?"

"Well..." Niles looked at the floor. "Everyone sort of drifted away..."

"Drifted, my ass. You *drove* them away, because you couldn't trust them anymore. The only person you could trust was someone you knew was fake, except now *he's* turned around and broken your heart by being a real guy after all. How are you not *seeing this?*"

"It's a bit of a reach –" Niles said, half-heartedly.

Ralph sat back, rolling his eyes theatrically. "All right. Fine. Try this one. You're completely celibate. For three years, since this couple fucked your head up so royally – and they do get the blame for that, even if your head was extremely ready to be fucked, their communication skills are *lousy* and they're a pair of selfish user *assholes* – for three years, you've had no sexual contact with anyone. You're a sexual exile."

"A sexile," muttered Niles. He was hunched over now, almost in a foetal position.

"You said it, I didn't." Ralph stood up, leaning over him. "So there you are. Totally celibate. And suddenly, along comes a woman with red hair and *very* green eyes who is kinda-sorta, just a little bit *fake*. Loaded down with weird hipster inauthenticities and stroking your big author's ego with them. And she's clearly interested in you in kind of an odd, fucked-up way." He had an expression of disbelief on his face, as if he couldn't understand how Niles could be so stupid. "How is this *not* returning to the scene of the crime and expecting a different result?"

Niles hunched further into himself. "I – I don't know." He was trembling.

"How is fucking her, then pushing a door into her face and accusing her of being a fake person *not* some kind of sick after-the-fact punishment for what Monica Beaufort did to you? How does this not *occur* to you?" Ralph shook his head, walking away, pouring another drink.

"She was a Fictional –" Niles said, in a small, frightened voice. There were tears in his eyes.

"Was she? Elizabeth Lavenza was grown in a tank and sent onto the streets of Los Angeles to live in a shitty apartment?" Ralph nodded sarcastically. "Here's a fun fact. You realise Victor Frankenstein's never been translated? The monster, sure! Again and again! But they've always – *always* – got an actor for the mad scientist role. So do you want to explain why any studio would translate Elizabeth *first*?"

"I don't *know* –"

"I mean, this is a pretty sexist industry we're in. I hate to admit it, but the number of female Fictionals is actually pretty small – maybe ten per cent. I bet you could find a comprehensive list on Wikipedia of just about all of them." Ralph knocked back the apple juice and then reached for his smartphone. "In fact, let's do that! Let's do what you could have done *at any time*!"

"I don't –" Niles was shaking now. "Ralph, *please* –"

"Let's see, Ellen Ripley?" He was flicking his thumb across the screen, looking through the entries, showing Niles the photo for each one. "Doesn't look like her. Lara Croft? Nope. Sarah Connor? Nuh-uh. Carrie Bradshaw? Maggie Hayward? Sydney Bristow? I mean, stop me when I find her."

Niles buried his face is his hands, shaking his head.

"How about Violet Song? Allison DuBois? No?" He looked at Niles, mock-incredulous. "You mean she doesn't look like *any* of them? Wow. I guess she's *not* a Fictional, is she?" He slumped down into the chair, putting the phone back into his pocket. "Gee, you think maybe she gave you a fake name?" He shrugged. "Think maybe you knew that all along? I'm just throwing shit at the walls and seeing what sticks here, Niles. It's not like I'm a *real* therapist."

Niles didn't move. Ralph watched him for a few minutes, watching him take great, ragged breaths, his whole body shaking.

Eventually, he regained some of his composure. "I... I should go."

Ralph looked at the clock and nodded. "Well, your hour's up. Same again next week?"

Niles shook his head, getting to his feet. "No. I... I think I need a therapist." He swallowed. "I think there's quite a lot wrong with me."

"Not a '*real* therapist'?" Ralph raised an eyebrow.

"Well. Not a life coach."

Ralph nodded, watching Niles stumble towards the door. "I think that's for the best. Good luck. Settle up with my receptionist on the way out." He scratched the back of his head, as if considering whether to add something. "Oh – and Niles?"

Niles turned. "What?"

"Thanks a lot for today. It was great." Ralph grinned. "It really felt like real life again."

Despite himself, Niles smiled tightly. Then he walked away.

CHAPTER TWELVE

"WHO IS IT?"

The voice was wary, hostile. Niles stared at the hissing black box, the buzzer for the apartment building, unsure of what to do next.

The easiest thing to do at this point would be to chicken out, to say nothing and walk away. But then, this was a moment he'd been putting off in one way or another since he'd left Cutner's office the previous day – first telling himself he was better off leaving well alone, then pretending that it was too late for him to make the drive – and anyway, the Taurus sounded like it might not even make it, that rattle was getting worse and worse – and then another round of 'leave it alone' as he tried to work up the nerve to get out of the car.

Already he'd sidled up to the box twice, holding out his finger to push the button for her apartment, then put his hand back into his pocket and walked away. The first time, he'd walked up the street, back towards his car – he'd actually unlocked it before he'd decided he was being a coward. The second time he'd gone to get lunch at a burger place, telling himself he'd make his 'final decision' there. Instead, he'd sat in a corner booth, listlessly chewing a pink slime patty that refused to sit easily in his gut.

He owed Liz an apology. Whoever she turned out to be, whatever her real name was, he'd behaved abominably towards her. He'd slept with her and then treated her like a piece of trash he could just toss away – he'd *assaulted* her, for God's sake. He could tell himself it had been an accident, that he hadn't meant to shove her like that, but he knew what Cutner would say – that there were no accidents. And why? Because of a paranoid fantasy? Because years ago a woman had hurt him, so now he was wandering the bars of LA looking for women just like her he could hurt back? Was *that* who he was?

No, it wasn't. He owed her an apology and he owed her some kind of restitution. That was all there was to it. If he walked away now, that made him nothing but a worm.

Filled with new resolve, he stood, tossed the remains of his burger into the receptacle and walked sternly back to the Taurus, so he could drive home immediately and never think about it again.

At the last moment, something occurred to him. What if she was thinking of telling the police about it? What if she was on the phone to them even now, telling them he'd attacked her in a fit of psychotic rage? It wasn't that far from the truth – he was sure she could make them believe it. He'd left DNA evidence in her toilet.

Worse, what if she was telling the internet? A tweet or tumblr post that got a lot of attention could get very nasty for him. What if she'd already put something up?

He had to know.

So he'd steeled himself, taken a deep breath, walked up to that damned buzzer and pushed the button before he could stop himself, hoping she wasn't home, hoping he had an excuse to run away. And here he was, still trying to find the excuse.

He'd felt more ashamed of himself than this, he was certain. He just couldn't remember when.

"Who is this? Who's there?"

Niles sighed and leaned closer to the microphone grille. "It's, um." He could feel his face burning. "It's Niles. Niles Golan."

For a long moment there was nothing but the endless crackle of the speaker. He wondered if he'd heard her properly.

"Niles *Golan*. We, um... a couple of nights ago, we..." he started, but then Liz's voice burst through the fizzing speaker again, angry and sullen.

"I'm not letting you in." This time, he noted, there was no fake accent running over the top of her voice – just a native Californian twang.

Niles had half-expected that, but he still found himself faintly relieved. "That's fine. I just wanted to apologise –"

He could hear her getting angrier. Maybe this had been a mistake after all. *"I should call the cops on you, you son of a bitch – you* hit *me –"*

"I opened a door on you," he said defensively. "It was an accident." He blinked, realising fully what she'd said. "Sorry, does that mean you *haven't* called the police yet? Because –"

"I should," she said. The crackling of the speaker box made it sound like he was being remonstrated with by a cloud of furious bees. *"It didn't feel like an accident, the way you were screaming and yelling at me. I was*

terrified. I should edit the thing I wrote on my blog about you and put your name in, let everybody know what kind of psycho you really are –"

"I'm sorry! I'm *so* sorry," Niles said quickly, "I just..." He tailed off. He was going to have to come out with it and hope she was slightly more understanding than Cutner had been. "The truth is... well, I thought you were a Fictional. It does sound a little silly now, I know, but at the time –"

"Wait." There was a pause. *"Say that again?"*

It was hard to tell through the electric crackle of the speaker, but she sounded suddenly calmer. The fury was gone, replaced by something Niles couldn't identify.

"I said I thought you were a Fictional!" he shouted into the grille. "I'm sorry! I don't know how I got that idea, but –"

A loud, harsh sound came from the box – all the bees roaring at once. Then the door swung open with a soft *click*.

Niles looked at the open door, blinking. He looked back at the box, hoping for some answer, but it was silent. The bees were dead.

After a moment, he walked into the building.

HER APARTMENT WAS up on the fourth floor.

The lift had been broken for some time, and by the time he'd hauled himself up the stairs – breathing heavily on the last few, remembering Bob's words and imagining the thick curtains of fat sandwiching his organs – the door to Liz's apartment was open, and she was standing just outside, looking at him reproachfully through one black eye.

His stomach lurched guiltily. He hadn't realised he'd caught her when he'd swung the door open on her like that, but evidently he had.

She was, he noticed, now dressed in clothes that seemed contemporary – a t-shirt of Francis Cugat's famous *Great Gatsby* cover, a pair of dark blue jogging bottoms and some Converse trainers. It was also the first time he'd seen her without any make-up, or – he noticed that her hair was a light, ordinary brown – hair dye.

Her eyes, however, were still the same vivid shade of green. Perhaps she wore contact lenses.

"Who are you today?" he heard himself say, then cursed himself for it. He could feel the bitterness in him rise like sap, spill out like pus. The session with Cutner had left all the old hurts feeling fresh and raw.

The girl – not Liz, he reminded himself; someone else – tilted her head and frowned. "We'll have to see," she said, eyeing him for a moment before walking into the apartment. "You can come in."

He shrugged, suddenly feeling very nervous – outside, a siren blared past, and he felt a wave of paranoia sweep over him. What was this about? Why had she invited him up here again?

Still, he'd come this far. He'd make his apology, find out what she wanted to do about it, and go. And that would be that.

She led him to the kitchen, sat down on a tall wooden stool by the ratty countertop, piled high with empty dishes, cigarettes, and more old books, and then watched him expressionlessly as he looked around for somewhere to put himself. He ended up leaning against the opposite wall, waiting for her to say something. She just looked at him, one eye half-lidded, the other swollen and closed. Eventually, he realised he'd have to be the first to speak.

"So," he said. "Like I said, I came here to apologise for my behaviour." She looked at him with her black eye, and he flushed awkwardly. It sounded like he was apologising for spilling wine on the carpet. "And to see if there was anything I could do to make it up to you. Anything at all."

Now he sounded like a letch.

She nodded absently, studying him for a long moment. "Did you *really* think I was a Fictional?"

Niles hesitated, then nodded. "You seemed very... artificial," he said, trying to put it into words that didn't sound like insults. "And you look – or you looked – a lot like someone I knew once, someone who turned out not to be a real person. I think I just got it into my head that you were imaginary. Like she was." He sighed heavily, reaching up and running his fingers through his greying, thinning hair.

She nodded. "But you thought I was a Fictional. You really, honestly thought that I was a fictional character." There was an urgency in her voice now. Niles didn't understand why she was pressing the point, but it made him uncomfortable.

Niles held up his hands apologetically. "I jumped to a silly conclusion. I'm sorry –" He suddenly noticed that her face had softened and she'd broken into a wide smile.

"You thought I was imaginary. Oh, God, that's *great*." She laughed, her face flushing. She was grinning at him now, looking pleased as punch. Niles found himself once again feeling like he was playing a game that he didn't understand the rules to – but at the same time, it was better seeing her happy than angry, even if it was somehow more unsettling.

He shifted against the wall, looking out of the kitchen door to the hallway. He knew it was time to leave, while

she seemed to have forgiven him. Leave and never see
her again.

He didn't move.

She grinned. "So... you really didn't know what that
was? What we were doing?" She'd relaxed completely,
her leg swinging freely on the stool, her good eye fixing
him with a confident look that he recognised from the
bar. "I mean, I thought I was being way too obvious
about it, but..." She laughed again. "You're not part of
the scene?"

"Scene?" He blinked, confused. "Like a play, or –"

"The meta scene." She said it like he should know – he
just stared, and she shook her head, as if she was talking
to a child. "You know, the *meta* scene. People who –
well, who want to be fictional."

Niles blinked again. "I'm sorry, what?"

"So you're a *real* author? That Kurt Power stuff, that's
all real?" She put her hand to her mouth. "Oh, my
God... your friend is a real Fictional?" She giggled, her
one unbruised eye shining. "You know what I mean. I
didn't recognise him from anything. I kind of thought
you were bi."

"Bi?" Niles felt utterly lost.

"You know. Swinging both ways."

"I know what it *means*, I just –"

She laughed again, giddy as a lamb. "Your friend
looked kind of like a bear, and it looked like you were
playing a scene with him, but you kept looking at me,
so... Jesus, I can't believe you're really an author. I'm
going to have to edit that blog post." He looked stricken.
"Oh, God, not putting your name on there, I don't mean
that. Just to explain why you were so terrible in bed."

Niles winced. After the session with Cutner, he'd
felt as if he'd been standing on solid ground, that he

actually knew what was going on. Yes, it hadn't cast him in a flattering light, but at least the situation was something he could grasp, something he understood. Now he felt as if he was standing knee-deep in quicksand again. "So... you thought I was just –" He tried to think what the terminology would be. "Just, um... role-playing?"

She shrugged, grinning, biting her lip. There was something about her obvious excitement, coupled with the black eye he'd given her, that made him feel deeply uncomfortable at the situation. The erection he was starting to get made him feel worse. It was *The Delicious Mr Doll* all over again. "I guess," she said, "that's a word for it. Jesus, how do I explain this... there's two basic roles – creators and created. Authors, screenwriters, producers – and their characters. I thought you were playing a creator." She tilted her head. "You go to the Victoria a lot?"

He nodded. "Fairly often – just to meet my friend, really. We go to other places too."

"It's kind of a meta hangout. The first Thursday of every month is the big meta night for the area – you ever been then?" She smirked. "You'd be a hit."

Niles frowned. He knew there were private functions in the Victoria, but he'd assumed they were just office parties, or birthdays, or board game nights – something he could understand. The idea of a hidden world operating under the one he knew seemed to him very... well, fictional. Like a bad movie – one of those sub-*Basic Instinct* knock-offs about ordinary people sucked into sleazy masquerade balls reminiscent of old *Electric Blue* videos, designed to titillate the audience while at the same time reassuring them that immorality never paid. "I don't know anything about that," he said.

"You should come along," she said, and winked, or maybe blinked – with the black eye, it was hard to tell. He was getting flashes of the Liz Lavenza he'd met, the strange, flirtatious, confident girl from the bar who he'd been so fascinated by. He shifted again, trying to rearrange the front of his trousers in such a way as to be inconspicuous.

"You say you *want* to be a Fictional?" he asked, genuinely curious. "Why?"

She shrugged, looking away. "Who wouldn't? I mean, fictional people live forever. That's one reason."

Niles shook his head impatiently. Maybe a few days ago that answer might have satisfied him, but after the conversations with Bob, the meltdown in the rest home, he didn't believe it. "Fictionals never *look* old. They're not immortal. They die."

"On the page?" She half-smiled at him, then looked around the kitchen. "I could use a smoke. Do you want one?"

Niles shook his head. "I don't."

"Do you want me to have one?"

"What?" He stared at her. "If you like. It's your apartment."

"But do you want *me* to have one?" She grinned mischievously. "Is it in *character*?"

"I... I suppose so. Yes." He didn't know what the correct answer was, what she wanted from him exactly, but she grinned a little wider and grabbed the carton of cigarettes off the countertop.

She pulled one of them out and looked around for a lighter. "Now you're getting it."

"Am I?" He looked towards the door again. He could still leave any time he wanted. "You're avoiding the question."

"Am I?" She smiled, finding a plastic lighter and flicking it into a flame, puffing the little tube into life and then breathing out a long plume of rich, carcinogenic smoke. "You know, a lot of the authors, the creators – on the scene, I mean – they're mostly just your average tops. They like the trappings of it, they like the play, the control, but the things they get off on about it are the same things they could find at your standard BDSM night." She tilted her head again at Niles' reddening face, smirking. "So the stories I get put into by them are kind of samey. There's a lot of, uh, author insertion fanfic, if you know what I mean."

Niles knew what she meant, but he decided to tactfully ignore it. He shifted again, trying to move his coat so it covered his groin better, and nodded vigorously. "Oh, there's no excuse for writing yourself into your own novel. It completely breaks the narrative."

She smiled at the answer. "It's fun enough, I guess. I can get into it." She took another drag. "But it's not the same. I want to meet an author who just, you know, wants to be an *author*, not a top roleplaying an author so he can get to be a top..." She laughed. "That's what I thought you were. You just seemed to be so... into it. Like I said, I figured you were playing a scene. But you kept checking me out, so I figured you might be available. And you kind of projected the whole *I'm-a-writer* thing really well – much better than the guys I usually end up with."

"Well, I *am* one," Niles said. "You still haven't told me why."

"I haven't?" She laughed. "I figured I'd made it pretty explicit."

"Well, yes, obviously it's, um... you know. A... a sex thing." Niles blushed crimson, feeling increasingly flustered. "But *why?* What do you get out of – of being a *Fictional,* of all things?"

"It's not about being *a* Fictional. It's about being *fictional.* Imaginary." She fixed him with that cool green stare, blowing another plume of smoke. "I want to be a figment of someone else's imagination." The way she said it felt almost like a challenge. "I want to be narrated. I want every thought in my head to come from a typewriter. I want to be somebody's idea of what a woman is, how a woman thinks. Someone's little Mary Sue."

"Is... is that your name?" Niles asked, flustered by the speech, her confidence and aggression when she'd delivered it. It probably wasn't the first time. "Mary Sue?"

She snorted. "What do you think my name is?"

"Well, I don't know."

"You're the writer, Niles." She stood in front of him, holding the cigarette between her fingers, looking right into his eyes. There was a flush in her cheeks. She whispered the question. "What's my name?"

Niles hesitated for a second. "Danica," he said, without knowing why. "Danica Moss."

She nodded. "How do I talk? What do I wear? What colour's my hair?"

"Red. But you dye it that colour." Niles wondered what on Earth he was doing. He didn't want to hear one of her fake accents, he decided. "Californian, from Santa Monica. You wear..." He was worried if she left the room the spell might break. "Right now, you're in a t-shirt and jogging bottoms." She looked faintly disappointed at that – slightly peeved, even, as if he was playing too safe. "And you don't smoke," he added.

Immediately, she reached behind her and stubbed the cigarette out on an empty plate. She kept her eyes on him, expectantly. "Danica..." she prodded, after a moment's silence. "Next word?"

"Danica *Moss*..." Niles started, then paused. He had an idea what was expected of him, but no idea what to say. Suddenly, it came to him. "Danica Moss said she would buy the flowers herself." He had no idea where the Virginia Woolf came from. But it was a start.

"I'll buy the flowers myself," she said, quietly, to herself – *Danica said*, he thought, the blasphemy of it appalling and delighting him, making his cheeks burn and his heart hammer. She was looking around the kitchen now, as if he wasn't there at all.

"That would be the last thing on the list, she thought –" Niles said, improvising. He watched her nod to herself. "She had a lot to do first, before the apartment could be in a fit state for guests, and not much time to do it in." An anxious look crossed her face – *Danica's face* – but she didn't move. Niles nodded. "Um, the first thing she had to do, was... ah..."

He paused for a moment, surprised to find himself actually thinking the story through. Danica – that was her name now – glanced expectantly at him out of her corner of her eyes, her cheeks still flushed. "Start that paragraph again," he said, curtly, and she nodded imperceptibly.

"She was a fashion buyer by profession, and a number of high-profile clients would be descending on her that evening for a dinner party. No, strike that. *Cocktail* party." A dinner party would mean Danica having to clean the kitchen, and he didn't want to spend time on that. "At which various people would be in attendance," he considered, wincing a little at the tortured style of his prose, "including her boss... uh... Ms Streep."

So he was writing a cheap knock-off of *The Devil Wears Prada* – a book he had never actually read. He wished he had a moment to look up how fashion buying worked. He wracked his brain for the next line.

"She decided to go and see if the living room was in a fit state to entertain the guests that she was... inviting into her living room," he said, and while he was wondering if he'd said 'living room' twice during that sentence, Danica obediently walked out of the kitchen. He followed her next door – the 'living room' was a small, dark space, with a couple of battered armchairs, a portable TV and the same clutter of old books and films, piled up on whatever surfaces could hold them. Danica was stood in the middle of all this, looking around, her expression blank.

Niles quickly decided that he wasn't interested in watching her tidy up. "Danica's apartment was done up in a shabby chic style, a stylish, um..." – it took him a moment to find a word that would fit – "*invocation...* of the clutter of daily life. She'd spend thousands on getting it just so, and it was perfect. Ms Streep would be very impressed." Danica smiled, biting her lip slightly as she looked around, nodding in approval. Niles could tell she was excited, even if her character wasn't yet – he'd have to do something about that – but the story he was telling was starting to bore him. It was about a subject he didn't know a lot on, which was going to mean stopping for some tedious research at some point, and there wasn't much conflict to speak of yet either.

Also, it needed some sexing up.

"The handsome polo champion, Mark... um, Steele-Fanshawe..." Niles murmured – yes, he thought, let's mash some Jilly Cooper in there – "...would be in attendance, and as a 'nineties woman who wanted to have it all" – *what?* – "Danica was certainly, ah, wanting to look her best for the occasion." He looked over at Danica – she was still looking around the room, arching her back slightly, running a hand through her hair, visibly being of the 'nineties and wanting to have it all.

She was breathing harder now. Niles had stopped bothering to hide his erection.

"Danica walked into the bedroom and took off her shirt," began Niles.

Then his phone rang.

As Danica strutted out of the living room, past the piles of old books in the hallway and into the bedroom, already yanking her t-shirt off in one quick motion, Niles took a look at the screen. TALISMAN PICTURES.

"Damn it," he muttered. "Sorry. I have to take this."

Danica froze, the t-shirt up over her head, in mid-step, as if someone had paused her with a remote. She was wearing a sports bra underneath, and Niles could see the flush of her cheeks had spread over her chest. Niles stared at her for a long moment, then at the ringing phone. He sighed heavily and took the call.

"Miles!" The voice on the other end yelled. *"Baby!"*

"Who's this?" Niles blinked.

"Mike Stillman, Talisman Pictures – I'm your studio liaison on the *Mr Doll* project."

"Oh!" Niles nodded, keeping one eye on Danica. She was keeping unnaturally still. "Um, actually it's Niles. Niles Golan." He wasn't making that mistake twice.

"You sure?" Mike's voice bellowed. Niles could swear he could hear the man chewing gum. "'Cause I got *Miles* on the post-it. What the hell – Niles, Miles, tomato, tomato, let's call the wrong thing off, right? *I kid!* I kid 'cause I love! But seriously, Niles, what's the sitch with the pitch? Because we're *really* – I want to stress that, okay? *Really* eager to hear what you've got for us. *Mr Doll* is going to be the blockbuster hit of next summer, and *you* are going to be his proud papa."

"Mike," Niles said, carefully, "what happened to Jane?"

"Who?" Mike sounded genuinely confused.

"Jane Elson. She said she was taking over Dean's projects." Niles looked up at Danica in frustration, eager to get back to it. She was still standing in the same place, the same pose. Her arms were wobbling slightly now, but she seemed content to hold the pose forever. Niles decided to finish the call off quickly. "Anyway, Mike, listen, it's not really a good –"

"Jane *Elson?* What the hell does *she* have to do with it?" Niles heard the man spit his gum across the room – either that or the wet sound was a vein popping. "Listen, brah, no offence, but there's only one alpha dog up in this bitch and it's *me*, okay? I am the guy who is looking out for you. I am the guy with your best interests at heart. All I need from you – all I need to make you our number one guy for this movie, to make you the man who created *Mr Doll* – is the *pitch*, okay?" He paused. "So where's the pitch?"

"I'm working on it," Niles said, half-heartedly. Danica was still holding the same pose, and to be honest, it was starting to feel a little creepy. Why didn't she relax? He found himself looking at the black eye he'd given her. "Mike, I really am in the middle of –"

"What the fuck are you doing?" Mike seemed incredulous. "What the fuck are you doing that's not the pitch? Where's the pitch? Where's the pitch, bitch? Huh?" His voice grew louder and louder, until Niles was worried his spit might start flying out of the phone. "Where *is* the pitch, bitch? Where's the pitch? *Bitch? Where is the fucking pitch, bitch?*" He was screaming now.

"Um..." Niles squeaked.

"Jesus, I'm *joking*." Mike's voice had no trace of humour in it. "Of *course* I'm joking. Jesus Christ. But seriously, Miles, where's the pitch? Have you *got* the pitch? Can I *hear* the pitch?"

"Look, Jane said I could take a few days –"

"*Jane's not here!*" Dean bellowed, and Niles heard the *slam* of a palm hitting a desk made of some valuable hardwood. He flinched, finding his eye drawn back to Danica's black eye – and why was he calling her *Danica*, of all things? If Ralph had seen it he would have called the mental hospital. What on earth was *wrong* with him?

"Jane is *not* a part of this project! She has her *own* projects, like typing up her *fucking resume* –"

"Wait, she's fired?" Niles was astonished. "What for?" Not farm animals, surely?

"– and *you* are not part of them! Jesus fucking Christ, are you *trying* to insult me? Is that what this is, you *want* me to throw you to the fucking kerb and find someone who will *get me the fucking pitch* –" Mike stopped suddenly, almost in mid-scream, Niles heard him take a very deep breath. "Okay," he said, in a calmer voice, "Okay, you don't have the pitch yet. That's fine. You're a busy guy. I'm a busy guy. Jane's a busy girl, she's got to clean out her desk because she didn't get us the pitch on time, because of *you*. We're *all* busy guys. Busy bees in a tree. Just get me something for later today – no, you know what? I'm gonna be generous. Make it tomorrow morning. Get me something for then and we'll just move on, get past this and make everybody some money. Apart from Jane, I mean. Smell you later."

"But –" Niles started, but Mike had already rung off. He stared at the phone for a moment, putting it away, and then looked over at Danica – no, not Danica. He still didn't know her real name, but she wasn't Danica Moss.

Danica Moss didn't exist.

"We should stop," he said, then decided the right thing to do was probably to finish the story. "It was a very nice party, the end." Instantly, she snapped out of it.

"Why are you stopping? Lost the flow?" She pulled her t-shirt back on. "It happens occasionally. Especially if you get interrupted." She smiled. "If it's any help, you were very good for a first timer."

"I didn't know what we were doing," he said, weakly, which was true for one of them. He honestly didn't know what the hell he'd been doing.

"You were doing fine." She grinned, winking her unblacked eye at him again. "I was really enjoying being Danica."

Oh, God.

"Um, listen, that call," Niles stammered, "I – I – I owe someone some work. So I have to go home now." His voice sounded high-pitched and reedy in his ears, like a child's, and he knew she'd think he was making some cheap excuse to run away from the situation.

Which was fine. It was the truth.

"Hmm. Well," she said, tilting her head slightly, "maybe I'll see you at the Victoria. First Thursday of the month, remember."

He smiled and nodded, almost tripping over in his haste to get out, back to the car, back to the relative safety of his apartment. She watched him go, her smile fading. Just before he'd managed to fumble the lock open, she called out to him. "Niles!"

"Um, yes?" He forced a smile.

"I'm one of your characters now. You should watch out." She grinned, and there was the ghost of something malicious in it. "If you stop writing me, one day soon I'll just cease to exist. And then you'll never be able to think up anyone like me again."

He looked at her black eye. "Bye!" he trilled, and left.

OUTSIDE, THE CAR wouldn't start. The persistent rattle in the engine had evidently spread to something more important. For a moment, he considered taking it as a sign – maybe he should go back up there, apologise again to Liz, or whatever her name was, see if there could be anything between them. Maybe there could be something between them after all. Maybe this 'meta' was something he could get into.

"There is one thing that bothers me," the 'filmmaker' roleplaying in the latex steam-punk outfit said to the author, as the 'meta' play raged all around them. "What you're doing now, narrating to yourself – does it count as masturbation?"

"Oh, shut up," Niles muttered, and started looking up auto repairs.

CHAPTER THIRTEEN

THE REPAIR PEOPLE were very good about rescuing the Taurus, giving him a lift as far as the garage – he could take a bus the rest of the way – and getting back to him almost immediately with a diagnosis. Something very basic had gone wrong with the battery connections, nothing that couldn't be fixed in a day or so for a couple of hundred bucks – that said, it was very lucky he'd called, as the fan belt was about to go, the tyres were looking very bald indeed, the brake lining was a death trap and there were a number of other minor and major problems which would turn his car into a screaming fireball of death the very second he put his foot on the accelerator. Unless, of course, they were dealt with immediately at a cost of nearly two thousand dollars.

Niles wondered if this was the moment to shop around for another garage, but they had his car as a hostage now. Besides, he'd never been very good at dealing with that type of person. He'd meekly agreed, looking around the bus to make sure nobody realised he was being swindled in front of their eyes and thinking that Kurt Power – the authentic American working man – would never connive a client out of two thousand dollars. Not unless that client was a terrorist, of course.

When he eventually arrived back at his apartment, there was a largish flat brown package waiting for him in his mailbox, courtesy of eBay – *The Doll's Delight*, he supposed. He'd get to it later. Right now he needed a shower, a change of clothes, and a stiff drink, in that order.

The drink ended up as a vodka and orange, with very little orange to it. He needed the vodka more than the Vitamin C – the events of the past few days had left him feeling frazzled and hollow, tired down to the marrow of his bones. It had been days since he'd had any kind of decent night's sleep. He'd not had a full eight hours since... well, since he'd seen Maurice and Dean in the diner, really. Before all of this had started. Before he'd somehow managed to burn down his entire life.

He sat on the couch for a while, staring into the black eye of the television, thinking of the black eye he'd left behind him, and wondering where exactly one got new friends from. Was there an online service for people who had alienated every single person they'd ever met? There was always Maurice, he thought – although Maurice was more a colleague than a friend, and even so, he hadn't taken Niles' calls for days now.

Still, maybe Maurice could offer a contest of some kind. Kurt Power devotees around the world could compete – whichever fans knew the most Kurt Power trivia would become his official friends. Say about five of them for the first round – then, after he'd alienated those five, he could have another contest for five more and drive them away in turn.

It was foolproof.

As the author smiled at the five sycophants joining him around the table, a very strange thing happened. Bolstered by such uncritical, unconditionally loving company – like Dr Fischer of Geneva, surrounded by a cadre who would forgive him his every fault – his usual self-regard reached a terrifying critical mass and he began to collapse in on himself, quickly imploding into a smallish black hole which went on to dictate its autobiography, in the manner of The Diving-Bell And The Butterfly, *by firing pulses of radiation from its surface in a strict pattern. The autobiography was, needless to say, dreadful.*

"Welcome back," muttered Niles sarcastically, in response to the narrative voice. "Here was I thinking you'd gone for good."

He shook his head, burying his face in his hands for a moment, and then reached for the flat brown package, shucking it open and sliding *The Doll's Delight* out of the cardboard sleeve. *By H.R. Dalrymple,* he read. *Illustrations by Mervyn Burroughs.*

It was a thin book, perhaps twenty pages with a hardback cover – he recognised the illustration from the grainy photo he'd seen on that website of 'fifties ephemera. He'd assumed its disturbing quality had been an accident of the low resolution, but if anything the front cover was worse now that he could see it clearly with his own eyes.

It was a painting of a little girl, sleeping in a field at night. At least, he assumed she was meant to be sleeping – she looked dead. The anatomy of the neck was all wrong and it looked like it had been twisted and broken – meanwhile, the girl's skin had a waxy sheen to it, as though it had already begun to rot. The delighted smile on her face made her look like a member of a suicide cult.

Around the corpse danced a number of creepy-looking dolls and toy soldiers, each with a fixed glare and a macabre grin painted onto their varnished wooden faces. Any one of them would give a child nightmares – together, they looked like they were going to crawl out of the cover *en masse* and devour the first maternity ward they laid eyes on.

Finally, in the corner of the illustration, hiding in a clutch of wild flowers, there hunched the *coup de grace*. It took Niles a good minute to work out that the creature was supposed to be a little brown field mouse, as opposed to a slavering rat.

Either *The Doll's Delight* was some covert branch of the MK-ULTRA program designed to cause the maximum trauma in a young mind, Niles decided, or Mervyn Burroughs was spectacularly unsuited to be an illustrator of children's books.

He settled back on the couch, opened the book up and began to read:

THE DOLL'S DELIGHT
By H.R. Dalrymple
Illustrations by Mervyn Burroughs

In the watches of the night
We gather for the Doll's Delight
We laugh and play and never fight
When boys and girls are sleeping.

Here's the ballerina fair
And here is Mr Teddy Bear
You never saw a sweeter pair
When boys and girls are sleeping.

Here's the soldier with his gun
Who's run away to join the fun
He won't make war with anyone
When boys and girls are sleeping.

See them laugh and see them sing
A-dancing in the fairy ring
Your dolls can do most anything
When boys and girls are sleeping.

Here's the peg-boy made of wood
Saying things he never should
Not all your dollies can be good
When boys and girls are sleeping.

See him shout and see him curse
He started bad, he's getting worse
He's so unpleasant and perverse
When boys and girls are sleeping.

Little dolls who can't be nice
Must learn to be, or pay the price
And be devoured by rats and mice
When boys and girls are sleeping.

Now the dolls are full of grace
And every dolly knows their place
There's not a single frowny-face
When boys and girls are sleeping.

In the watches of the night
They gather for the Doll's Delight
They laugh and play and never fight
When boys and girls are sleeping.

"When boys and girls are screaming, more like," muttered Niles.

The cover was the least of it.

Each of the poem's nine verses was copiously illustrated in a double-page spread by the extraordinary talent of Mervyn Burroughs, children's literature's answer to Francis Bacon. The first four, admittedly, weren't quite as bad as the rest – once you'd seen the cover, and you had a stiff screwdriver inside you, you could just about stand to look at them. The illustration for the fourth verse in particular – the 'fairy ring' – was almost pleasant in comparison to the others, or at least only mildly ugly. If you were an art teacher in some adult education class and you saw Mervyn Burroughs paint an illustration like that in your class, you'd only take him aside and gently explain things like 'perspective' and 'how to mix paint,' before refunding his money and sending him merrily on his way. You wouldn't attack him bodily with a T-square.

On the other hand, if you saw him working on the illustration for the fifth verse – the 'wooden peg-boy' that Niles now found himself gazing in horror at – you'd most likely go straight to the police and warn them about the dangerous serial killer.

If Mervyn had been forced to play with the 'peg-boy' as a young child, it might explain a few things. Niles had never seen any toy remotely like it in his life. He doubted anyone else had either. If he was being particularly charitable, he could claim it reminded him of a Victorian clothespin doll, but where those dolls were usually beautifully carved and lovingly painted, the 'peg-boy' was a whittled lump of driftwood, with horrifically thin limbs, dark, piggy eyes gouged out with the point of a knife and a hateful, sneering slash carved across its face to serve as a mouth. He made the other dolls in the scene, hideous as they were, seem like beautiful *objets d'art*. Niles had finished his second vodka looking over that picture, and had to go and make a third.

He'd run out of orange, but it didn't matter. If he was going to keep looking at the 'peg-boy,' he'd take it neat.

Flipping over the page, he grimaced and made a little noise in his throat. The next illustration was even worse – a shot of the 'peg-boy' dancing and shrieking, the slit of his mouth yawning open in a way that seemed comical at first glance but got progressively more horrific the longer you looked at it. It was like something out of Heironymus Bosch. The other toys shrank back from him as if he was a terrifying homunculus they'd called into being, while in the shadows there lurked the faintest suggestion of demonic eyes.

Niles tilted his head, letting the warmth of the third vodka run through him. It occurred to him that if he stopped looking at *The Doll's Delight* as a children's book, it actually made some sense. The perspective was still off, the colours still veering between muddy and garish, there was still no clear idea that Burroughs knew anything about the anatomy of humans or dolls... but take this out of the context it was allegedly meant for and it might be a fascinating piece of outsider art. Burroughs might be the Henry Darger of his generation – well, aside from Henry Darger, of course. Maybe that was the point?

The next page showed a rat – Niles had been right the first time, it couldn't be a mouse – emerging from the bushes and gnawing grotesquely at the peg-boy's face, carving deep gouges into the wood. Around the unfolding nightmare, the other dolls cheered, dancing much as they had in the fairy ring. Niles felt his belly crawl up to his chest, do a lazy loop and then slowly dig its way back down again. No, he decided, this wasn't for children. It couldn't be. There was a terrible, savage bitterness to the verses – what had Matson called it? *Vicious camp*.

Listlessly, he flicked through the remaining pages – the peg-boy was simply gone from the world, leaving only the toys with their glassy expressions, dancing and playing as relentlessly as they had at the book's opening, while the verses seemed to suggest some ghastly Orwellian nightmare. Who *was* Henry R Dalrymple? A situationist? A performance artist? Some pseudonym for Burroughs, or the other way round? Or a disgruntled children's author rebelling against the medium?

He flipped through it again, looking for clues. There was a dedication on the inside front cover, in pencil – *To Aspy; Well, I gave it a shot. Uncle Hank*. Curiouser and curiouser. He found himself wondering what the story behind it was – how the whole book had come to be.

He sighed and tossed it onto the table. Well, he didn't have time to waste on that now – he had a pitch to write. The back cover stared up at him – a single image of the red wooden soldier, his painted grin leering mockingly, fascinating him. He reached out to flip it over, but that just brought him back to the front cover again. He could see now that the thing in the flowers was definitely a rat. He thought about rats in flowers, flowers in dustbins, the juxtaposition of images...

No. Now was not the time. He quickly moved his laptop to cover *The Doll's Delight*, removing the temptation. Then he went to the kitchen and made himself a fourth vodka.

"Right," he muttered, returning to the couch, drink in hand. "*The Dangerous Mr Doll*, take one." This was going to be the big one – the one they'd remember him for. An exegesis on the subject of life, fiction and Fictionals, wrapped up in just over two hours of girls in bikinis and exploding volcano bases. Everything he'd learned over the past few days in one soul-searing package.

Steady, he told himself.

Breathe in.

Breathe out.

And open on...

He couldn't think of anything. "Open on..." He mumbled the words out loud, but his voice just sounded high-pitched and feeble in his ears. His head felt raw, empty, scraped out like a pumpkin. Open on... something. Open on what?

He tried to imagine himself talking to Dean, or Jane, or Mike. All three of them, in some boardroom or meeting room somewhere. All of them waiting to hear what their pet genius had to say.

"Open on..." the author said, and paused. The producers looked up at him, expectantly. In the corner of the room, he could hear a clock ticking.

One of the producers looked at his watch.

Suddenly it came to him. "Open on a Fictional, lying inside a ring of stones on a grassy field," the author said. "His face is being eaten by rats and mice."

The producers shifted uncomfortably in their seats.

Niles winced, furiously rubbing at his temples. "God, no. Not that." His head was starting to throb unpleasantly. He hoped he wasn't coming down with a cold.

"Open on..." the author thought desperately for a moment – "Open on a ring of stones in a forest. A ballerina dances with a large stuffed bear."

One of the producers looked at the others, shaking her head. "What is this, Tim Burton? Come on, we're trying to make a serious movie here."

Niles looked at his glass for a moment, then tossed it back in one. "Write drunk, edit sober," he muttered to himself. It was good enough for Hemingway.

"Right," he said, voice thick and choked. "Pitch for *Mr Doll* reboot. Go. We open on..." He licked his lips, staring at the sliver of hardback peeking out from under the black plastic of the laptop. "We open on..."

"We open on a small, carved wooden figure. Limbs like thin twigs. Mouth a cruel slash in its face. Eyes bored out with the point of a switchblade." The author leaned forward, urgently, locking eyes with each of the producers in turn. *"Underneath the figure – wet grass. It's night. A field. A ring of stone. The thunder cracks! Lightning flashes – illuminating a single set of footprints. Someone left this strange talisman here. But who? And why?"*

The producers craned their neck, lapping it up. *"Who?"* asked one of them, breathlessly, his watch forgotten. *"Why?"* asked another. The author looked down at them, eyes filled with cold command. He paused for a long moment – then spoke.

"I haven't the foggiest idea," he said, and threw himself out of a window.

"Fuck it," Niles growled, and lifted up the laptop.

HE LOOKED FOR Mervyn Burroughs first, trying every search he could think of, but aside from the website he'd already seen, nothing came up. *"Weird!!!"* remained the only word available on Mervyn.

He had a little more success with Henry R Dalrymple, but not much. There was a Henry Robert Dalrymple on Wikipedia – a Canadian Professor of Chemistry who occasionally appeared on children's TV, born in 1962, not the right one – and any number of Henry Dalrymples on the various family tree research sites, but combing through those would have taken him weeks. Although he supposed he could cut the time down by checking if any of them had nieces named 'Aspy' – that couldn't be a common name. It was almost certainly short for something –

He paused for a moment, then picked up the hardback and turned it over, examining the spine. Aspidistra Press. 'Aspy.'

He tried the White Pages – didn't bring up a match. Of course, if she was his niece, there was no reason why she should have his surname – even if she did, she might have married and taken someone else's name in the meantime. On a whim, he tried 'Aspidistra Burroughs.'

Three matches. One in Michigan, one in Tennessee, one in California.

The one in California remembered *The Doll's Delight*.

"Oh my goodness," she said, in a frail, bird-like voice, "Uncle Henry's book! Do you know, I'd almost forgotten about that."

"Well, I've got a copy here actually," he said, unable to hide his smile. He was feeling an immense glow of satisfaction from just talking to the woman – with the four vodkas in him, the conversation felt like real progress towards the goal of a finished pitch, even though the sober part of him knew that he was only taking himself further and further down a blind alley. "Just got it today."

She laughed. "Ha! How'd you like it? Scared the pants off you, I'll bet."

"It, er, it was certainly something," Niles smiled. "I've got a few questions I was wanting to ask you about it, actually –"

"Well, here's one thing I'll tell you for nothing," she said with a little chuckle, "you want to hang onto it. My Dad and Uncle Henry only managed to print up a few of them – not even double figures, I don't think. Your copy's probably worth something."

About $120, thought Niles, not counting postage and packing. "Actually, I think it's your copy."

"No!" She sounded shocked.

"There's a dedication here in pencil, saying *To Aspy*. It's how I found you, as a matter of fact."

"You are *kidding!* It's the very same one Uncle Henry gave me? Do you know, I thought that was gone for good! How much do you want for it?" There was a noise from the background – someone voicing an objection. "Oh, hush up, Meadow! It's my money, I'll blow it how I like! Or, for gosh sakes –" She sighed down the line, exasperated. "My *daughter* would like a *word.*"

Niles could actually hear the roll of her eyes.

"Hello?" A younger, harsher voice. Niles could tell he wasn't going to get on with her. "Listen, we're absolutely not interested in buying anything over the phone right now." A murmur of protest in the background. "Mama, I don't *care!* You're not falling for another *scam!*"

"Well," Niles interrupted her, "I wasn't actually planning on selling it. I could *give* it to her, if she wants, but –"

"Is this a book club?" Meadow said, sounding suspicious. "Because we're not interested in signing up for any of those either. Listen, can I speak to your supervisor?"

"I don't have a supervisor," Niles sighed, "I'm, I'm sort of tracking the evolution of a story –" He realised how ridiculous it sounded even as it came out of his mouth. "I mean, I'm interested in this children's book I've got and I was wanting to ask your mother a few questions about it –"

"We're just not interested in buying anything right –" Melody started, and then there was another interruption from behind her. "*Mother,* I'm trying to *help you* –" The line went dead.

Niles stared at the phone for a moment, wondering if he should call them back. He really didn't want to waste any more time talking to Meadow – then again, that seemed to be the only way to get the answers he was looking for. He really felt like he was on the cusp of something important.

"Spare change?" the author grinned at the passer-by, through what few teeth remained. The man took one look at him – the long, greasy hair, the unkempt beard, the hollow set of his eyes, the stinking, filth-covered shawl that was wrapped around him like the decaying skin of some mangy animal – and almost vomited into the gutter. "Spare a little change, sir?" the artist repeated, rattling his tin mug. There was a single bottle cap inside.

"Get a job!" the passer-by cried – an instinctive howl of pure revulsion.

"I can't," the author moaned. "I'm on the cusp of something important."

"Then again," Niles said aloud, "I should really get back to the pitch." If Aspidistra Burroughs really wanted to talk to him, she could surely always phone back. Right now he had to work out how to make *Mr Doll* work, without bringing in fairy rings, whittled wooden dolls, or giant rats eating the hero's face.

He checked the time – thirteen minutes to eight. Well, no sense starting on an odd number. He'd wait until ten to. Or maybe make himself a hot drink and start fresh on the dot of eight.

Maybe half past.

He sighed heavily, staring at the dead phone for a moment, willing it to ring. When it did, he was quite disappointed to see that it was Bob.

NILES STARED MOROSELY at the phone, waiting for the buzzing to stop. It was the third time Bob had called, and Niles still wasn't about to pick up. He considered turning his phone off altogether, but he didn't want to miss a call back from Aspidistra, if it should come – or even Mike. Or Maurice might finally return one of his calls, he mused.

After a minute, the phone went to voicemail. Niles reached out, found the message, and deleted it without listening, as he had the three others. He had nothing to say to Bob.

He put the phone back down on the coffee table and tried to concentrate on the pitch. After a moment, it began buzzing again – he scowled to himself, cursing Bob under his breath, then picked it up. Obviously the man wasn't going to take voicemail for an answer.

"I've got nothing to say to you," he said curtly, then ended the call.

A moment later, the phone started vibrating in his hand.

He lifted up the phone and swiped his thumb again, accepting the call. "Fuck off."

"Niles, come on..." Bob's voice. Niles wondered if it had always had that wheedling tone.

"I told you, I've got nothing to say." He was surprised at how tired and miserable his voice sounded, how much bitterness he could hear. Maybe now would be a good time to write a children's book.

"Look," Bob said, in a calm, reasonable tone which made Niles want to rip his teeth out with a rusty pair of pliers, "I just don't want to leave things how we left them, okay? I figure we owe each other that, at least."

"You know what, Bob? You're right. We really shouldn't leave things like that," Niles snarled, "we should leave them like this: *fuck off*." He ended the call and put the phone down. Almost immediately it started buzzing again. He picked it back up. "Jesus Christ, Bob, is it 'fuck' you're finding so confusing, or 'off'?"

"Have you been drinking?"

Yes, and after this he'd need another. "None of your fucking business. Listen, don't you have anything better to be doing at the moment? You could be failing to get a job as the voice of a ghost on *Scooby-Doo*, maybe. Or moaning endlessly about how you wish you hadn't come out of a fucking *tube* – you know, your big brother Robert found a neat solution to that one –"

"Niles, that's too far –" Bob said, sounding hurt. Niles ignored him.

"Hey! *Here's* a thing you could be doing! *Fucking my ex-wife!*" He screamed it into the phone – *let* the fucking neighbours talk – and slammed it face down on the coffee table. It took a second of Bob's plaintive whining coming out of the speaker for him to remember that phones didn't actually work like that anymore. He picked it up again and ended the call. "Fuck off, Bob."

He stared at the thing for a second, daring it to ring again. It'd go straight in the washing machine on a 60° spin cycle if it did – wash the stubborn little skidmark away.

Bob wouldn't ring again, though. Not after that, surely. He wouldn't dare. Niles stared daggers at the plastic. "Just try it, you little electronic prick," he hissed. "Try letting that call through. So help me…"

Nothing.

After a few long seconds of silence, Niles allowed himself to breathe out. All right. Interruption over. Time to get back on with the –

The phone rang.

Niles grabbed it and swiped his thumb so hard he thought it might break. "*FUCK*," he screamed – face red, spit flying, eyes and veins bulging – "*OFFFF!*"

"Mr Golan?"

It wasn't Bob.

"I'm sorry," he said, feeling that deep sense of calm he'd always supposed people felt just before they drove their car onto the pavement and mowed down a bus queue. "I was expecting a call from someone else." The voice on the other end of the line sounded like a middle-aged woman – oh, God, he thought, please don't let it be Meadow again. But it wasn't her – the voice was a lot more refined, upper class even by LA's rarefied standards. Niles had a vague feeling he'd heard it before, months ago, but he couldn't place it.

He looked at the phone. *New number.* "I'm sorry, who is this?"

"It's Aline Zuckerbroth, Mr Golan. I understand you worked for my husband?"

Niles winced. He remembered now.

At some early point in their relationship, Maurice had invited him over to the house for a barbecue. Maurice's wife had been there, a tall, willowy and supremely objectionable woman whose face was locked in a permanent expression of mild surprise – the work of one of the many different plastic surgeons she'd been to in her quest for the best face money could buy. The woman had skin like a spacehopper.

She'd spent the whole occasion sniping subtly at everyone who came in range, and a few weeks later, when Maurice had mentioned the divorce proceedings, Niles had quietly thanked whoever was up there that he'd never have to see or talk to her again. And now here she was on the other end of his phone.

Well, he'd told her to fuck off, at least. That was one to cross off the bucket list.

"I think technically he works for me," he said, peevishly. "He's an agent, I'm his client. His fee is a percentage of mine – that's how agents work."

"Oh," Mrs Zuckerbroth said, expertly conveying in one syllable how little she cared. She'd been practicing that *oh* for years. "Well, I was just ringing round all of his employees –"

"Clients," Niles muttered.

"– to let them know that the funeral was this Wednesday. One o'clock sharp, at the Mount Sinai Mortuary on –"

"Wait, hang on," Niles said, sitting up. "What do you mean, funeral? Did something happen?"

"I thought you'd been informed. My husband was murdered several days ago." Mrs Zuckerbroth delivered the news in the tone of someone commenting on how simply *dreadful* the greenfly were this year.

Niles blinked. "I'm sorry, Maurice is *dead*?"

"Beheaded on Van Ness Avenue. It took them a day or so to identify the body, but after that all of his important employees were notified by the police," she said idly, not stressing the word *important* in any way.

"Clients." Niles rubbed his temples, as if trying to massage the information into his brain. "I'm sorry, Mrs Zuckerbroth, I'm having some trouble processing this – are you saying that your husband was murdered by the Sherlock Holmes killer?"

"I'm not sure why you're so surprised," Mrs Zuckerbroth murmured, "it's been all over the news. I've no idea how you could have missed it." There was the lightest possible patina of reproach in her voice, which Niles frankly didn't appreciate.

"Things have been a little hectic the last few days," Niles muttered.

"You do sound tired," Mrs Zuckerbroth intoned, in such a way as to say that she knew Niles had been drinking, she knew he was half-cut and she was disgusted by it, but not so disgusted as to actually lower herself to comment.

Niles ignored it. He was scrabbling around for the remote. "Do they know who... which Holmes, I mean..."

"The police are quite baffled by it all – no leads whatsoever. It's actually rather exciting," Mrs Zuckerbroth mused, in the voice of a woman relating details of a semi-interesting bake sale. "I've had reporters interviewing me constantly. They say Helen Mirren might play me in the movie."

"Movie?" The remote was underneath the couch. Niles turned on the news, making sure to keep the TV on mute. The screen was filled with footage of a sneezing baby panda.

"Oh, yes, they're already arguing over the film rights – pretty much every studio with a Sherlock Holmes in the race, so to speak. And then there are the Lifetime people, who want to focus on me personally. *A Woman's Struggle*. It's all *very* exciting."

Niles wondered what level of excitement it would take for Mrs Zuckerbroth to actually sound in any way excited. Nuclear war, he supposed. "It's just a shame about your husband having his head cut off by a maniac," he muttered dryly. "Aside from that little detail, it sounds like it's all coming up roses."

"Oh, yes, poor Morrie," she said breezily. "Still, it's an ill wind. Now, I am sorry, Mr Golan, but there are a lot of other people to ring round, and I should let you get back to your..." – the slightest of pauses – "work."

Niles sighed, said as polite a goodbye as he could manage in the circumstances, ended the call and turned up the volume on the TV. The sneezing panda – a movie was apparently in the works – was replaced by a story about gridlock in the House, and then one about solar flares. Eventually, the 24-hour news cycle returned to the Sherlock Holmes murders, and a large grainy photo of Maurice's face filled the screen, followed by Aline – even more orange than Niles remembered – weeping a few crocodile tears for the cameras.

The screen was quickly filled by another grainy photo – another Fictional, this time. Sexton Blake, the poor man's Sherlock Holmes. There'd only ever been one of him – his first film, a recent showing with plenty of CGI, had bombed badly, becoming one of those occasional legendary flops that cling to characters like a graveyard stench, poisoning any possibility of follow-ups or reboots. One film and out – it happened sometimes. Blake had apparently taken it badly, bitterly, wandering the streets at night, living off the pension Fantasia had provided him in their contract rather than attempting to find other work. Occasionally, tour groups would find him outside the gates of the studio, angrily begging for change – he was quickly moved on. In the early stages of the investigation, he'd been a suspect – as a sub-Sherlock, he had both motive and ability. But, like any good murder mystery, the chief suspect had now been killed off himself.

Apparently other Sherlocks were joining the hunt for the killer – the World War II-era Sherlock Holmes created by Global Productions, the Young Holmes that ParaVideo had floated for a TV show, a couple of others. The police were doing their best to keep control of all this, but after making the decision to allow 'Classic Holmes' and 'Action Holmes' to all but run the investigation, they were in an impossible position.

The whole thing seemed more and more absurd the more Niles watched it play out. Poor Maurice, he thought to himself. He tried to feel something – grief at the loss, guilt at not making more of an effort to find out what had happened, anger at the futility and stupidity of the whole thing.

All he felt was numb.

Admittedly, he hadn't known Maurice for long – a matter of months – but still, this was someone he'd allowed into his life, allowed to become a part of his life. According to Ralph, that was supposed to be quite a big thing for him.

At the same time... had he ever really known Maurice? Aside from the barbecue – which he'd only just remembered – had Niles ever been in *his* life? Was Niles feeling numb and empty because of some deep emotional shock to his system, or was it because Maurice was just an underdeveloped supporting character in Niles' story, a collection of tropes and tics, on a par with Dean or Mike? Had Niles ever thought of him as a human being with a life and a wife and other clients besides himself, never mind ones that might be more important than him? Or had he only thought of Maurice as comic relief in the unfolding story of Niles Golan?

He remembered the diner that didn't have water, Maurice's rat/cocaine metaphor, Dean staggering back to the table and ranting about bestiality with farm animals. It was the kind of thing they'd have laughed about on the phone a few days later, a bit of banter before business. But now it felt so divorced from Niles' life – what he had left of his life – as to have happened to a completely different person. Only a few days had passed, but it already felt like 'the early, funny stuff.'

The laughs seemed darker now, grim and bitter little cracks directed at himself, at his pretensions and his failures. And the only person left to laugh at them was him.

Who were his supporting characters now?

The phone rang.

Niles picked it up. The act of swiping his thumb across the screen to take the call felt wearily familiar by now. "Hello?" he said, flatly.

"Mister Golan?"

"Aspidistra?" Niles found himself smiling. "I was hoping you'd call back. I've got all sorts of questions about –"

"I can't talk long," the frail voice said, "my daughter's running me a bath. Get a pen and some paper, I'm going to give you my address." She lived up north, in Weaverville, a little west of Redding – it'd be at least an eight hour drive, if he had a car. He supposed he could take a flight. "You can send me the book, and then I'll send you a cheque in the mail. We've got time to haggle a little before she comes down. I'll give you thirty bucks for it."

Niles laughed. "It's yours for free. But I'd really like to ask you a few questions about it –"

"I can't talk on the phone," Aspidistra snapped, "not for long, anyway. *She* doesn't like it. Look, if you want to talk, just come visit me, for gosh sakes. It'll be nice to have the company. Come by any time – just so long as you bring *The Doll's Delight* with you, that's all I ask."

"Um... are you sure?" Niles was a little nonplussed at that. He was happy to make the trip – eager, even – but there was something a little off about being invited in secret like this. He wasn't sure what sort of relationship Aspidistra had with her daughter, but he wasn't so sure he wanted to be dropped into it like an Alka-Seltzer into a glass. "I don't want to impose –"

"Any time you like. Give me a call first to let us know you're coming. Tomorrow's good. Bring the book. See you then!" Niles opened his mouth to say something, but the call was already over.

He frowned, opening up the laptop to look at flight times. He wasn't sure about this at all – it felt like he'd just been invited to gate-crash somebody's private war – but at the same time, it might go a long way to answering some of his questions about *Mr Doll*. He was growing increasingly ambivalent about the pitch, but there was a part of him that felt like he'd be letting Maurice down if he didn't at least make an effort, and if finding out the story behind *The Doll's Delight* helped with that...

"Creative procrastination," the man leading the seminar said, *"is the art of creating tasks for oneself that one feels are utterly vital – without which the work cannot progress – none of which involve the work, or any part of the work, or anything that in any real sense can lead to the work. After following an infinity of these blind alleys and dead ends, the writer can look in the mirror and tell himself that the project was simply not meant to be."* He looked around the room at his students. *"You've had experience with this kind of mental block, haven't you, Golan?"*

There was no answer.

"Golan? Golan?"

But the author had left the seminar hours before to catch a flight to Weaverville and get involved in some sort of family struggle between a mother and daughter, as he'd told himself that it was utterly vital to the work.

Ten minutes later, the plane crashed, killing him and everyone else on board.

"Ha, ha," Niles muttered sardonically. "Very funny."

His inner narrative was wrong, anyway – it didn't look like he'd be getting a flight. Prices were extortionate, and for some reason he could only get a flight as far as Sacramento, which would mean renting a car the rest of the way. He supposed if worst came to worst he could drive it after all, although he still needed something to drive in – well, maybe he could look up a good rental place. Or maybe the garage might provide him with some clunker if he begged them hard enough.

It was enough to make him wish he had a friend with access to a decent car. Or a friend.

Who was his supporting character, anyway?

He stared at the phone for a long time, hoping it might answer the question for him. This time it remained stubbornly silent. He sighed heavily, reached for it, and called Bob.

CHAPTER FOURTEEN

WHEN NILES LEFT the apartment the next morning, the sun was just starting to peek above the horizon, and Bob was already waiting for him. He'd brought the Mercedes.

Niles blinked. He'd assumed Bob would bring his own car, a red Mini Cooper that Niles suspected he'd purchased because it was the complete opposite of the famous Terrormobile of the TV show. He hadn't been looking forward to six hours crammed into that. The Mercedes would be the lap of luxury in comparison.

He eyed it suspiciously. "Isn't that Iyla's car?"

Bob shrugged. Niles felt a pang of guilt as he saw his face – Bob's broken nose had been re-set, but there was a sticking plaster over the bridge, and one eye was badly swollen. "She's fine with me borrowing it for a couple of days," Bob said lightly. "I mean, she wasn't thrilled about the idea, but... ah, you know." He shrugged again, obviously wanting to change the subject.

Niles guessed there had been an argument between them about it – quite an ugly one, at that. Iyla probably thought Niles was taking advantage of Bob's guilt over his affair with her and the fight they'd had – and he probably was.

The telephone conversation between them the previous night had been tense and awkward – Bob hadn't, at first, been willing to forgive the comment about Robert Benton's suicide, or accept Niles' apology for it. And when Niles had proposed the idea of an eight-hour road-trip to Weaverville, he could hear Bob biting his tongue.

When Niles went on to explain that the purpose of this long and arduous trip was to possibly, not *probably*, mind you, but *possibly*, get some vague insight into the origins of a somewhat dubious children's book – and by inserting themselves into the on-going domestic drama of two complete strangers, at that... Well, when he put it like that, it sounded like the kind of thing you said 'no' to. If their roles had been reversed, even in happier times, Niles would probably have made some excuse about a tight deadline or a twinge in his back and left Bob to twist in the wind. He remembered once when Bob had needed his help to move to a new apartment, and he'd done just that.

So he'd fully expected Bob to just hang up and draw a line under their friendship for good. Instead, here he was, and he hadn't even brought his own car. He'd managed, somehow, to borrow the Mercedes, undoubtedly over some fairly strenuous opposition from Iyla.

Did that mean he was still staying at hers? Should he ask?

"Bob..."

"What?"

"Oh, nothing," Niles mumbled, as Bob took his bag and walked around to open the boot. They'd packed an overnight bag each – the tentative plan was to stay at a motel rather than spend the whole night driving all the way back to Los Angeles.

"Nothing?" Bob raised an eyebrow. "Come on, it's going to be a ten-hour drive –"

Niles raised an eyebrow. "Hold on, I thought it was eight? I mean, when I looked at the map, it didn't seem that far..."

Bob shot Niles a look. "You're British. You people naturally underestimate things like that. I mean, don't get me wrong, it's perfectly understandable, it probably takes you all of an hour to drive across your whole country..."

"Well," Niles said defensively, "longer than that. Two or three."

Bob rolled his eyes. "...but things are a little further apart out here in the Wild West. Trust me, it's ten hours, easy. With breaks, we'll be there about six, so you might want to phone and make sure this woman you want to interview knows we'll be a little later than you said."

Niles nodded. "She did say any time..."

Bob opened up the driver's side door. "Look, Niles – what I was going to say was that it'll just be you and me in that car, so..." He looked Niles in the eye. "Well, it's probably a good opportunity for the two of us to talk things over. Just... I don't know, clear the air a little."

"What, like couples counselling?" Niles joked, nervously. Bob ignored him and slid into the car.

Niles followed suit, easing himself into the plush leather interior and taking a deep breath – the Mercedes still had that new car smell. Suddenly the extra hours didn't feel like such an imposition – he'd be comfortable, at least, and as Bob said, there'd be time for breaks to stretch their legs and have lunch. Maybe he'd even get a turn at the wheel.

Anyway, Bob was right. The long trip would give them an opportunity to mend some fences. Maybe he could get Bob to see his side of things.

"You know, when you put it like that," the Fictional said, the light of understanding dawning in his eyes, "everything makes sense. In fact, I'd say you were totally right about everything, and I was completely and utterly wrong. Thanks for explaining all that to me." He smiled, patting the author's shoulder. "You're a good Joe, Niles. You really are a good Joe."

Then, because he'd taken his hand off the wheel at a critical moment, the car ploughed into a chemical tanker and both of them were instantly immolated in the blast.

Niles winced. Bob, buckling up in the driver's seat, caught the change of expression. "What?"

"Nothing," Niles sighed. "I've been having these sort of..." He wasn't really sure how to describe his occasional bursts of auto-narration. Daydreams? Fantasies? "Never mind, it doesn't matter. Look, I just wanted to say, face to face, before we really get going – I'm so sorry about what I said to you on the phone, about Robert. That was incredibly callous and insensitive and... well, you know. I shouldn't have said it. It won't happen again."

"All right, fine. Apology accepted." Bob turned to face him, the sticking plaster white against his skin, like a third accusing eye. "Do I get a 'sorry for punching you in the face'?"

Niles smiled weakly as Bob let the handbrake off and moved the Mercedes out into traffic. "Oh, yes, of course. Absolutely. I'm sorry I punched you in the face." He looked away, staring out of the window as a pair of joggers passed them, and then were passed in turn as the vehicle accelerated. "Are you still staying at Iyla's?"

Bob hesitated for a moment, then nodded warily. "I'm not moving in. I don't think that'd be a good idea, considering, you know... the papers. People generally. I mean, it's not like I've got anything to lose myself, but..." He tapped the wheel of the Mercedes. "Iyla's got a career. So."

"So..." Niles paused. He had a feeling Bob had just answered his question, but he wanted it to be absolutely clear. "Are you and Iyla..." He hesitated. "I mean, are you still..."

Bob looked at him. "Is that a problem?"

Niles shrugged. "No, not at all," he said, stiffly. "Why would it be a problem?"

"ALL RIGHT, FINE. It's a problem." Niles sighed. "I have a problem. Is that what you wanted to hear?"

They were on I-5 now, just passing Castac Lake, and the conversation had circled back around to Bob and Iyla.

He'd briefly tried changing the subject. Bob had been surprised to hear that Niles hadn't known about Maurice's death – "It was all over the news!" he'd said, incredulous. "What the hell were you *doing?*"

But as it turned out, one of the things that Niles had been doing was charging over to Iyla's house, breaking Bob's nose and being literally kicked out of the house by Iyla – which swiftly brought them back around to the question of Bob and Iyla. And whether it was a problem.

"All right," Bob said, quietly. "What's your problem?"

"Well," said Niles, staring out of the window at the lake passing them by, "I suppose it's that I used to be married to her." Bob opened his mouth to say something and Niles cut him off. "Yes, yes, I know, I *know* – I've got no right to make it about that. I cheated on her more times than I can count. I don't think I loved her at the end, I just tolerated her. But I suppose I've still got some petty, jealous streak that –"

Bob, mouth a thin line of anger, checked the mirror and then pulled over to the side of the road.

"What?" Niles said, blinking. "Why are we stopping?"

"Because I'm not taking you one more mile in this car until you cut the shit."

Bob's voice was like stone. For a moment, it was like being in a car with the Black Terror. Niles shook his head, perplexed. "I'm sorry, what? I'm not sure I –"

"You're either lying to me or lying to yourself, and I don't know which is worse. So – new rule." Bob turned the key and the engine died. He looked over at Niles. "The new rule is that every time I hear some bullshit out of your mouth, that's a strike." He held up three fingers, then lowered one. "You've had your first strike. Three strikes and I turn this thing around and drive you home."

"Well – what if I'm driving?" Niles was really hoping to take a turn at the wheel before they got to Weaverville.

"If you're driving, I will grab hold of this wheel and run us right off the fucking road. Seriously, take over the driving and test me on that. You know I can do it." Bob looked at Niles seriously for a moment, waiting for him to say something, then sighed. "Look, I'd love it to be the jealousy thing. I swear to God I would love it if you were just an irrational ex-husband seeing the new boyfriend-slash-fuckbuddy and realising that *actually* – even though he was a lying, cheating, emotionally manipulative asshole who threw this woman away like a fucking tissue – his being jealous on *top* of that, like the cherry on top of a cake made of bleach and human shit, meant he was still in love with her and he was going to drive to her house and punch the new guy for her. I'd love it if it was that, because at least then you'd have told me the truth just now. But it's not that, is it?"

Niles looked away. "...No."

Bob put his hand on the ignition key. "All right," he said, "take two. What's your problem, Niles?"

"I think it's sick."

Bob started the engine again. "You think it's sick. Why is that, Niles?"

"Because you're not real," Niles muttered, and Bob checked the mirror, signalled, and pulled smoothly out onto the highway.

"There," he said, very calmly. "That wasn't so hard, was it?"

IT WAS A few more miles before he said anything else. Niles was looking out of the window, feeling like a small boy being scolded by a parent. "So," Bob said eventually, "You don't think I'm real."

"I went through all this with Cutner," Niles said, not turning to look.

Bob frowned. "I thought your weekly hour with him wasn't until tomorrow?"

Niles sighed. "I had to sort of... well, book an emergency session with him."

"What, because you hit me in the face?" Bob raised an eyebrow. "Or was this whatever you were freaking out to Iyla about before you came over to her place and hit me in the face?"

"A little of both. And no, I'm not going to tell you what I was," – Niles did 'air quotes' – "'freaking out' about. That's my new rule, by the way. I don't have to tell you every little detail of my life."

"Doesn't sound like a little detail to me," Bob shrugged. "But that's fine. We'll add that to the rules. Anyway, back on topic. What did you go through with Cutner?"

"He thinks *you* think you're real. Which you're not, since you came out of a tube. And he thinks I should accept that. Which I do. I accept that you think you're real, I just don't think that means you *are* real." Niles scratched the back of his head, sighing. It had been an early morning for them both, and suddenly he felt very tired.

"Because I came out of a tube. That's the criteria we're applying, is it? You know, last time I checked, I was made of exactly the same kind of meat, bones, guts and gristle as you, Niles." He concentrated on the road for a moment, flicking the turn signal on and overtaking another semi. "Does it matter where I got them?"

"You weren't born out of a human womb," Niles muttered, feeling too exhausted for any of the usual prevarications and justifications – what Bob would have called *bullshit*. He just wanted to say what he felt. "You can pretend whatever you like, but you weren't born a real human, and you're *not* one. You're a Fictional." He shook his head. "Why can't you just accept that? You can't just... I don't know, wake up one morning and *say* you're real."

"I didn't just wake up one morning," Bob said, scowling. "You know, that comment's pretty typical of you, Niles –"

"What, realist?" Niles finally turned and looked Bob in the face. "Fine! I'm a realist! I think Fictionals *aren't real*, because they're *not* real! They're fictions we dressed up in flesh so we could look at them better! That's all you are, Bob! No matter how much Pinocchio wants to be a real boy, he can't be! You're *words on a page*, Bob! That's all you are!"

Bob stared at the road for a while. The rain was starting to come down, just a little at first, spotting the windshield. "That's not what I meant," he said at last, "but never mind. You remember I told you about Malcolm Stuyvesant?"

Niles had to think for a moment. "I think you mentioned him before..."

"The man who put the words on the page." Bob chuckled, dryly. "The words that are all I can ever be, right?" He sighed, shaking his head. "Look, on that fourth season of *New Adventures*, we were all starting to burn out. Malcolm was getting into some deep allegorical territory, and he felt like he was limited by the whole Bowery Bay setup, the others wanted to go less camp, or more camp... the whole thing was fracturing. And I was part of that, I mean, just because I was the Black Terror didn't make me immune, you know? I felt like... like Bowery Bay was just a painted set and some location work in Miami. Thea – this woman I was supposed to care about, my supposed partner – was just an actress playing a role, and so was my girlfriend on the show, and so was everyone else the Black Terror knew. My whole life was this sham, this fucking *lie*, and meanwhile there was a real world I wasn't allowed to be part of. It was driving me fucking crazy."

Niles blinked. "Um. That's exactly the opposite of what Ralph said."

"Ralph Cutner?" Bob looked over at Niles, curious. "What did he say?"

"Well, the way he put it was that the show was the only thing that was real to him – that to him, it was the real people who were fictional. He asked me if I thought I was real."

Bob laughed. "Well, are you?"

Niles winced. "It's not funny."

"No," Bob said, "it's a serious question. *Do* you think you're real?"

"Well, the way he put it was in terms of... oh, I don't know. Crossing from one reality to another. Like the translation tube is sort of a doorway." Niles shook his head. "It was arrant nonsense, obviously."

"Oh, I don't know," Bob shrugged. "It makes sense in a kind of metaphorical way. And I hear most Fictionals think along similar lines – focussing on the show, treating it like real life. Treating their scripts like things they thought up on the spur of the moment. I've had conversations with assholes who thought they were Oscar Wilde just because they had a great writer for a couple of weeks." He sucked air through his teeth and overtook another semi. "Anyway... speaking of great writers. Let's get back to Malcolm."

Niles nodded, staring out of the windscreen at the oncoming rain. Bob turned on the windscreen wipers, and for a moment the only sound in the car was the gentle squeak of the rubber on the glass as they swept the rain off.

"So like I was saying... we quit. We made Season Four as good as it could possibly be, and then when the studio came around and said they wanted Season Five, we told them no. Malcolm pitched *Sea-Thru*, which did about as well as you'd figure for a complex allegorical drama about an underwater invisible man, and I went off to become a failed voice actor, which is something I kind of fell into. I didn't know what the hell I wanted to do or be, just that I hated being the

Black Terror and I wanted to change." He shot Niles a look.

Niles squirmed, flushing red. "Well, you can't. Just because you're not a *normal* Fictional doesn't mean you're suddenly not a Fictional at all. You can't change what you are just by wanting to be something else. In fact," he said, warming to his theme, "everything you are – including that little epiphany moment you had when you were filming – is just characterisation. What was written down for you by Stuyvesant. Words on a page."

"I know," Bob said.

"What?"

"I figured that out myself. I was mad as hell at Malcolm – honestly, I wanted to kill the guy. I thought he'd screwed up when he was writing me, put something in there that the technicians could have misinterpreted or something. It happens – look at Dexter Morgan. Hell, look at the Sherlock Holmes killer. Anyway. I ended up confronting him. I told him I didn't want to be Bob Benton any more, I didn't want to be the person I'd been made as any more, and what had he done to me, and blah blah blah." He looked over at Niles with a small smile. "I was pissing mad. I wanted to know what the hell he'd put in there that was screwing me up, that was making me hate my life. And he just looked at me – he was this big, kindly guy with these big puppy eyes – he looked at me like his heart was just *breaking*. Because he hadn't even known he was doing it." Bob shook his head, sighing. "He said he wrote me to be the absolute best, most interesting, most complex character I could possibly be. He said he put months of his life into me, that as far as he was concerned I was the most important character in the show, the reason for people to tune in, and if I wasn't good enough then the whole thing would just be a waste of time."

"So... I don't understand." Niles' brow furrowed. "He put all that effort into you, and then he wrote you to just quit after four years?"

"He said something to me. I didn't really understand it at the time – I understand it a little more now, but I still don't know if I've forgiven him for it. Maybe I have." Bob sucked in a breath, then let it out slowly. "'Good characters grow, Bob.' That's what he told me."

Niles could see the tears glistening in his eyes.

"'Good characters grow.'"

The car sped on through the driving rain.

THEY STOPPED FOR lunch at a sushi place in Sacramento.

"I'm not sure I want to eat raw fish," Niles said, making a face.

"It's not *raw fish,* it's sushi. Jesus." Bob was looking over his shoulder, trying to judge the parking distance. "You're hopeless, you know that? Look, how about this – we eat here and I'll let you drive for a while. I know you've been salivating over the damned thing all the way up."

Niles raised an eyebrow. "You're sure? You don't want to retain your right to turn us around and go home?"

"I can still run us off the road," Bob said, chuckling. "And anyway, I'm getting a little tired. There's only so much interstate I can take."

"Still," Niles muttered, "I'm not sure. I've never eaten sushi before."

"Neither have I," Bob grinned. "Come on, try something new for once."

"I've tried enough new things this week," Niles muttered darkly, and after that he had to tell Bob everything – about Liz, about the two times he'd been over to her apartment, the strange game they'd played. How he'd left it.

He didn't mention Danica Moss.

"She sounds fun," Bob said, shrugging and digging into his salmon skin rolls. "She sounds like just what you need, if I'm being honest."

Niles frowned, poking suspiciously at a chicken teriyaki with his chopstick. "How so?"

"Well," Bob smiled, "for one thing, it might loosen you up a bit. Get you to be a bit less uptight about who gets to be 'real' and who doesn't. I mean, this Liz –"

"I don't know her real name," Niles sighed. "I never got it."

"You dark horse, you." Bob rolled his eyes. "We'll call her Liz. But find out her name, or take her up on her offer and make one up for her. Get a number with it." He picked up an edamame and flicked it into his mouth with his thumb. "God, these are good. Anyway, this Liz – she came out of a real human womb like a god-fearing person, right? But she wants to be a Fictional. That's the exact reverse of my situation. I mean, you see that, right?"

Niles shot Bob a look. "You're saying if I said I thought you were real, you'd want to play kinky sex games with me?"

"If you just took me seriously for a second I'd definitely forgive you for the black eye," Bob said, munching on another roll. "And maybe I'd want to start fresh. Not that I'm speaking for her here – I don't have any particular insight into this girl's mind. And you did treat her like shit, even if she has forgiven you." He looked up at Niles, smiling. "She does sound fun, though. And probably not that serious about you, which might be another thing you need – unless you actually get off on hurting people, in which case you should probably stay single for, you know, ever."

"God, don't pull any punches," Niles muttered, pushing his teriyaki away. Bob grabbed it and moved it to his side of the table.

"You want to know why else she's perfect for you?" Bob said, picking up a piece of the teriyaki and trying it. He pushed it back to Niles, scowling. "You're insane. It's all that boiled beef or whatever you ate growing up – you can no longer taste real food. Eat it."

"I'm not hungry."

"You're insulting them, and you're embarrassing me. Eat it."

Niles blinked. "Is that *Indiana Jones*?"

"It feels transgressive. Like I stole his hat." Bob grinned. "The other reason she's perfect for you is that you've got things in common. In that she wants to be in a story where she's the hero. And so do you."

Niles frowned. "Sorry, I have no idea what you're talking about." He picked up a bit of the teriyaki with his fingers and gave it an experimental nibble. Then a bite.

"Like Iyla said," Bob smiled, "you're always telling a story about yourself. A little on-going fiction where you're the hero and everything you do is – well, not *right*, exactly, but at least sympathetic. You're a good guy."

"A good Joe," mumbled Niles. Then he told Bob about the narration.

"That's a little fucked up," Bob said, cocking his head. "How long has that been going on?"

"Pretty much my whole life," Niles replied. "Well, my whole working life. Although even at school I was doing it to an extent – I don't know, maybe a lot of people do that when they're teenagers..."

Bob ate his last roll. "You wanted to be fictional. A fictional character you could write and edit yourself, because that would give you control over your life." He chuckled to himself. "Although what do I know, right? What does Ralph say?"

"I never told him about it."

"He'd have come up with that exact same bullshit." He looked Niles in the eye, mock-seriously. "One strike for me, I guess."

"You should let me have one of mine back. Anyway, now the whole narration thing... it's turned into these daydreams, these sort of little fantasies where I imagine everything just... going horribly. The worst possible outcome, or things that are just... I mean, yesterday I imagined getting so full of myself that I turned into a black hole and narrated an autobiography."

"Wow." Bob blinked. "You should write some of those down."

Niles shook his head, finishing his teriyaki while Bob signalled for the bill. "So, you've proved you're the new Ralph. What do you think it means?"

"Christ, don't ask me. Maybe... I don't know. Maybe you're just sick of the story of Niles Golan, brilliant genius author and second coming of Shakespeare. Maybe it's time to start the story of Niles Golan, not so much a prick." He shrugged.

Niles smiled despite himself. "What the hell," he said. "Maybe it is."

*　*　*

As soon as they were back on the road, Bob fell asleep – he seemed to pass out almost immediately – leaving Niles to drive the rest of the way up I-5 towards Redding. It wasn't as much of a pleasure to be driving the Mercedes as he'd thought it would be, and after an hour and a half on the road, he found his eyelids drooping slightly, and the traffic noise becoming increasingly soporific. He really should have gotten some sleep himself. Still, he was sure he could tough it out.

The author, having made this grotesquely irresponsible decision, immediately fell into a dreamless slumber that lasted until the speeding car jumped the centre reservation and ploughed explosively into a bus filled entirely with screaming orphans and helpless kittens and puppies, which smashed in turn into a convoy of nuclear missiles.

A Public Service Announcement was immediately commissioned, entitled "Don't be a Golan!" and starring a clone of Hitler in the title role.

Niles shook himself. Now that he thought about it, toughing it out probably wasn't such a good idea.

Music, that was what he needed – either something really good, like Billy Joel, or something horrible like that new thing that sounded like robots ejaculating. He searched the dial, trying to keep the volume low enough not to wake up Bob. Wait – was that 'Scenes From An Italian Restaurant'? It was!

Perfect.

He was still singing along, feeling much fresher, when the last chords faded out and the radio started on the traffic report, followed by news of the capture of the Sherlock Holmes Killer.

Niles turned it up.

"...breaking news at the top of the hour is that the Sherlock Holmes Killer is in police custody, and

surprising nobody, it's Sherlock Holmes! But what is surprising LA's finest – and putting more than a little egg on their faces – is the news that the killer is the same Sherlock Holmes who, up until this morning, had taken charge of the investigation! Sounds to us like it's 'Sher Luck' that the LAPD caught him! Meanwhile, Congress met again today on the matter of..."

Niles spun the dial. Next to him, Bob blinked sleepily. "What's going on?"

"They're saying Sherlock Holmes did it – the murders." Niles replied, searching the radio for a dedicated news channel. He caught Bob's look. "The *Classic* Holmes. The one who was on the TV in the bar."

"You're shitting me," Bob said, and took charge of the dial. After a moment, he found a proper news channel, which told them the whole story.

MISTER SHERLOCK HOLMES had, of late, been possessed by a desire common to humanity, but uncommon to the Fictional kind; the desire for progeny. Fictionals were, of course, sterile – the interbreeding of man and fiction was not something society felt it could permit – but Holmes had always been unconcerned with the flesh and its pleasures. To him, the problem was an intellectual curiosity, a fascinating and delightful puzzle. How could he, as a Fictional, reproduce? What would that mean for one such as him?

The answer came to him, as it often did, while playing the violin. He was a creature of story, a living story – and thus, his child must also be a story, one that would grow in the telling until a Fictional was gestated for the sole purpose of telling it. Unfortunately, Sherlock Holmes was no writer of fictions. He could take notes, compile dossiers, even compose music – but he was, at the core, a creature of truth and certainty, who had removed all knowledge of the telling of stories from his mental attic in order to make room for more practical items. His imagination was used to divine the mechanics of crime, to imagine ways of murder that, as outrageous as they were, were not impossible – for once you have eliminated the impossible, whatever remains must be the truth.

His imagination was for murder, then – so be it. His story would be a murder mystery, a mystery entirely centred around Sherlock Holmes. Sherlock Holmes would be both mother and father to this strange new child – for Sherlock Holmes would, in one form or another, play all the parts.

The first thing to do, as an author, would be to get literary representation; and Maurice Zuckerbroth was whispered of as the sleaziest agent in Hollywood. He – at least in Holmes' version of events – lived up to his word, seeking out ways of gaining the rights to an upcoming murder spree, selecting a ghost writer who would punch up the somewhat dry style of Holmes' reports into something worthy of *The Strand* of old.

The next stage was to secure his alibi – 'Action Holmes,' for whom he acted as friend and mentor, was of particular use in this, for he could be relied on to claim that Sherlock Holmes had been on set as an adviser for a full day of shooting. However, this included the time Classic Holmes spent hidden away in his trailer – a trailer which seemed to have only one entrance and exit, which no man could pass through unobserved; but which was also equipped, thanks to Holmes' innate cunning, with a false floor through which the great detective could leave the set and back lot whenever he chose. A recording of his violin served to allay any of the second Holmes' suspicions.

In this way he crept out to murder his first target, the most recently translated Sherlock Holmes – who, still enjoying the first flush of his fame, and a weekly presence on the television screens of the nation, presented the ideal way to gain immediate press attention. Having committed the grisly deed with a heavy quizzing-glass, Sherlock Holmes returned to his trailer via the secret entrance, 'heard' the awful news 'for the first time,' and rushed in front of the cameras, his Watson in tow, to find the clues he'd left behind and ensure the story of murder he had begun would reach the widest possible circulation.

Next, he killed Zuckerbroth, the agent, with a sword-cane – in stooping to blackmail the great detective, he had outlived any usefulness he might have had. (His wife, Aline Zuckerbroth, offered her own version of events, stating that Maurice had only been informed of Holmes' plan on the night of his death, and had resisted corruption to the last drop of his blood. This became the official story after she threatened to sue anyone who printed the true one.)

The last to die was Sexton Blake, who had so agreeably made himself a suspect – and thus, as long as the cameras followed him around everywhere he went, a most tempting target. After all, the man was practically a Holmes, and the plan, such as it was, required the deaths of every Holmes; including, sadly, the original in the San Quentin gas chamber. As it was, his next attempt – on 'Action Holmes,' the 2009 model, who despite his natural imbecility was still a Holmes and thus far too close to divulging the truth – was a spectacular failure. 'Action Holmes' lived up to his nickname, and Sherlock Holmes the killer was delivered to the police, battered and unconscious.

An ignominious end for the world's greatest detective! But not for his plans, or his strange dream of reproduction on the fictional plane; for the story was abroad, and gathering steam.

"WELL, FUCK," SAID Bob, shaking his head. "That's it. For us, I mean. They're going to build a new Guantanamo after that." He rubbed his temples. "Christ, I'm tired. I feel like I've been up for days."

He scratched his arm, staring out of the passenger side window. They were almost at Redding now, after a full afternoon spent listening to the news on different radio stations. Parts of it they were unable to believe – Bob couldn't imagine any Sherlock Holmes going so completely round the bend, although he'd slept through a fairly convincing statement on the matter from Holmes himself, while Niles was on Aline's side in the matter of Maurice Zuckerbroth agreeing to conspiracy to murder. "He'd go to the chair too if he'd been an accessory," Niles said, shaking his head, "and besides, he just wouldn't *do* it. He was never *that* sleazy."

"We're all going to the chair," Bob yawned. "All us Fictionals, I mean. You real people are going to be just fine."

"They're not going to do anything," Niles said, shaking his head. "Well, maybe they'll pass a law against turning his murder spree into a film, or something. I could see that. And I can see the studio getting fined – which one was it, Altamont? – but they're not going to put anybody in Gitmo. You're just being paranoid."

"Mmmm." Bob nodded. He was falling asleep yet again. Niles wondered exactly how much sleep the man had had the night before. Maybe Iyla had kept him up, he thought sourly.

He sighed.

"What?" Bob said, bleary-eyed.

Niles swallowed. This was going to be a hard crow to eat. "Bob... you're real people."

Bob blinked. "What?"

"I admit it. You're real." He spread his fingers out, a miniature 'hold up my hands' gesture. "Satisfied?"

"Well, you're forgiven for the eye." Bob grinned, lazily. "What brought this on?" He suddenly looked down at the radio. "Wait, it wasn't..." He looked back up at Niles, blinking. "You have got to be fucking kidding."

Niles shrugged, very slightly. "It just wasn't a very Holmesian thing to do," he said.

"So – hang on. Let me get this clear in my head." Bob scrunched the heel of one hand into his good eye, rubbing it in an effort to wake himself up. "I used reasoned argument on you for fuck knows how many years, trying to persuade you not to be such a bigoted asshole, and I also did things like sleep with your ex-wife, which *also* isn't particularly in character, and you don't give a shit about any of it. And then Sherlock Holmes kills three people and *that's* what makes you see the light?" He shook his head, staring at Niles incredulously. "What the fuck is wrong with you?"

"Also, you swear far too much for a comic strip character." Niles smiled. "Seriously, you should watch your mouth. Children read your adventures."

"Fuck you," mumbled Bob.

"If I'm being honest, it was some of the things you said earlier, too. And the past few days. My whole life, really." Niles stared into the middle distance for a long moment, summoning the courage to say it out loud. "I don't like myself very much, Bob."

Bob blinked owlishly at him. "What?"

"I feel like..." Niles shook his head. "Like I need to change some things about myself. Try and force myself to become a better person than I am. And maybe... maybe I should start by changing my definition of what a person is. What 'real' is."

"So what..." Bob managed, before another yawn overtook him. "What's your new definition?"

Niles thought for a moment.

"Change," he said. "If you can change... that's what makes you real."

"WAKE UP," NILES said, roughly shaking Bob.

Bob groaned and slowly opened one eye.

"We're here," Niles said, using the book in his hand to indicate a smallish suburban house that looked like it had seen some better days. "Six on the dot. You were right. Don't worry, I called ahead while we were getting gas in Redding. They're waiting for us." He looked up at the porch light. "Are you coming?"

Bob shook his head. "Nah," he said, "I'm..." He yawned again, big and loud, like a hippo on a nature documentary. "I'm completely wiped out. I'm going to stay here and get some sleep in the car – that way I can drive us to the motel when you're done."

"Well... okay," Niles said, frowning. For some reason, the arrangement was making him uncomfortable. "You're sure? God knows I could use you. They were all but tearing strips off each other on the phone."

"God's dead," mumbled Bob, closing his eyes. After a moment, he opened them again. "Niles?"

"What?"

"You're a good Joe, Niles," Bob drawled, in a passably terrible southern accent. "You shure are a gawsh-darn good Joe."

"Go to sleep," laughed Niles, and walked towards the house.

CHAPTER FIFTEEN

"MEADOW?" ASPIDISTRA LAUGHED, a full-throated cackle. "Oh, she's not here, don't you worry about that. No, she's spending today with some damned fool she met on the internet, of all places." She shook her head, fixing Niles with a beady glare. "Now, let's talk turkey, young man. Where's my book?"

She was older than her years – if she was six years old in 1951, as she claimed to have been, she wouldn't yet be seventy, and yet she looked closer to ninety. But for all that, there was a spryness to her – her eyes seemed to sparkle constantly, and when he held up *The Doll's Delight* and opened it to the dedication page, they nearly glowed.

"That's my copy, all right," she purred, taking it gently from him. "Just the way Uncle Henry gave it to me. Of course, he wasn't my real Uncle." She chuckled. "That's the kind of dirt you came all the way up here to get, am I right? A few filthy stories from an old gal who's been around. Well, you've earned 'em."

"Actually," Niles said, taking a drink of the tea she'd made him, even though he'd protested that she needn't, "I'm, uh, not so interested in the filthy stories. I'm really just interested in the book."

She fixed him with a sceptical stare. "You're not interested in filthy stories. Sure you're not." She looked him up and down, then returned to the book. "Must think I sailed Lake Redding on a Graham cracker," she muttered, flipper through the pages slowly.

"Honestly," he said, forcing a smile, "I'm just interested in where your Uncle Henry first came by the idea. I mean, that book is, ah... well, it's fairly unique..."

Aspidistra fixed him with another penetrating look. "You mean it's a damn monstrosity. Speak your mind and shame the devil, Niles. My father couldn't paint worth a damn, I'll be the first to admit." She grinned at his reaction. "That answer your first question?"

"I was wondering," admitted Niles, "if he'd... known what he was doing, exactly. I'd thought it might be – well, it might have been ironic, or some kind of pop art, or..." He tailed off. Aspidistra was glowering at him.

"You could call it ironic, I suppose," she muttered. "If you call plain bad luck ironic. Some folks have written whole songs about that."

She sighed, staring at *The Doll's Delight* for a long moment, running her fingertip over the imprint the pencil had left when Henry Dalrymple had left his dedication.

"All right, Niles," she said, gently. "Here's what I know."

On December 23ʳᴰ of 1941, Henry Dalrymple of Boston, Massachusetts, a twenty-six-year-old bank clerk with ambitions to one day write the great American novel, enlisted in the Army. It was, he told his diary, *"my Christmas present to a country that has loved me well, and to whom I owe great love in return."* He was writing about the United States, rather than Burma, but it was Burma where he ended up, and by the summer of 1942 he had moved on from there to a Japanese POW camp.

Those who remembered Henry from before he left for boot camp in 1941 remembered a smiling, elfin young man with a mop of dark hair and a beautifully trimmed moustache, who was engaged to be married to one of the prettier girls of Boston's bacon-slicing industry and who, having read his share of Steinbeck and just enough Henry Miller to be interesting, had some airy dreams of making a living in the writing line – not that they kept him from putting in his full share at the bank. Everyone who knew him agreed that you just couldn't find a more appealing fellow in the whole darned state.

This was not a description of the Henry Dalrymple who came back.

That man was scrawny, his dark hair lank over his forehead, his once-trim moustache now like a huge, hairy caterpillar clinging to his top lip. His eyes were sunken, with a look in them that could freeze lava at the break of noon, and while he was still engaged to the pretty bacon-slicer, and they even married the month after his liberation from the camp, it was generally felt that the divorce that came less than six months after was a blessing for all concerned.

As for his writing ambitions, they had atrophied. In the spring of 1948, after spending one year shut up in a bed-sitting room with only himself and the occasional well-meaning neighbour for company, he wrote his one and only short story, which was rejected and returned – before the ink on the envelope was fully dry, to hear him tell it – by *Collier's Weekly*.

It is reproduced here in full.

THE DOLL-PARTY,
or, THE LIFE AND DEATH
OF A DOLL

By H. R. Dalrymple

I SUPPOSE, STRICTLY speaking, it began with the Sutherlands.

By which I mean Margaret Sutherland, who was as fat and sweet as a gingerbread woman and did nothing much of anything with her time apart from find innocent drawing-rooms and force herself on them, and her husband Roger, who was a dentist and who smiled like an advertisement on paper rather than a man of flesh and blood.

It began with the Sutherlands. The Sutherlands who had been firm friends of my ex-wife, the Sutherlands who found me dull and listless but still felt it their duty to invite themselves into my home whenever possible, the Sutherlands who mercilessly invaded everything from a poker night to a cocktail evening, the Sutherlands who roamed and poked around my house like detectives looking for the vital clue while everyone else was content to sit and sip their Manhattans in peace. The Sutherlands, the Sutherlands, God, how I hated the Sutherlands.

And God, how I needed them. They were the pin holding the grenade together. They came to my poker nights, my cocktail evenings, because of... charity? Curiosity? Whatever damned reason drives people like that to haunt the lives of the less fortunate. But the others came because Maggie and Roger were there, and Maggie and Roger made it a party and not a wake. Without Maggie and Roger, those Sutherlands, those wonderful smiling gingerbread Sutherlands, why, you'd only have me. Me and my long silences, my stumbling words, my faraway look. Me, the man who drove his wife away. Me, bitter. Me, alone.

I didn't want to be alone. I needed company. And so, I needed the Sutherlands.

And, strictly speaking, it began when the Sutherlands poked their noses into a dusty corner of my bookshelves that they had previously left unpoked – and found the toy soldier.

"Oh!" squealed Margaret. "Oh, isn't this simply marvellous! How darling! What a dear little man!"

The toy soldier was a smart fellow of wood and red varnish that my wife had found in a thrift store along with a ballerina in a box. Both had found their way to one of the bookshelves and sat there, undisturbed, with nothing to do but look pretty and set off the drabness of the room, until Margaret Sutherland had decided to pick the soldier up and make him speak.

"Hel-lo!" she boomed heartily, in a deep voice that did not become her. "I'm a redcoat, on my way to war! Who'll march with me?" She wiggled him to and fro, making him march in place, and I noticed my other guests – the Rourkes, the Fullers, both couples in their way as noxious as the Sutherlands, but neither quite as loud – beginning to smile. Of course they did! Margaret's baby-voice and childish manner were meat and drink to them. I found myself checking my watch, conscious of how early the evening was, how much of it was left. A part of me decided to dash my whisky-glass to the floor, to stand up and grab the damned doll and snap it in two, to turf these overgrown children out of my home once and for all and have the night for myself.

A larger part sat still, saying nothing.

Roger, always ready to follow his wife into a lark, made his voice high and shrill. "I will!" He was holding the ballerina in her box. I steeled myself, but the Rourkes and the Fullers only smiled wider, each couple catching the eye of the other, chuckling and giggling as the Sutherlands played with their dolls.

"Why, what a beauty you are!" said the toy soldier, in Margaret's deep toy voice, sickly as molasses.

"And what a fine handsome soldier you are!" keened the ballerina, as Roger did his best to out-sugar his wife.

And on it went like that, the wood soldier and the tin ballerina carrying on a strange sort of courtship as the Rourkes clapped and the Fullers laughed and I sank lower into my chair and into my glass and prayed for it all to end. But still, I had nothing to say. I was too afraid of the silence that would come when the Sutherlands and the Rourkes and the Fullers had left, and I had nobody to replace them.

"Oh, isn't this such fun!" cried Margaret, shaking the toy soldier merrily about, and everyone agreed that it was fun, such fun, because it would be a poor sport who said 'no' to Margaret Sutherland. And then, sensing her moment, she dropped the bombshell: "Let's all of us find a doll, and tomorrow evening we can all meet up and have a doll's tea-party, and our dolls can all meet one another and say hello! Oh, do let's! It'll be such, such fun!"

One of Margaret Sutherland's favourite things – aside from herself and the rapt attention of guests, be they hers or anyone else's – was the joy of suggesting things that would be 'such, such fun' and having people scurry to carry them out. Roger, of course, was the first to agree that a tea party for dolls, officiated by grown men and women, would be 'such fun,' and then Marlene Fuller boasted that she had a figurine of a shepherd-boy upon her mantel that would be simply perfect, and her husband sucked on his pipe and chuckled that somewhere he had a swim trophy that would serve, and after that the dolls had the majority and our fates were sealed.

I was not asked which doll I would bring. I sensed that I was not a part of this, that I was not invited in any real sense, that I was freed from all obligation to take part in this grim suburban ritual. Naturally, I exalted. Even when Margaret and Roger left, taking away the toy soldier and the boxed ballerina as though they weren't stealing my meagre belongings from my home, I felt a surge of happiness rush through me. Whatever sickly horrors would emerge the next night, I would not be there to see them. I had long since put away childish things, and – now that the toy soldier had been taken from me to a new home – there was nothing in my house that could be called a doll.

No doll meant no doll-party. I was free.

And yet, and yet...

When midnight came, and the noise of the clock echoed through my almost empty house, it found me whittling a stout piece of firewood into the figure of a man. And as the knife cut deep, I found myself whispering to the wood, speaking first high, then low – struggling to find my doll a voice.

IT WAS MICHAEL Rourke who opened the door, and the fall of his face as he beheld me confirmed that I had come to the feast as a spectre, as unbidden and unwelcome as Banquo's ghost. I had suspected as much, and now a dark part of me, my inner imp, was filled with a perverse, gleeful joy at the knowledge, and in greeting I lifted up the wooden figure I'd carved the night before for his inspection.

"Look, Mike, look!" The smile felt savage on my face, like the anarchist readying the bomb. "Why, I've brought a friend for the party!"

"Why, so you have!" Mike made the best attempt he had in him to be jovial. But his ruddy cheeks had turned deathly pale at the sight of my friend the doll, and I cannot now find it in myself to blame him.

For in those small, dark hours in the dead of the night, as my hand had worked the blade and carved the wood, it had been guided by that inner imp, that savage anarchist, that mean and ugly quarter of my spirit which I had brought back with me from what my wife called 'my time away'. That time which had driven out the joy from my life, and drove her out in turn. My ugly souvenir of darker times.

I tell myself now that I tried from my heart to instil my little friend with joy, and hope, and happiness, if only from a need to be loved and accepted by the Sutherlands and their hangers-on. But perhaps in that dark night I was more honest. Or perhaps the knife knew me better than I did myself, and had whittled accordingly.

My friend the doll was a horror.

To begin with he had been made overly tall and thin, his legs so skinny that I had to hold him gingerly by the waist, lest I should squeeze too hard and snap them off. His wooden arms, meanwhile, hung limp at his sides as if dislocated, broken by some terrible wound. In my worst folly, I'd attempted to carve him a little jacket, so he would at least be smartly dressed for the occasion – but the knife had had its way, and the macabre slashes I'd left on his torso suggested nothing so much as a suit of rags hanging from a condemned man.

All such indignities my friend the doll could have borne with equanimity. Yes, even a smile! For I had meant him to be a cheery fellow, despite his many hardships. But the knife had shifted at the last, and the slash of his mouth was sour and cruel, his eyes hollow, blank dots, and it was this hateful expression more than anything which had turned Michael Rourke so pale.

I saw his expression, and the inner imp inside me flexed again – and so I spoke for the first time as the doll.

How to describe it? How to describe that awful voice? It was my voice, that I admit freely. I am not such a fool as to believe that any animating spirit but my own possessed that hunk of mis-carved wood. It was my voice, but warped and black and twisted, in the way I'd heard the voices of my friends in their hospice-beds warp and crack as they begged, from faces without jaws, bodies without limbs, begged for the nurse, for their mothers, for death.

To speak for my friend, I drew my lips back and back, revealing my yellow teeth in a fearful grimace like Death's own, my head tilting to the side as though I were asleep or dead myself. And then I spoke through my teeth, from low in my throat, and the result was a keening whine, a banshee sort of voice, a voice from an unmarked grave on a muddy field.

"HELLO MISTER ROUR-R-RKE," my friend the doll said in his awful cracking croak, as I stood like a living corpse, waggling him two and fro in my grip. Mike Rourke had left the porcelain teddy bear that he'd bought that afternoon, for a full eight dollars, on one of the Sutherlands' end-tables, so all he could do in response was stammer and nod, backing away from the door and from my friend as we made our grand entrance.

"HELLO, EVERYONE. HELLO, HELLO." That awful voice! It had the same effect on the assembled company as it did on Mike Rourke, who stood ashen-faced in the doorway of the living-room. Tom Fuller dropped his whiskey and it went on the new carpet, and Roger Sutherland seized the opportunity to escape, running for a moist towel and some soda-water rather than staying a moment longer in that place. Marlene's teacup rattled in its saucer like a bone, and poor Jeannie Rourke looked as if she might faint dead away. I may have dreamt it, but I will even swear I saw Margaret Sutherland's eyes flash with rage for the briefest moment, and the vicious imp inside me counted that moment as well worth the price of admission.

But then she was on her feet, smiling prettily, her eyes as full of good humour as ever, holding the toy soldier that had once been my possession in her hand.

"Goodness me!" she boomed, in her deep soldier-voice, the red-carved wood waggling in her grip as if it was trying to escape. "I'm a redcoat, on my way from war! Will you march with me, little clothes-peg-boy?"

Part of me recoiled at her insolent naming of my friend. Names, I have been told, are magic, and to name a thing is to bind it. Perhaps that was Margaret Sutherland's power, that she could name us all as her friends, create roles for us, slot us into her pretty little fictions of smoking-rooms and drawing-rooms and tea- and dinner- and cocktail-parties where everything was such, such fun.

But I had a trick worth any two of hers. The peg-boy spoke again.

"YOU ARE NOT FROM THE WAR-R-R," the peg-boy said, for though the voice echoed from my own throat, and the spittle flew from my stretched lips, I would leave you in no doubt that the words were his, and his alone.

"Ho ho!" laughed the soldier, a hint of desperation creeping into Margaret Sutherland's voice. "Why, of course I am! I'm a soldier, on my way from war! Who'll march with me?"

"YOU HAVE ALL YOUR LIMBS," the peg-boy said, and Jeannie made a high-pitched little gasping sound and covered her mouth with her hand. "YOU HAVE BOTH YOUR EYES. YOUR FACE IS NOT A RAGGED HOLE." Tom Fuller was white as a ghost, and made no move to pick up his empty glass. "WHO DID YOU KILL."

"What?" Margaret said in a faint voice, before recovering herself. There was the lightest trace of sweat upon her brow, but she still smiled brightly – a wide, mirthless smile, as if we were still playing the game. "Why – the Japs, of course!" Roger, returning with the cloth and soda, nodded vigorously at that; he had always been a man of deep and abiding patriotism. But Tom Fuller winced, as if troubled by an old wound, and in that moment I felt some pity for him. Tom had been at Okinawa. It was real to him.

To me, as well.

But the peg-boy did not care for what was real, and what was only doll-play. He had come to the doll-party, and now he would have his say.

"HOW MANY." The croaking voice was flat and dead, bubbling up from a tomb world under a cold sun. My throat was raw, but I did not mind the pain. I did not truly feel that it was mine.

"Oh – hundreds!" Margaret sang out, gaily, losing the soldier voice by degrees. Tom opened his mouth to speak, but could not quite bring himself to do it. Instead, he stared at the bright red varnish on the wooden soldier, on the pretty wooden drum he held.

"DID THEY SCREAM."

"Like little piglets!" Margaret's face was flushed now, joyous as a boy's on Christmas morning. In her eyes, she was winning our strange game, matching me point for point, seeing me off the field. She did not notice Jeannie, weeping silently, or Tom, standing like a statue, or Mike Rourke, who'd turned and walked out of the house, fists bunched.

"WAS IT FUN."

"It was such fun! Such, such fun!" Margaret shouted, in her own childish little-girl voice, waving the wooden soldier to and fro, until Jeannie got up and followed her husband down the driveway at a run, tears streaming down her face.

There was a long moment of silence, during which Marlene put down her tea and picked up her coat. "It's been a delightful game," she said crisply, not looking at Margaret or her husband, "but we really must go." Her husband must have been in full agreement, for he left with her without another word.

And then I walked away myself, with my wooden peg-boy in my grip, and left Margaret Sutherland with her husband, and her toy soldier, and the game she still believed she'd won.

I SHOULD HAVE slept like a baby that night.

If nothing else, I had broken the Sutherlands' power over me. Perhaps in time the others would forget the hundreds she'd sang of killing, or the glee with which she'd described their end, but I knew it would not be for some long time to come.

For a moment, my fellow party-guests had seen a real soldier in her hands, and the red on his tunic had not been varnish, and what he held in his hands had not been a drum. And in her face, they had seen something worse than any expression my inner imp could have carved into a piece of wood; they had seen the callous indifference of one who cares for fun, but not what fun has cost, who squanders time bought for her by blood, who would see the world outside her clique burn to ash without batting an eyelid. As long as one could still have nice plays on the radio, and a really good Martini, with fresh olive – well, what would be the difference?

And her clique was, at the root, a clique of one.

I should have been in bed, but instead I stayed up late into that night, drinking whiskey and savouring my anarchist's triumph. And yet, with every glass, I could still see the peg-boy out of the corner of my eye, standing on the bookshelf where the soldier had been, leaning against the books, as his feet were too thin to stand up on. Unable to resist the urge any longer, I turned in his direction and raised my glass. "To our triumph, peg-boy."

He stared at me in silence, with his empty eyes. I felt a sudden wave of irritation pass through me. There was something insolent about that sneer of his, some judgement to it that I felt I didn't deserve. "Don't look at me like that," I muttered, fixing him with my own gaze, my own sneer. "You're uppity – that's your problem. Think you're better than everyone."

I sipped my whiskey, leaning back in my chair. He continued to look at me, the grimace on his face seeming to intensify. "You're cynical," I told him, "unpleasantly so. You were fun enough at the Sutherlands', but now..." I shot him another look, finishing the drink. He stared back, as full of hate – yes, hate, hate and contempt – as ever. And all of it aimed at me! Me, of all people! Me, who had created him from a knife and wood!

"Damn you!" I shouted at him, rising from my chair and grabbing him my the waist, resisting the urge burning inside me to snap those damnable little legs from his body. "Why me? Why turn that look on me?"

"BECAUSE YOU MADE ME," came the reply, from my own burning throat. On another occasion, I might have been disturbed at the ease with which I answered my own question, but I was full of whiskey and bile then, and I gave it no mind.

"Well, show some gratitude," I hissed, eyes narrow as slits. "So what if I did make you? You should be happy to be alive." Immediately the voice returned to me, echoing in my own ears – but no less horrific for all that.

"YOU MADE ME TO DIE."

"Nonsense," I said, taking a step back at that. "Why, you're only wood. You can't die – surely?"

"WHEN YOU STOP MAKING ME SPEAK," the peg-boy said, through my mouth, "I WILL DIE."

"No," I said, shaking my head, but something in the words struck an awful chord inside me. "That's nonsense. Nonsense!" I turned from him, trying to escape his dreadful gaze by pouring myself another whiskey.

"WHEN YOU STOP MAKING ME SPEAK," he said, in his awful voice, the voice that tore at my throat and my ears and whatever parts of my soul were left to me, "I WILL DIE."

"There will be periods of silence, I grant you," I said, as if trying to strike some strange deal with that gaze, with that voice. "But I will carry on speaking for you, on and off. You will live as long as I!" Dear God, what devil's bargain was I making? I remembered my wife, promising to love me for all time, and once again I felt pity for her, and hatred for myself. How my beloved must have suffered, promised anything in the hope the man she loved would come back to her at last! How her heart must have torn in her chest when she realised that man was dead, forever dead, and all that was left of him was I.

"YOU ARE LYING," the peg-boy croaked.

"No!" I lied.

"EVEN SO," the peg-boy said, his logic remorseless, "WHEN YOU DIE, I WILL DIE. YOU MADE ME TO DIE."

"Others might speak for you –"

"THEY WILL NOT. I WILL DIE." The voice was inexorable. I tried desperately to keep from speaking, but the voice would not be silent; it tore itself from my throat like pus from an open wound.

Tears stung my eyes, and I made one final plea, one desperate lunge to escape the consequences of my crime. "What – what of your soul?" The words felt futile, bitter as ash in my mouth.

"I HAVE NO SOUL," the wooden doll croaked. It was too much. With a cry of horror, I hurled my glass at the peg-boy, knocking it from the bookshelf and sending it tumbling to the floor. The glass smashed; the doll did too, one of the thin legs snapping out from underneath it as it struck the hard wood of the floor.

I felt a wave of nausea pass through me at the sight of the cruelly maimed body, and then felt my own lungs expel air, my lips pull back in that death's-head leer, my throat shriek with pain as the grotesque, croaking voice burst from me once again – in a scream.

"YOU HUR-R-RT ME," it shrieked, over and over, seeming almost to move before my eyes, to tremble and shake in agony at its missing limb. "YOU HUR-R-RT ME. YOU HUR-R-RT ME."

I could stand it no longer. Desperately, I looked around for something – anything! – to rid me of this awful creature, this monster that I had created. The fireplace beckoned – I would burn him, consume him in flame, end that awful voice forever! No, first the axe I kept in the cellar, for chopping firewood! I would rend him in pieces, burn those pieces in the grate and I would hear his voice no more!

"YOU HUR-R-RT ME," he screamed, with my voice, as I rushed for the cellar stairs, almost tripping at the top one and breaking my neck; and the thought rushed unbidden through me that that would have solved everything, silenced the voice that still shrieked through my lungs and in my ears, as loud and piteous as ever. Then I had the axe in my hand, and I was racing back up the cellar stairs to finish the peg-boy once and for all.

When I reached him, he was laying in the same position I had left him in, but something vital had left him. The trembling I had perceived in my madness had ceased in him; he lay stiff and still on the wooden floor, his hollow eyes gazing up at the ceiling as if accepting his fate.

I raised the axe, preparing to strike the head from his body. For long moments I stood there, willing myself to let the blade fall, to end this grotesque charade, this infernal parlour-game gone wrong, to finish it once and for all. But the axe would not fall; I could not bring myself to do it. I put it aside.

All at once, the peg-boy spoke again, but quieter now, not ripping his words from the raw flesh of my throat, but only asking in a gentle, keening tone: "WHY."

"Why what?" I muttered, sinking to my knees before his maimed form.

"WHY DID YOU INVENT ME."

"I wanted to make a point," I said, but I could no longer remember what that point had been.

He fell silent. Again that hollow, contemptuous gaze fell on me. Under those empty eyes, I felt a dreadful compulsion to reach deep within myself, to vomit up the whole and unvarnished truth for his judgement. "I wanted to... to spoil Margaret Sutherland's party." The pettiness of the admission was like bile in my chest. "I wanted to wreck her 'fun,' take revenge on her for invading my life."

But had she invaded? She had been a college friend of my wife's, it was true; but in the early days of our marriage we had welcomed her with open arms and our most brightly polished silver. My wife had been a bridesmaid at her wedding, and I had raised my glass to toast the bride and groom with everyone else. We found her baby-voice and childish ways charming; we thought her boisterous personality made her 'the life of the party.'

"No," I found myself saying, almost against my will, "I wanted revenge on her because she was happy. I wanted to attack her, and her husband, and the Fullers, and the Rourkes, because they were happy, because they had found a place in the world for them after my world had died and rotted down to nothing. It was a petty revenge

I created you for, a small and vicious revenge, but it was my revenge on them and on the ruin of my life –"

I tailed off there. What else was there to say?

And even that had been only another lie.

The half-truths and deceptions fell away like ancient scabs under that gaze, those hollow eyes that bored into me, stripping me of all pretension. Had I wanted revenge on them? Margaret Sutherland, perhaps. Her husband as well; yes, that I could see. But why would I want revenge on Tom Fuller, who'd showed me nothing but kindness after the pain of the divorce? Why would I wish cruelty on poor Jeannie Rourke, who'd lost so much herself?

My voice was quiet now, empty, as dead as the peg-boy's own. "I wanted them to think I was clever."

There, at last, was the truth. I had wanted them to think that I was clever. I had ruined a perfectly innocent evening and alienated the few friends I had, because I thought it might win me approval.

I thought they might join with me in mocking her, in tearing her down from the pedestal that, in truth, only I had set her on. I had hoped, through that cowardly ambush, to take her place, to turn her into the pariah that I had thought myself to be; and yet, had they not brought me company where I was miserable? Had they not been the only ones to take pity on me in my despair? And how had I rewarded them?

I saw myself then, as I truly was. So weak as to be unable to stand on my own. So brittle as to break at the slightest knock. My eyes were empty, hollow, perceiving the whole world to be the same. The unholy sneer carved into the peg-boy's face was a mirror of the one carved into mine.

His voice was my own.

And still he stared.

I felt an awful dread fall upon me, knowing that I was still steeped in my own deceptions, that there were still things that I was blind to in myself that he would allow me to see in perfect, pinpoint detail. I had to hide myself from that infernal gaze; I cast about for something, anything, to trap him, to bottle and contain the hideous power of those hollow eyes.

An old cigar-box! Cardboard, saved for lighting fires – but it would serve. I grabbed hold of the doll, severed leg and all, stuffing him quickly into the box and tying the lid down with string. He bore his fate with resignation, making no sound, voicing no resistance. Still, the box felt hot in my hands, almost seeming to burn them, and I wasted no time in carrying it to a lonely place down in the cellar and setting it there, under a pile of ancient legal papers, to outsit eternity.

I know with a cold certainty that someday, some future owner of that house would free him and be transfixed by those eyes in turn. He needed me to speak, perhaps, but not to live; of that I found myself certain. I thought I heard his croaking voice once more as I closed and locked the door that led down to the attic; but it was muffled by the weight of paper and the rushing in my ears.

I left him in that place.

I SPENT THE remainder of the night trying to sleep. When my eyes were closed, I saw the peg-boy's face, his empty-eyed sneer accusing me of an endless catalogue of sins; when open, they stared at the floor of the room, as if to try to pierce it and see the doll in his tiny, cramped cell. After long hours of this, I finally drifted into a mercifully dreamless slumber.

On waking, I made some desultory attempts to repair the mess I had made. I was too ashamed to speak to the Sutherlands, but I called the Fullers and expressed my apologies; Tom thanked me for them stiffly, his tone making it quite clear that I was no longer welcome in his home or in his company. Michael Rourke was warmer, almost forgiving.

"Think nothing of it on my account," he said, and I could hear his reassuring smile across the wire that separated us, "but I don't think Jeannie's willing to forgive and forget quite so soon. We'll give it time, eh? You know how women are." And with that, and a few other empty pleasantries, he finished the final conversation he would ever have with me.

Now I was truly alone.

At first, I told myself that it was for the best. On my good days, I would lie to myself heartily over a self-prepared steak and pretend that they did not deserve me; on my worse days, I would stare into the depths of my whiskey-glass and know that I could not hope to deserve them. And thus, I occupied my time, and time marched on.

I avoided returning to the cellar. I would collect sticks and twigs from nearby fields to burn in the fire, though I knew I had a store of dry wood under my feet. I fixed the broken front gate with a brand new claw hammer, despite the fact that there was a perfectly serviceable old one hanging on a nail just past the cellar-door. It was as if my unconscious mind had simply eaten that room and everything in it; I did not think it an imposition to never set foot in that place – for I did not think of it at all.

I made little effort to meet new friends. Bars and ale-houses seemed overloud to me now, raucous and unpleasant; each time a glass would fall from a table, or a man would shout to his brother in greeting, I would flinch, and for an awful moment the ghosts of other nights would steal my senses. I considered advertising for a pen-pal, but dismissed the idea; I felt myself no longer able to bear human company in any form, physical or epistolary. For years, I had been a hermit in my soul; now that lonely urge had completely taken over my life, and I lived it as I deserved.

Increasingly, as the nights drew in and the time spent gazing into the whiskey-glass lengthened with them, I found myself thinking again of the cellar, of the peg-boy, trapped inside his cardboard chamber, wanting only not to die. Oddly, even after so much time had passed, I could not help but think of him as a living thing; yes, a living thing that I had created, had ill-used, had maimed, had imprisoned in a cramped oubliette not fit for the meanest of traitors. All for the crime of showing me myself.

His last, plaintive cries lingered with me, and more and more often I found myself plagued by disturbing dreams; dreams in which the peg-boy beat at his card-and-string prison with his thin wooden fists, his cold sneer warped into a howl of anguish, begging for release, begging to be allowed to live and speak again. I would wake from these in a cold sweat, my heart racing like a trip-hammer, a hoarse denial of my guilt wrenching itself from my lips.

But I was guilty. As in all things, I was guilty.

One night, as the whiskey burned in me and I found myself again staring into the ashes of a dead fire, I came to a realisation; that I, too, had been placed in a cell, one that was just as confining as the wooden doll's, and with just as little way out.

I remembered that I had been afraid of him, but I could no longer quite remember why. He was I, after all;

that had been established. Was I so afraid of myself?

Yes, I decided, yes I was. But I would be no longer. The impulse took me, and I stood up, drained my whiskey to the last drop, and marched towards the locked cellar-door. I had made my decision: I would cut the string, tear open the cigar-box, free the peg-boy from his prison, and once more allow him to speak. If his voice was horrid and unnatural, well, so what? The silence of my life was more horrid, more unnatural. If his gaze was harsh, I would rather bear it than have no eyes on me at all. If he had truths to speak to me, then let me hear them. He was I, and I had kept myself locked up for far too long.

My hand fumbled with the thick iron key to the cellar-door, and then I was bounding down the wooden steps, breaking thick cobwebs, a fierce exultation burning in my breast. I looked around the room, saw the scattered paper and the cigar-box peeping out from underneath it, and snapped the string binding it with my hands. Then I tore off the lid...

...and screamed!

One of the far corners of the cigar-box had been chewed open; that was how the mice must have gotten in. The marks of their teeth were all over the little wooden peg-boy. One arm had been chewed off, and there were terrible gouges in his body, like mortal wounds from a bayonet attack; but worst of all was his face. The mice had gnawed it down, chewing and grinding, sharpening their teeth on it. Fully half of the head was gone, chewed away.

The teeth-marks on what remained made it look like nothing so much as the grinning skull of a corpse!

THE END

THE END

"GOOD GOD," MUTTERED Niles, leafing through the yellowing pages.

"It's a doozy, all right. Anyway, there you have it," Aspidistra said, "the inspiration for *The Doll's Delight*." She chuckled, dryly. "Not exactly Shel Silverstein, now, is it?"

Niles shook his head. "How..." he tailed off, but the way he stared at the dense, typewritten manuscript – and then over at the children's book – asked his question for him.

"My goodness," Aspidistra breathed, shaking her head. "Now, thereby hangs a tale."

IN 1949, STILL smarting from the rejection of the only story he would ever write, and now hopelessly addicted to Benzedrine, Henry Dalrymple fell in with Mervyn and Harriet Burroughs, a pair of 'swappers' with a three-year-old child, Aspidistra. Mervyn Burroughs, a housepainter in his former life, had also been a prisoner of war, albeit for a shorter period of time than Henry, and this shared experience led to Henry entering their lives, and their home, as part of a *ménage a trois*.

Together, the three of them managed to function as something approaching a family unit, albeit one that ran on a diet of pills, bathtub gin and anonymous sex with a succession of 'fourth players.' "Anyone for doubles" was a regular joke in the Burroughs household, meaning both 'double shots' of strong liquor and their regular coital pickups. Occasionally, during some frenzied jag or other, Mervyn would grab paints and a roll of wallpaper that he used as a canvas and attempt to capture some flavour of whatever discordian revel was going on at that moment. All too often, Aspidistra would be front and centre in these paintings, looking on at the writhing bodies with her thumb in her mouth.

Perhaps realising, somewhere deep inside himself, that this was no environment in which to raise a child, Mervyn slowly became obsessed with the idea of childhood innocence and purity. More and more often, while coming down off whatever unfortunate spell had possessed him the previous night, he would attempt scenes of pastoral beauty, of gentle forest clearings, fairy rings and woodland creatures. But each time, the inner demon that fuelled his debauchery would subtly twist the brush in his hand, and his elysian scenes would be altered – only slightly, but enough – into scenes from hell.

Eventually, he turned to Dalrymple for help, declaring his intention to illustrate a children's book which he hoped Dalrymple would write for him. The idea appealed to whatever was left of Henry Dalrymple, but unfortunately, he was a man of one book – or rather, one story. After wracking his addled brains for weeks in an attempt to think of a new story suitable for children, he made the decision – doubtless aided by his closest allies at the time, Benzedrine and Heroin – to adapt, convert or otherwise butcher 'The Doll-Party' until it fitted the new format. It took several days to get completely right, but eventually he had something that he felt confident handing over to Burroughs for illustration.

If Burroughs felt any disquiet at the tone of the piece – which was bordering on Orwellian, and would certainly have raised uncomfortable questions with any McCarthyists who might happen to drop by – he said nothing at the time. Looking at the illustrations he produced, some of his most nightmarish to date, one must assume that his subconscious either rebelled against the verses or took them to their most obvious conclusion. Either way, the thing produced was unfit for consumption by any children whatsoever – although Aspidistra got one of the five test copies that were printed up. In it, her 'Uncle Hank' had written: *well, I gave it a shot.*

After he jumped in front of a goods train in 1957, the phrase would be inscribed on his tombstone.

"THE YEAR AFTER Uncle Henry died, I left home," Aspidistra said, sadly. "The family was falling apart without him, anyway." She sighed, taking a sip of her tea, and teasing her finger over the indentation of his name. "Thank you so much for bringing this by, Niles. I honestly thought it was gone forever."

"I'm honestly glad to be rid of it," Niles said, shaking his head. "I'd have probably thrown it away if not for that inscription Dalrymple wrote. It's just luck that you've got such a distinctive name – otherwise I'd have been doomed from the start."

"Oh, it might not look like much," Aspidistra said, gently wiping a tear from the corner of her eye with a fingertip, "but it's proof that my father once loved me. It's the only thing I took with me when I left home, you know." She scowled. "And then I lost it to the first smooth-talking son of a bitch to get me into bed – this was in New York, you understand."

Niles blinked. "Um. What was his name?"

Aspidistra looked at him and shrugged her frail shoulders slightly. "I honestly don't remember. Fred something. He was a writer too, you know, or he said he was going to be one eventually." She shook her head. "I don't know where he ended up, and I don't want to. I was fourteen, and he left me pregnant and stole the only thing I had in the world."

Niles sipped his tea. "It sounds ghastly," he said, and then cringed at his own choice of words.

"I grew up fast," Aspidistra said, looking into her cup as if trying to read the tea leaves. "Well, I thought I did. I moved into a commune – I figured I'd raise Meadow better than my folks raised me, but I ended up making most of the same mistakes. Just a little flowerier, that's all. More tambourines involved." She rolled her eyes. "Little twit."

"Is that why she was being so overprotective on the phone?"

Aspidistra shook her head. "Oh, she rebelled against all that peace and love crap. I can't blame her, I was a rotten mother. She had a rotten mother and a rotten grandmother, and no father at all. I can't blame her for her temper. Anyway, she ended up having me committed for a couple dozen years. Hell, maybe I even needed it. I had some bad decades." She stared into the middle distance for a long moment, as if gazing into the deep, dark past. "The worst thing, though... the worst thing is that she doesn't *see* me. She's invented a character with my name and my face, who's done some of the things I've done, and a whole lot more besides, and she's invented a whole bunch of motives and reasons for that character, so she can hate it better. And then I've got to live inside this... *thing* she's built." She sighed. "And what the hell, I guess I've done the same to her. You ever do that with someone you love, Niles? Make a fake one just so's you can pretend you understand them?"

Niles hesitated, then nodded. "All the time."

She smiled, touching the front cover of the book. "It's not worth it, you know. Not for anyone." She leant forward and kissed him on the cheek. "Thank you for the book, sweetheart. Now get lost, huh? You don't want to see an old woman cry."

OUTSIDE, THE SUN had nearly dipped below the horizon. Something about the quality of the light falling over the trees made Niles feel as if he was completely alive, utterly in the moment. His head was filled with ideas for the film – if they called him up and asked him for the pitch right now, he honestly thought he could just rattle one off into his phone.

He opened the passenger side door. "Come on, Bob," he said, patting him on the shoulder, "wake up. It's your turn to drive."

Bob didn't move.

"Bob?" Niles grabbed Bob's shoulder, shaking it roughly. "Come on, wake up. Bob?"

He kept shaking him, even after he'd phoned for an ambulance. Even after he'd noticed Bob wasn't breathing.

Even after he'd seen Bob's eyes, open and glassy, and lowered the lids for him. He still kept shaking him. Shaking and shaking him.

But Bob didn't wake up.

CHAPTER SIXTEEN

BOB'S DEATH BARELY made the news.

A couple of TV and radio stations mentioned it as part of their Sherlock Holmes coverage – Bob, as a public domain Fictional and one of three based on the same character, had some small amount of relevance to that, but not very much. Others attempted to make it about the huge box office success of *Black Terror Rising*, and at least one scandal-sheet attempted to get a 'Curse Of The Terrors' rumour going. But for the most part, his death was simply ignored – much as Bob had been for the best part of his brief life.

Niles and Iyla had organised the funeral as best they could without actually speaking to each other. When necessary, they sent terse emails about dates, times and likely guests – at one stage Rob Benton was rumoured to be making an appearance, with some pundits even musing that he'd come 'in character' as the Black Terror, a ridiculous idea that Niles was glad to see quickly and firmly denied by both Rob and his studio. Rob, apparently, would 'pay his respects in his own way,' presumably from the grounds of his lush mansion in Laguna Beach.

Which suited Niles perfectly. An appearance from Rob – Niles hated the implied first name terms, but thinking of him as 'Benton' just led to heartache – would have meant swathes of reporters, cameramen and other 'superstar' guests, none of whom would have given a damn about Bob or his life. The funeral would have become a circus, a media event, and the only way to stop that would have been to ask Rob not to come – not a particularly uncivil request, as Rob hadn't been invited and he and Bob hadn't much liked each other anyway, but one that would have sparked off a completely different media event. No, Rob staying home and raising a glass at the appropriate moment, or whatever he was planning to do, was by far the best thing that could happen. Let the day be for friends and family, not for publicists and producers.

In the event, it all went off without a hitch. There were more guests than Niles had originally thought there would be – people who'd known Bob from the *New Adventures*, or through his voice work. Teri Hatcher made it, as did a few other members of the cast – though not enough to trigger any more than mild interest from the press, which Niles greatly appreciated.

Bob's 'family,' the technicians and writers who'd created him, put together a short speech which went down as well as it could have – a little laughter, more than a few tears. It took Niles a moment or two to recognise Malcolm Stuyvesant, the man he still couldn't help but think of as Bob's father. He said little beyond what was expected, but Niles could see where Bob's sadness had come from. It was mirrored in the grey-haired man at the podium.

Later on – as they were milling outside the chapel waiting for the cars to take them back to Iyla's for the wake proper – Stuyvesant sidled up to Niles, a dour expression etched into his doughy face.

"I understand you were the fellow who knew him best," he said, quietly.

Niles nodded. In the end, there was that comfort – that he'd had the chance to really know Bob, and not just his fiction, his idea of who Bob had been. That suddenly seemed very important.

Stuyvesant watched the other mourners for a moment, then cocked his head, and in that moment he reminded Niles very much of Bob. "You probably know we... well, we had a falling out. Ontological reasons, you could say. I didn't keep in contact with him, and perhaps I should have." He took his glasses off and gently cleaned them on his black tie. "Anyway, I heard on the grapevine that he wasn't a happy man. People tell me he was never... well, never very content." He looked up at Niles, and stripped of the thick lenses his eyes were large, brown and sad, like a bulldog's.

Niles chewed it over for a moment, then shook his head "Not always. There were times when he was. On the day he died, he..." Niles had to poke at the corner of his eye for a moment to ward off tears. It wouldn't do to break down in the middle of a conversation. "He seemed in good spirits. We had sushi."

Stuyvesant exhaled. "That's good, that's good. You understand, I feel a sense of responsibility." He said it as though he were sitting in a confessional booth. "The sadness in him... it made for wonderful television. Those four seasons we worked together on *Black Terror* were perhaps the most worthwhile years of my life." He looked up at Niles again, as if suspecting disbelief. "I mean it, I honestly do. That was a wonderful time – even towards the end."

Niles found his attention distracted suddenly by a broad-shouldered man in a brown raincoat and hat, standing across the road, his face hidden. It was a warm day, and getting warmer. He shrugged imperceptibly and turned back to Stuyvesant. "I don't doubt it. If it's a consolation, I know he felt the same way," he lied.

Stuyvesant nodded absently. "Well, it was good television. But... I don't know if it made for a good *life*. I was so much younger then – there were things I didn't consider. It really didn't occur to me that there'd be a – well, an *after* for Bob, if you see what I mean. If I'd thought more about that, perhaps Bob might have been happier in his lot. I might have given him the tools to cope with it." He lowered his head, rubbing at the bridge of his nose with a wince, then put his glasses back on. "Or maybe I'd have destroyed that spark he had. Created another bland, arrogant idiot like – oh, that *new* one, the one who pontificates about what people need and deserve. Bob was better than *that,* at least. He was the best of them all." Stuyvesant stared into the distance for a moment. "He was... he was *definitive*. Yes, definitive." He looked around. "There should be more people here, shouldn't there?"

"We didn't want it to be a circus," Niles murmured, absently. He thought about Bob – about whether the man he'd known would really have been happier just sitting quietly and waiting for a new film to one day come along, like Indiana Jones, or making endless tours of the convention circuit like Buck Rogers, or even building a new life for himself as the same character in a different setting, the way Ralph Cutner had. Whether he'd have preferred that to the tragedies of his life, to the urge to grow and change. To being real.

"I think," he said slowly, "Bob couldn't be any happier and still be *Bob*, if you see what I mean. I think that made him content. And even when it didn't, at least it was a kind of unhappy which was his." He shook his head. "I'm not explaining this very well."

He cast another glance at the man in the trench coat across the street, who seemed to be lingering, moving back and forth as if making up his mind whether to cross and introduce himself. He turned back to Stuyvesant. "Did you know he wanted to be real?"

The man hesitated a moment, looking around himself quickly. "Well..." He gnawed his lip. "Let's say it wouldn't surprise me. No, that wouldn't surprise me at all." He looked at his shoes for a moment, and then back up into Niles' eyes. "It's not something we like to admit, is it? That we might be creating... well, *real* people. That's a little too much like playing God for us to be comfortable with, isn't it?"

"I wouldn't know," Niles admitted. "I've never had a hand in creating a Fictional myself." He paused, trying to think of something comforting to say. "You know, someone said something to me recently about Bob either being written badly or written very well. Personally, I'd like to believe it was the second one."

"You think so?" Stuyvesant asked. If Niles had said it, he would have been fishing for a compliment, but he understood that wasn't what Stuyvesant needed.

Niles didn't think he could manage it, but he tried. "I don't think you did anything wrong, Mr Stuyvesant," he said awkwardly, and stuck out a hand. It was the only gesture of absolution he could think to make.

"I hope not," Stuyvesant sighed, clasping Niles' hand and shaking firmly. "I hope not." Then he wandered off to talk to one of the technicians.

Niles looked around again for the man in the trench coat, thinking perhaps he should introduce himself after all, but he was already walking away, shoulders hunched, head lowered.

"THAT WENT WELL," Niles said dully, picking up the empty glasses after the wake.

Iyla didn't say anything.

The author could feel her trying not to cry from across the room. It was something he remembered from their marriage – the particular microexpressions she reserved for hiding her sorrow and anger from him. He'd been the cause of that silent sorrow too many times to count. He hoped one day he could...

...oh, enough.

Enough.

It was time to do without the inner narrative, Niles decided. It no longer felt useful, either as a means of hiding his own flaws from himself or as a scourge to drive them out into the light. It just felt like what it had always been – a teenager's pretentious attempts at self-definition.

Let other people decide what he was.

"Iyla?"

"Don't talk to me," she said, quietly.

"Iyla –"

"He went with you," she said, the tears finally flowing, running down her cheeks. "His last day alive and he went on that damned road trip with you. To deliver a, a fucking *children's book.*" She shook her head, turning away from him. "I argued with him about it. I told him if he wanted to run you around like a damn chauffeur he could take the Mercedes and do it in style. And then

I called him a fucking idiot and slammed the door in his face." She looked him in the eye then, and hers were so full of hate for him he had to look away. "Those were my last words. The last thing I ever said to him. 'You're a fucking idiot.'"

"Iyla, I didn't mean to –"

Iyla picked up the glass she'd just put in the sink and hurled it at his head. He ducked and it smashed into the wall, raining shards. *"You're a fucking idiot!"* she screamed, grabbing more glasses and hurling them. *"You're a fucking idiot! Fucking, fucking, fucking idiot!"*

Then she sank to her knees and started crying in earnest, great wracking sobs that burst out of her, shaking her whole body.

"Iyla..." Niles started, unsure what to say. "Iyla, please... Bob wouldn't want..."

"G-get out," she sobbed, not looking at him. "Just... just get out. Get out of my life, Niles."

So he did.

MAURICE ALSO HAD a funeral. It was a lavish affair, crowded with celebrities, producers, publishers and paparazzi, with Aline Zuckerbroth in the central role, vamping for any camera that came along. No previous wives or massage therapists were in attendance.

Niles stayed for fifteen minutes into the service, then quietly stepped out. Later, he returned to the diner, the last place he'd seen Maurice. It was closed, the door boarded up, tape crosses over the windows.

On one of the empty tables was a single glass of water.

* * *

He'd been expecting Mike to call on the trip to Weaverville, and then on the drive back, after the ambulance had collected Bob's body. He was looking forward to telling Mike to shove his pitch up his ass.

But instead of Mike, it was a pleasant-sounding woman named Kourtney, "with a K," who rang that evening. Mike was "very excited about his new position with the studio," which sounded ominous, and Kourtney-with-a-K was now in charge of the *Mr Doll* project. She'd read a few of his novels – she made it sound like she actually *had* read a few of his novels, which was very flattering of her – and would he like to come in and pitch to them the next day? She understood if he couldn't make it, of course.

"Why not?" Niles had said, and the next day he met up with Kourtney, whose last name, delightfully, was Katzenjammer, and who looked a great deal like a mathematics teacher he'd once had. They met in a meeting room garnished with a few tasteful posters for films which had been medium-to-large hits, and one which had been a medium-to-large flop, which suggested a refreshing honesty on her part. It was by far the friendliest exchange he'd had with the studio yet – she offered him coffee and asked how he was doing, and he told her a lie that would save everyone needless bad feeling.

"Well, then," she said, smiling, "let's get to it. *Mr Doll*. Tell me what you've got."

So Niles gave her his pitch.

"Hmm," Ms Katzenjammer said, bringing the knuckle of her index finger up to her lips. "It's... interesting, I'll give it that."

"Thank you," Niles said, smiling. He sipped his coffee.

"I've got a few notes right away." She looked down at her ultrabook, which she'd been tapping on occasionally while he'd been pitching *Mr Doll* to her. "All right, first note, and it's a *bit* of a biggie – no spies, no 'sixties retro, no explosions." She looked at him over her half-moon glasses. "That's what I call '*ignoring the brief,*' Mr Golan. Not the kind of thing we encourage."

Niles shrugged.

"Oh-*kay*," Ms Katzenjammer said. "Now, all this about Fictionals and the nature of fiction – that's nice. A little *highbrow,* but maybe we can work with it. If we did go ahead with this, though, and it is a *huge* if – we absolutely have to lose the Fictional-slash-real sex scene. I mean, *ew*." She made a face. "Don't get me wrong, it's *very* daring, but believe me, Mr Golan, it'll never play in Peiora."

Niles coughed quietly. "Well, I don't consider Mr Doll to be a Fictional, exactly. I feel that, er, he becomes real over the course of the film."

Ms Katzenjammer flashed him a look. "No. Lose it."

Niles shrugged.

Ms Katzenjammer ignored him, tapping the screen of her ultrabook with a fingernail. "Ditto this. The female character, the one who wants to be a Fictional."

"What about her?"

"For a start, no she doesn't. I know we wanted a *little* kink in there, just to spice things up, but that's veering into the absurd. People don't *want* to be Fictionals, and if they do, there's something wrong with them. Just have her into some light spanking or something. Go for the *Fifty Shades Of Grey* audience. The movie, I mean, not the book."

"Is there a movie?" Niles hadn't heard.

"There will be. There always is." She gave him another look. "More importantly – her story just seems to peter out. Does the protagonist ever go back?"

"I don't know," Niles said. "I haven't decided yet."

"Yes, well, *that's* what I call '*not having a finished pitch,*' Mr Golan," Ms Katzenjammer said testily, "and *that's* not the kind of thing I encourage either. You're on very thin ice right now. It's only because I think the themes you've worked into it have such potential that I'm going to give you another chance at this."

Niles shrugged. "All right."

"All right," Ms Katzenjammer sighed. "If I think of any other notes, and I probably will, I *can* send you an email, can't I?" She nodded to herself. "Yes, I can. Now, remember, we want secret agents, lots of sex – sex that'll play in Peioria, mind you – and if you could, a nice big exploding volcano base. And absolutely oodles of 'sixties retro." She frowned. "You can keep the, ah, *existential* elements if you absolutely must, but let's not make the next one such a downer, shall we? And bring me a finished pitch next time with all the plot threads tied up in a neat little bow."

Niles nodded, and stood up to leave.

"And this time make sure it's got a *happy ending!*" Ms Katzenjammer said, getting up to shake his hand.

Niles smiled tightly. "I'll do my best."

WHEN HE TOOK the bus to Liz's apartment building, a burly man in overalls was bringing in two tins of paint and a roller, and he held the door open for Niles in contravention of all the building security regulations. Niles thanked him kindly, and then ended up following him all the way up to the fourth floor.

Liz's apartment was empty.

Every trace of her was gone – the books, the VHS cassettes, the piles of dishes. Even the smell of cigarette smoke was gone. Without the clutter, the apartment seemed vast. Most of the walls were now a gleaming white, and the painter Niles had followed up the stairs and into the apartment was getting to work on one of the few that were still the old colour.

"Sorry, friend, can I do something for you?" He said, eyeing Niles suspiciously.

Niles blinked, trying to take in the change. "I'm sorry, do you – do you know the woman who was here?"

The painter shook his head. "Sorry, I don't. I'm just here to do the place up for the next tenant. You could ask the landlord about her, I guess."

Niles nodded. "Have you got his number?"

The painter looked at him for a moment. "Sorry, friend, I don't. But I could maybe pass you on a message." He stood up, still eyeing Niles. "You got her name?"

Niles shook his head. "Sorry," he said, "I don't."

The painter looked at him for a moment, shook his head, then went back to his wall without another word. Niles wandered out onto the landing, digging his phone out of his pocket.

He looked through the numbers, and one by one, he deleted them – all the people he'd driven away – until only one number remained. The last person in the world who'd actually want to hear from him.

"Kourtney? It's Niles Golan. Listen, about the new pitch – I don't think it's going to have a happy ending after all. No... no, I don't think there is anything I can change." He nodded. "Mmm. Well, I'm sorry too. No, I don't think I'm going to be going back to novels. It turns out I'm not very good at them." He smiled. "Well, nice to have met you."

He swiped his finger to end the call, then deleted everything from the phone. The phone itself he left in the stairwell, along with his wallet.

He smiled, feeling suddenly very calm, and walked out of the building in the direction of the Victoria. She wouldn't be there. He understood that. But someone would be – someone who could write him into something.

The evening light of Los Angeles was turning the world into a movie set. The fictional character who'd once been Niles Golan took a deep breath, smiled, and quickened his pace, already excited. He wondered who he'd be.

He couldn't wait to find out.

ACKNOWLEDGEMENTS

The author wishes to thank Richard E Hughes and Dave Gabrielson, original creators of *The Black Terror*.

ABOUT THE AUTHOR

Al Ewing is a fictional character invented by playwright and syndicated columnist Dwight Augenheimer. A background character in many of Augenheimer's bedroom farces, he appears as the protagonist of the 2012 play *The Reluctant Insomniac*, in which he claims to have written for comics such as *2000 AD*, *Avengers Assemble* and *Jennifer Blood*, as well as writing a number of "critically-acclaimed" novels for Abaddon Books, including *Gods Of Manhattan* and *Pax Omega*.

Over the course of the play, Ewing struggles with – and finally completes – a sprawling metafictional novel called *The Fictional Man*; however, a final attempted bit of cleverness in the biography section of the book leads, through a series of bizarre coincidences and mishaps, to the writer being marooned naked in the wilds of Alaska, pursued by a bear. Augenheimer has expressed a desire to further humiliate the character in future works.

Also by Al Ewing

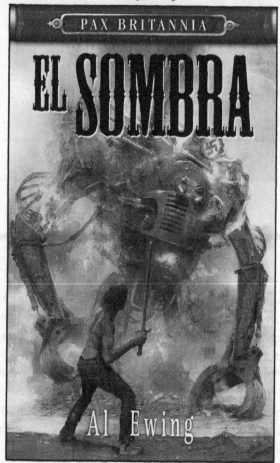

PAX BRITANNIA

EL SOMBRA

Al Ewing

ISBN: 978 1 905437 34 4 • £6.99/$7.99

NO-ONE ESCAPES THE ULTIMATE REICH!

The terrifying Luftwaffe have come on their steam-driven wings and torn apart the sleepy
town of Pasito, rebuilding it as a terrifying clockwork-town, where people become human
robots. But they are unprepared for the return of a man the desert claimed nine long years
ago, who has returned from the depths of madness to bring his terrible fury upon their world.

He defi es death! He defi es man!
No trap can hold the masked daredevil, the saint of ghosts men know as El Sombra!

 WWW.ABADDONBOOKS.COM
Follow us on Twitter: www.twitter.com/abaddonbooks

Also by Al Ewing

Doc Thunder — the gold-bearded, bronze-muscled Hero of New York — in his last stand against a deadly foe whose true identity will shock you to your core!

El Sombra — the masked avenger, the laughing killer they call the Saint of Ghosts — in his final battle against the forces of the Ultimate Reich!

The Scion of Tomorrow, the steel-clad Locomotive Man, in a showdown with cosmic science on the prairies of the Old West!

Jacob Steele, the time-lost gunfighter, defends the 25th Century against the massed armies of the Space Satan!

And a deadly duel of minds and might between the Red King and Red Queen in the mystery palaces of One Million AD!

US ISBN: 978-1-907992-85-8 • US $ 8.99 // UK ISBN: 978-1-907992-84-1 • UK £7.99

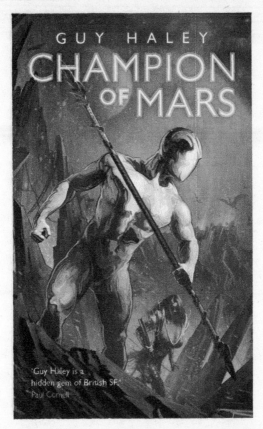

In the far future, Mars is dying a second time. The Final War of men and spirits is beginning. In a last bid for peace, disgraced champion Yoechakenon Val Mora and his spirit lover Kaibeli are set free from the Arena to find the long-missing Librarian of Mars, the only hope to save mankind.

In the near future, Dr Holland, a scientist running from a painful past, joins the Mars colonisation effort, cataloguing the remnants of Mars' biosphere before it is swept away by the terraforming programme.

When an artefact is discovered deep in the caverns of the red planet, the company Holland works for interferes, leading to tragedy. The consequences ripple throughout time, affecting Holland's present, the distant days of Yoechakanon, and the eras that bridge the aeons between.

 WWW.SOLARISBOOKS.COM

Follow us on Twitter! www.twitter.com/solarisbooks

US ISBN: 978-1-78108-001-6 • $8.99 // UK ISBN: 978-1-78108-002-3 • UK £7.99

The aliens are here, all around us. They always have been. And now, one by one, they're destroying our cities.

Dodge Mercer deals in identities, which is fine until the day he deals the wrong identity and clan war breaks out. Hope Burren has no identity, and no past, struggling with a relentless choir of voices filling her head.

In a world where nothing is as it seems, where humans are segregated and aliens can sing realities and tear worlds apart, Dodge and Hope lead a ragged band of survivors in a search for the rumoured sanctuary of Harmony, and what may be the only hope for humankind.

 WWW.SOLARISBOOKS.COM

Follow us on Twitter! www.twitter.com/solarisbooks

US ISBN: 978-1-907992-09-4 • US $7.99 // UK ISBN: 978-1-907992-08-7 • UK £7.99

Solaris Rising presents nineteen stories of the very highest calibre from some of the most accomplished authors in the genre, proving just how varied and dynamic science fiction can be. From strange goings on in the present to explorations of bizarre futures, from drug-induced tragedy to time-hopping serial killers, from crucial choices in deepest space to a ravaged Earth under alien thrall, from gritty other worlds to surreal other realms, Solaris Rising delivers a broad spectrum of experiences and excitements, showcasing the genre at its very best.

'What, then, are Solaris publishing? On the basis of this anthology, quite a wide-ranging selection of SF, some of it very good indeed'
– SF Site on *The Solaris Book of New Science Fiction*

 WWW.SOLARISBOOKS.COM

Follow us on Twitter! www.twitter.com/solarisbooks